PENGUIN BOOKS

New Penguin Parallel Texts: Short Stories in French

Richard Coward was born in 1955 in Barrow-in-Furness and educated at Lancaster Royal Grammar School and Sidney Sussex College, Cambridge, where he read French and Spanish. He taught at Bishop's Stortford College and Sherborne School before moving to Eton, where he is now a Housemaster. He is married to Anne and they have three sons, James, Edward and Matthew.

NEW PENGUIN PARALLEL TEXTS

Short Stories in French

Edited and translated by Richard Coward

PENGUIN BOOKS

PENGUIN BOOKS

Published by the Penguin Group
Penguin Books Ltd, 80 Strand, London WC2R 0RL, England
Penguin Putnam Inc., 375 Hudson Street, New York, New York 10014, USA
Penguin Books Australia Ltd, 250 Camberwell Road, Camberwell, Victoria 3124, Australia
Penguin Books Canada Ltd, 10 Alcorn Avenue, Toronto, Ontario, Canada M4V 3B2
Penguin Books India (P) Ltd, 11 Community Centre, Panchsheel Park, New Delhi – 110 017, India
Penguin Books (NZ) Ltd, Cnr Rosedale and Airborne Roads, Albany, Auckland, New Zealand
Penguin Books (South Africa) (Pty) Ltd, 24 Sturdee Avenue, Rosebank 2196, South Africa

Penguin Books Ltd, Registered Offices: 80 Strand, London WC2R 0RL, England

www.penguin.com

Published in 1999
13

Introduction, notes, this collection and translations
copyright © Richard Coward, 1999
Copyright in the original stories remains with the authors,
unless stated otherwise in the Acknowledgements on p. 215
All rights reserved

The moral right of the editor has been asserted

Set in 10/12.5 pt PostScript Monotype Baskerville
Typeset by Rowland Phototypesetting Ltd, Bury St Edmunds, Suffolk
Made and printed in Great Britain by Clays Ltd, St Ives plc

Contents

Introduction

This collection of twelve short stories, representing the work of eleven different authors, is an eclectic choice on my part. No collection of this length could ever hope to be representative of the work that is being published, so it seemed to me pointless even to try to distil the essence of the modern short story being written in French. In the broadest of terms, it was my intention to select stories that had literary value but were accessible to as broad a panoply of readers as possible. As their translator, at all times I remained as faithful to the French text as possible, though considerations of English style and the difficulty of translating idiom had to be taken into account. The first volume of stories, edited by Pamela Lyon and first published in 1966, contained work emanating only from France. Its sequel, edited by Simon Lee and published six years later, contained two stories from Switzerland and one from Belgium, but the remaining five again emanated from France. The main emphasis of my brief was to produce a collection of short stories that had been published after 1970, and very early in the course of my researches it became clear to me that the country that is the birthplace of the language is no longer the main source of the genre. The decision not to include Belgian or Swiss authors was made on the undoubtedly dubious basis that work from these countries had been included in a previous volume. The stories in this edition appear in order of increasing linguistic difficulty, which may not necessarily reflect the difficulty in literary interpretation the reader may experience.

Reference to the two previous editions of parallel texts reveals a broad range of authors, but none is thought of specifically as a short-story writer, and the same is true for many of the authors included in the present volume. When one thinks of the French *conte*

one's mind immediately goes back to the nineteenth century and to the Naturalist work of Maupassant (1850–93). He was the undoubted master of his craft at that time, writing short, sardonic narratives in which one always looks for the sting in the tail. In 'La Parure', for example, the already impoverished Mme Loisel works in drudgery for ten years, thereby sacrificing her youth and beauty, to repay the loan of 36,000 francs she was forced to take out to replace a diamond necklace that she once borrowed and lost. Maupassant reveals in only the last two lines of the story that the original was a fake and worth only 500 francs. Further back in time one thinks of Voltaire (1694–1778) and his *contes philosophiques* of the mid-eighteenth century. Yet because Voltaire's intentions were to overtly satirize aspects of contemporary society, comparison with modern fiction cannot be made. Indeed, the almost surreal nature of Voltaire's narrative invites a cerebral rather than an emotive reaction to his writing. Even further back, in the seventeenth century, is the work of Charles Perrault (1628–1703), famous for his *Histoires ou Contes du temps passé*, usually known simply as the *Contes*, which defended and praised contemporary culture. These drew heavily upon the tradition of oral story-telling, though their narrative style was greatly adapted to meet the polite tastes of Perrault's society, dictated by the *bienséances* that so greatly influenced literature in the latter part of the seventeenth century.

There are no such restrictions upon literature today, but in seeking out modern writers of short-story fiction in French one comes to the conclusion that the genre has lost for the modern French reader much of the appeal that brought so much success to Maupassant and his predecessors. By contrast, there has always been a strong tradition of short-story writing in English, both in Britain and America, and this may be the reason why the genre is enjoying something of a renaissance in French-speaking Canada. However much they seek political and cultural autonomy, the French-speaking Canadians cannot avoid the influences and attitudes that bombard them from outside their boundaries, be they in newspapers, on the television or the radio.

The stories in this collection were all written by authors from

Quebec or France and the majority were published after 1990. I would have liked to include some of the Creole literature from the Caribbean but the tradition of story-telling there remains principally an oral one, with a strong emphasis on moral tales, often using animals as characters, very much in the style of Aesop or La Fontaine. The simplicity of the language means that they can be read easily by anyone with a basic knowledge of French, and the themes with which they deal are so markedly different from those of the stories I have chosen that it seemed inappropriate to include them. The same may be said for Francophone African literature, which also reflects a mainly oral tradition.

The subtitle of this volume, Short Stories in French, seeks to emphasize that literature written in French is more global than would be conveyed by the pithier 'French Short Stories'. In French we have the terms *récit*, *conte* and *nouvelle*, which are all translatable by the English 'short story', yet what is a short story as opposed to a short novel? One is tempted to write that, if there is a distinction, it is one of length, but reference books are not clear on the point and it is beyond the scope of this introduction to take the matter further. Nevertheless, it is immediately apparent from this collection not only that short stories can vary greatly in length but that they do have a common element, which is justifiably where the short story, however long, cannot be thought of as a short novel. All short stories focus upon a small number of characters, in some cases only one, and the author allows us to know only those traits of personality that are pertinent to the tale being told. All the stories focus on specific incidents in the characters' lives, and the sheer concentration of that focus is at times redolent of the Unities of Time, Place and Action that conditioned the neo-classical tragedies of the seventeenth century. There is no room for lengthy development of setting or of character relationships *à la Balzac*, and extraneous detail would only detract from the author's specific intention. An exception to this may possibly be J.-M.-G. Le Clézio's 'David', which I included precisely because some may consider that it sits on the fence between short story and (very) short novel. However, there is no doubting the narrowness of the story, which is marked by an absence of any

subplot and an all-pervading sense of obsession in the main character's search for his brother, Édouard.

It could perhaps be argued that obsession is a notion common to all the stories, thus binding them into a thematic whole. It is certainly the case that in all the stories the characters focus on a single target or are held trapped within a specific place, but this is surely inevitable, given the conciseness with which the author is forced to observe his or her characters. This is true of Louise Cotnoir in 'Accursed Notebooks' ('*Les Cahiers maudits*'), in which an anonymous woman scribbles endlessly away in an attempt to make sense of a horrific moment during the Second World War. Without the detail that gives a three-dimensional feel to a character, and because of the need to limit the range of activity due to the length of the genre, it is inevitable that the characters will seem to lack any sense of peripheral vision. In order to appreciate the stories more fully it is necessary to look beneath the obvious and to question the motives of the characters. In 'The Third-rate Film' ('*Le Navet*'), it is loneliness that prompts the central figure to go to the cinema in an attempt to escape the sense of isolation that has led her, almost obsessively, to use the plural pronoun when referring to herself. In 'Self-destruction' ('*Autodestruction*'), the man is sucked into a spiral of terror that destroys him as he hallucinates because of the solitude that he fears so much. There are echoes of Dostoevsky's 'The Double', or even a Dickensian ghost story, as he picks up a book and begins to read a text that appears to be about himself. Terror and panic take over until eventually he reads that he is going to die in the black waters of the river. The story succeeds precisely because it is so concise, offering no hope of escape to its protagonist because René Belletto has focused exclusively upon the fear of being alone.

Revenge and the desire for recognition are the driving forces in 'The Hunters' Café' ('*Le Café des Chasseurs*'), as the patriotic old soldiers seek retribution upon the Scandinavian who cooked himself an egg on the flame of the Unknown Soldier beneath the Arc de Triomphe. Daniel Boulanger, possibly the best known of all the authors in this collection, treats his subjects with a lightness of touch that allows him to paint a comic picture of the old soldiers in their

wheelchairs, holding up the traffic in the Champs-Élysées. The subject matter is serious, and the soldiers' sense of outrage is never devalued, but the author's sense of the comic allows him to engage his reader without ever mocking his characters. There is a similar sense of the unreal in 'The Occupation of the Ground' ('*L'Occupation des sols*'), in which Jean Échenoz brings together a father and son in their attempt to preserve for ever the large mural painting of a dead wife and mother. The writing is tense and economical but at the same time descriptive and the reader should be alive to Échenoz's use of neologisms to appreciate fully the humour in the writing. In 'You Never Die' ('*On ne meurt jamais*'), it is the preservation of memory and sensations evoked by a particular place that is the subject chosen by Alain Gerber. Of all the stories in the collection this is arguably the most moving, for its brevity and conciseness force the author into poetic evocation rather than description.

The feeling of emptiness that follows the end of a twelve-year romantic affair is the driving force in 'The Object d'Art' ('*L'Objet d'art*'). Here the young woman transfers her affection for a lost lover on to a work of art, sacrificing by its purchase a sabbatical trip to the West Indies. Heady from the effects of alcohol, she walks home late at night, after the private view, and has to battle with the elements in the sub-zero temperatures of Montreal. On a first reading, one wonders where the story is going. Is it merely an evocation of obsession with an object? This proves hardly to be the case as we examine the power of art to evoke within us powerful emotions and reactions that, in this case, appear to take the character to the edge of insanity. The story could succeed on this level alone but Jean-Paul Daoust takes his art one stage further and the final paragraph adds a grim twist, which is satisfying both on the level of plot and in forcing us to reflect on the power of suggestion. The introspection of the woman finds a parallel in the obsessive search for a former lover that drives on Pierre in 'The Character' ('*Le Personnage*'). To the end, we are never totally sure if the object of his search is a real person or a fictional character, and it is this interplay between the real and the imagined that takes us into Pierre's mind in such an engagingly fascinating, and yet haunting, manner.

'Héloïse' is a moving account that begins by evoking the tenderness shown to a she-donkey by a woman unable to bear the child to whom she wants to give the name Héloïse. There are elements of black humour in the subject matter, but Sylvie Germain treats it with great sensitivity and prevents it from descending into melodrama. Marthe, the woman in the story, is killed by lightning when attending to the donkey and her husband blames the animal for her death. Cruelty follows and it is only when it is too late that he realizes the significance of the donkey to him.

The stories of Frédéric Fajardie and Sylvie Massicotte come closest to the sardonic twist of the typical Maupassant story, though neither author employs the terseness of expression of their nineteenth-century predecessor, who at times appeared to have worked with the same economy of expression as the Impressionist painters, of whose work he greatly approved. Yet the stories do focus on brief moments of time in the lives of their characters and suggest much about specific feelings and emotions, whilst leaving us breathlessly expectant for more. Irony plays an important part in their success, for it forces us to think back over the story, or even to reread it, in order to discover those hints which could only be glossed over at a first reading. In 'The Third-rate Film' ('*Le Navet*'), for example, it is not until the man appears outside the cinema that we realize why he had to change seats using only his arms. And it is only then that we fully appreciate the woman's repugnance at what she has seen on the cinema screen. In 'All Lights Off' ('*Tous feux éteints*'), Joachim can only give meaning to his life by killing himself; in 'Learning How to Live' ('*Apprendre à vivre*') two characters come briefly together before one is killed. The young boy has his new roller-skates and in a naively adolescent way wants to avoid an encounter with a girl with whom he is desperate to go out; the man in his thirties has an old Renault 4 and is cursing the fact that his wife has been having an affair. Two diametrically opposed experiences collide and, ironically, it is despair that kills hope, thus leaving us wondering at the relevance of the title and the outcry of the car driver.

Learning How to Live

FRÉDÉRIC FAJARDIE

Apprendre à vivre

Il venait d'avoir seize ans et sa seconde paire de patins à roulettes – un modèle très supérieur à la première – offerte par ses parents afin de récompenser une année scolaire particulièrement brillante.

Il se prénommait Patrick. Les fils à papa du lycée disaient qu'il s'agissait là d'un «prénom de prolo»[1] mais Agathe, avec laquelle il aurait flirté depuis longtemps s'il n'avait été si timide, Agathe trouvait ce prénom «sympa» et même «plutôt cool».

Patrick ne savait pas très bien ce qu'il voulait. La période lui semblait brouillée: plus vraiment l'enfance et ces grandes peurs vite exorcisées par un câlin maternel ou la voix bourrue et tendre de son père.

Pas encore l'âge adulte, cette horreur qu'il pressentait: le chômage, les inutiles diplômes, un patronat agressif, cupide et cynique, bref, le cauchemar. Mais peut-être aussi une vie merveilleuse . . .

Il se trouvait dans un no man's land de la vie, en quelque sorte. D'où les patins à roulettes, une manière de prolonger l'enfance, de tenir l'angoisse à distance.

C'était ridicule et enfantin, il le savait, n'étant pas sa propre dupe mais il avait envie de se faire plaisir.

Sauf que ce plaisir risquait de tourner à la confusion: n'était-ce pas Agathe qu'il apercevait, sortant du métro Arts-et-Métiers?[2]

Antoine Lopez, au volant de sa fourgonnette 4 L, maudissait la terre entière. Il avait l'impression d'une vaste conspiration visant à son malheur. Descendant la rue de Belleville à toute allure, il faillit écraser un vieil Arabe qu'il injuria, une jeune Chinoise à qui il montra son index dressé, un chien efflanqué qui fit un saut de côté . . .

Learning How to Live

He had just turned sixteen and had been given his second pair of roller-skates – of a design that was much superior to his first pair – by his parents in recognition of a particularly glowing school year.

His Christian name was Patrick. The daddy's boys at the *lycée* said that it was a 'pleb's name', whereas Agathe, with whom he would have flirted long since if he had not been so shy, said that the name was 'nice' and even 'rather cool'.

Patrick did not really know what he wanted. This period in his life seemed confused: not really childhood any more and those great fears were no longer quickly exorcized by a maternal cuddle or the gruff yet tender voice of his father.

It was not yet adulthood, that time of horror that he sensed lay ahead: unemployment, useless certificates, aggressive, money-grabbing and cynical employers, in short, a nightmare. But perhaps also a marvellous time of life . . .

He found himself to some extent in the no-man's land of life. Hence the roller-skates, a way of prolonging childhood, of holding anguish at bay.

He knew that it was ridiculous and childish, for he was no fool to himself, but he wanted to please himself.

It was just that this pleasure could turn into confusion: wasn't that Agathe that he spotted coming out of the Arts-et-Métiers metro station?

Antoine Lopez, at the wheel of his Renault 4 van, was cursing the entire world. He felt as though there was a great conspiracy which sought to bring him misfortune. Driving down the rue de Belleville at full speed, he almost ran over an old Arab at whom he swore, a young Chinese girl at whom he made a rude gesture with a raised index finger, a skinny dog which jumped to the side . . .

Quoi, c'est vrai: rien ne marchait. D'abord, pourquoi était-il chauve à trente ans? Ensuite, pourquoi roulait-il en 4 L, avec son ancienneté, alors que des chauffeurs moins expérimentés avaient droit à des Golf tôlées? Et sa femme, de dix ans plus jeune, comment se payait-elle toutes ses fringues soi-disant en solde? Et les coupes de cheveux de chez Mod's Hair? Et le parfum Dior? Et les bijoux? Avec ses 6 000 francs mensuels de secrétaire ou bien s'était-elle trouvé un amant fortuné?

Et pourquoi inventait-elle des griefs contre lui – il n'y en a que pour tes parents, tu ne m'emmènes pas en voyage, tu passes trop d'heures au travail et d'autres choses encore, aussi insensées? Pourquoi sinon pour se donner bonne conscience lorsqu'elle le trompait? Pourquoi s'inventer des motifs, pourquoi toute cette ignoble lâcheté?

Désespéré, il hurla «Salope!» en traversant la place de la République[3] à toute vitesse, empruntant la direction Châtelet par Arts-et-Métiers.

C'était Agathe, pas de doute! Et elle venait vers lui . . . Patrick hésita puis se souvint de ces types en patins à roulettes qui s'accrochent à l'arrière des camions.

Il avait toujours trouvé cela dangereux et stupide mais, cette fois, cela semblait le moyen idéal pour s'éclipser avec discrétion et célé-rité. En l'absence de camion, il choisit une vieille 4 L fourgonnette arrêtée au feu rouge. Avec ce tas de boue, peu de chance que le chauffeur se prenne pour un pilote de formule 1.

Il s'accrocha à la galerie.

– Tu crois que je t'ai pas vu, p'tit connard? gronda Lopez qui démarrasur les chapeaux de roue en faisant hurler les pneus de sa 4 L.

Le cœur de Patrick cognait très fort, peut-être parce qu'il allait cesser de battre à tout jamais dans moins d'une minute, qu'il était encore tout neuf et débordant de choses douces et tendres . . .

Patrick pensait que cela allait vite, trop vite. Il n'osait pas lâcher la galerie, le vent lui arrachait des larmes, la terreur l'envahissait tout

So, it was true: nothing was working. First, why was he bald at thirty? Then, why was he driving such an ancient Renault 4 when drivers with less experience than him had the right to soft-top Golfs? And how did his wife, ten years younger than he, manage to afford all those clothes which she claimed to get in the sales? And the hair-dos at Mod's Hair? And the Dior perfume? And the jewels? And all on her 6,000 francs a month as a secretary or had she found herself a rich lover?

And why did she hold so much resentment against him – you only think of your parents, you never take me on your trips, you spend too long at work, and other things which made just as little sense? Why other than to clear her conscience when she was deceiving him? Why make up such reasons, why all that horrible cowardliness?

In despair, he yelled 'Bitch!' as he drove at full speed across the place de la République, turning towards Châtelet by Arts-et-Métiers.

It was Agathe, there was no doubt! And she was coming towards him . . . Patrick hesitated, then remembered those guys on roller-skates who grab hold of the backs of lorries.

He had always considered that dangerous and stupid but, this time, it seemed the ideal way to slip out of the way with discretion and speed. In the absence of a lorry, he chose an old Renault 4 van that had stopped at the red light. In that heap of mud there was little chance that the driver would take himself for a Formula 1 driver.

He grabbed hold of the roof-rack.

'Do you think I haven't seen you, you little sod?' muttered Lopez, who shot off at top speed, making the tyres of his Renault 4 scream.

Patrick's heart pounded, perhaps because it was going to stop beating for ever and ever in less than a minute, perhaps because it was still brand new and overflowing with sweet, tender things . . .

Patrick thought that he was going quickly, too quickly. He did not dare let go of the roof-rack, the wind was snatching tears from

entier tandis que les gens se retournaient sur les trottoirs, stupéfaits ou pressentant le drame.

Libérant une main, Patrick tapa sur la vitre arrière en répétant:

– Arrête . . . Je t'en supplie . . . Je t'en supplie . . .

Lopez n'était pas qu'un simple salaud. Salaud, il l'était, c'est évident, mais ce dernier cohabitait avec un être blessé, humilié, crevant de solitude dans son malheur et qui venait dans sa misère et son délire de trouver une victime expiatoire.

Il maugréa:

– Je vais t'apprendre à vivre, moi!

Puis il freina brutalement au carrefour des rues du Renard et de la Verrerie.

Le choc foudroya Patrick qui conserva une expression d'horreur et d'incompréhension sur son visage jeune à tout jamais.

Quant à l'épitaphe, elle tomba des lèvres dures d'un lepéniste en vadrouille:

– Il avait qu'à pas s'accrocher.

Sauf que Patrick ne s'accrochait pas vraiment. Dans une société à vomir, il se raccrochait simplement aux branches de cet arbre de vie qu'un autre appela les «Grandes Espérances».[4]

him, terror was running right through his body whilst people on the pavements were turning round, dumbfounded or foreseeing tragedy.

Taking one hand off, Patrick tapped on the rear window and shouted repeatedly:

'Stop . . . I beg you . . . I beg you . . .'

Lopez was not just a mere bastard. Bastard he was, that is obvious, but that bastard was in the company of a wounded, humiliated man, dying from loneliness in his misfortune and, in his wretchedness and his madness, he had just found a victim to atone for it all.

He grumbled:

'I'm going to teach you how to live!'

Then he slammed on the brakes at the point where the rue du Renard crosses over the rue de la Verrerie.

The impact immediately killed Patrick, who kept a look of horror and incomprehension on his face that would remain for ever young.

As for the epitaph, it fell from the harsh lips of a fatalist out for a stroll:

'He just shouldn't have held on.'

Except that Patrick was not really holding on. In a nauseating society, he was merely hanging on to the branches of that tree of life which someone else called 'Great Expectations'.

All Lights Off

FRÉDÉRIC FAJARDIE

Tous feux éteints

C'était en 1976, l'an III[1] des années de crise. Le rêve d'un monde plus juste commençait à battre de l'aile: dans l'ombre, les fossoyeurs de l'espérance affûtaient leurs longs couteaux, qu'ils fussent politiciens sociaux-démocrates ou directeur d'un quotidien soi-disant «gauchiste». Les grandes écoles[2] déversaient leurs promotions de fieffés salopards, chiens de garde du Kapital[3] qui devaient «mettre à la raison» la «canaille ouvrière», la «masse de manœuvre immigrée» et transformer les purs produits d'une université critique en intellectuels déclassés, isolés et désespérés. Les charognes de la pub s'apprêtaient à entrer sur la scène de l'Histoire, les crevures du patronat devenaient oublieuses des petites suées de la Libération[4] ou de Mai 68.[5]

Le tourniquet de la démobilisation tournait à plein régime: à quoi bon être solidaire des Chiliens, des Palestiniens ou des derniers Indiens d'Amérique? Chacun pour soi, comme en 40: Giscard[6] n'a-t-il point le charisme de Daladier?[7]

Joachim Dioudonna était une sympathique fripouille.

A sa naissance, l'été 1944, les fées ne s'étaient pas penchées sur son berceau. Pas de fées mais toute une troupe de héros de la vingt-cinquième heure armée de ciseaux et de tondeuses. Une troupe qui cracha sur le nourrisson et «mit la boule à zéro» à la jeune maman coupable d'avoir succombé au charme d'un soldat du roi de Prusse, un pauvre grifton[8] de la Wehrmacht en pleine déconfiture.

«Fils de boche», dans les années cinquante, cela vous avait la saveur de «fils de Rital» dans les années vingt ou «fils de Polack» dans les années trente: il faut bien un exutoire à la haine que les cons portent en eux comme la nuée porte l'orage.

Exclu plus que marginalisé, Joachim trouva sa voie peu après

All Lights Off

It was in 1976, year III of the crisis years. The dream of a fairer world was beginning to crumble: in the shadows, those who were going to bury hope were sharpening their long knives, be they social-democrat politicians or editor of a so-called 'leftist' newspaper. The *grandes écoles* were disgorging their output of consummate bastards, guard-dogs of Das Kapital, who were to 'bring to their senses' the 'working-class rabble', the 'immigrant work-force', and to transform the pure products of a critical university into socially outcast, isolated and hopeless intellectuals. The publicity vultures were getting ready to come on to the stage of History, the damned employers were becoming forgetful of those moments of angst of the Liberation or May '68.

The turnstile of demobilization was spinning round: what was the point of showing solidarity with the Chileans, the Palestinians, or the last American Indians? Every man for himself, as in 1940: does not Giscard have all the charisma of Daladier?

Joachim Dioudonna was a pleasant enough rogue.

When he was born, in the summer of 1944, the fairies had not leant over his crib. No fairies but a whole troop of heroes from the twenty-fifth-hour army of scissors and clippers. A troop that spat on the infant and 'shaved the hair' of the young mother, found guilty of giving in to the charms of a soldier of the King of Prussia, a poor squaddie of the Wehrmacht, which was in total defeat.

'Son of a Hun' in the fifties had the same ring as 'son of an Eyetie' in the twenties or 'son of a Polack' in the thirties: there has to be an outlet for the hatred that stupid bastards have inside them as a cloud carries a storm.

Excluded rather than marginalized, Joachim found his way in life

ses vingt ans. Pendant douze années d'un parcours bref mais
étincelant, il allait donner des cauchemars à tous les flics du
Calvados.[9]

Lorsque l'automne s'apprête à céder le pas à l'hiver, le Calvados est
une bien belle région. La brume s'attarde sur les herbages mouillés,
le givre étincelle sous la caresse d'un pâle soleil, une odeur de
pommes flotte sur tout le département. Une odeur de pommes
fortement alcoolisée . . .

Depuis Mendès France,[10] il devient difficile de faire «bouillir la
goûte» : attirés par l'odeur de la distillation, des flics et des agents du
fisc traquent les serpentins de cuivre des alambics. Non que l'État
réprime l'alcoolisme mais plutôt la volonté, pour celui-ci, de taxer les
alcools. D'où la fin d'une liberté ancestrale: produire sa propre gnole
avec ses propres fruits.

Cependant, l'oppression engendrant la résistance, l'auteur de ces
lignes peut témoigner que les nouveaux gabelous[11] sont des caves:
lorsque cent cinquante mètres de tuyaux souterrains débouchent
dans une prairie battue par les vents, le premier agent du fisc qui
sentira la gnole en distillation gagnera le «nez d'or» du ministère
des Finances!

Mais reste le transport . . .

Et c'est ici que Joachim entrait en scène avec son break DS 19[12]
au moteur gonflé par tous les garagistes du pays portés sur le calva.
Chauffeur hors pair, Joachim avait un autre don: rouler à 100 km/h
sur des départementales TOUS FEUX ÉTEINTS. A côté de cela, Prost[13]
dans sa F 1 vous a un petit air de travelo enfourchant un balai de
sorcière . . .

Douze ans de rodéos, de flics trépignant de rage ou pleurant dans
leurs talkies-walkies avant ce barrage de fourgons, en 1976, près de la
Croix-d'Heuland et Joachim, royal, choisissant d'entrer dans la
légende en percutant volontairement un platane à 120 à l'heure pour
être aussitôt incinéré par l'incendie de cent cinquante litres de gnole
pure . . .

Fin d'un monde? Qu'on se rassure, mais . . . «Silence, le R.P.R.[14]
guette vos confidences!»

shortly after he turned twenty. For twelve years of a short but glittering career he was to give nightmares to all the coppers in Calvados.

When autumn gets ready to give way to winter, Calvados is a most beautiful region. The mist lingers over the damp pastures, the frost sparkles beneath the embrace of a pale sun, a fragrance of apples floats throughout the *département*. A very alcoholic fragrance of apples . . .

Since Mendès France, it has become very difficult to 'make oneself a drop of the hard stuff': attracted by the smell of distillation, coppers and inspectors from the Tax Office track down the copper coils of the stills. Not that the State curbs alcoholism: it is more that it has a desire to collect a tax on spirits. Hence the end of an ancestral freedom: making one's own hooch from one's own fruit.

Yet, since suppression begets resistance, the author of these lines can bear witness to the fact that the new customs officers are cellars: when one hundred and fifty metres of underground pipes come out into a wind-beaten meadow, the first inspector from the Tax Office who smells the hooch being distilled will win the 'golden nose award' from the Treasury!

But there is still the matter of transport . . .

And that is where Joachim came on the scene with his DS19 estate car whose engine had been souped up by every garage mechanic in the district who was keen on calvados. A driver who knew no equal, Joachim had another gift: driving at 100 km per hour on the secondary roads WITH ALL LIGHTS OFF. Beside that, Prost in his Formula 1 looks as ridiculous as a drag-queen sitting astride a witch's broomstick . . .

Twelve years of free-for-all, of coppers stamping their feet with rage or weeping into their walkie-talkies until that barrage of lorries, in 1976, near the Croix-d'Heuland, when Joachim, majestic, chose to become the stuff of legend by deliberately driving into a plane tree at 120 km per hour in order to be instantly incinerated by the fire from 150 litres of pure hooch . . .

The end of a world? Not to worry, but . . . 'Quiet, the RPR is listening to your secrets!'

David

JEAN-MARIE-GUSTAVE LE CLÉZIO

David

Quelquefois, il croit que la rue est à lui. C'est le seul endroit qu'il aime, vraiment, surtout au lever du jour, quand il n'y a encore personne, et que les voitures sont froides. David voudrait que ce soit toujours comme cela, avec le ciel clair au-dessus des maisons sombres, et le silence, le grand silence, qu'on croirait descendu du ciel pour apaiser la terre. Mais est-ce qu'il y a des anges? Autrefois sa mère lui racontait de longues histoires où il y avait des anges aux grandes ailes de lumière, qui planaient dans le ciel au-dessus de la ville, et descendaient pour porter secours à ceux qui en avaient besoin, et elle disait qu'on savait que l'ange était là quand on sentait sur son cou un passage de vent, rapide et léger comme un souffle qui vous faisait frissonner. Son frère Édouard se moquait de lui parce qu'il croyait ces histoires, et il disait que les anges, ça n'existait pas, qu'il n'y avait rien d'autre dans le ciel que des avions. Et les nuages? Mais pourquoi les nuages prouvaient l'existence des anges? David ne s'en souvient plus, et il a beau faire des efforts, rien ne lui revient.

Mais le matin, maintenant, c'est libre, trop libre, parce qu'il n'y a plus rien, plus personne qui attend. Pourtant il voudrait que cela ne cesse jamais, parce que c'est après que c'est terrible, après, quand le jour est vraiment commencé, et que roulent les voitures, les cars, les motos, et que marchent tous les gens, au visage si dur. Où vont-ils? Que veulent-ils? David préfère penser aux anges, à ceux qui volent si haut qu'ils ne voient même plus la terre, seulement le tapis blanc des nuages qui glisse lentement sous leurs ailes. Mais il faut que le ciel soit toujours du matin, très grand, et pur, parce que c'est l'instant où les anges doivent pouvoir planer longtemps, sans risquer de rencontrer un avion.

La rue, à six heures du matin, est belle et calme. Dès qu'il a

David

Sometimes, he thinks that the street is his. It is the only place that he loves, truly loves, especially at daybreak, when there is still no one about, and when the cars are cold. David would like it always to be like that, with the bright sky above the dark houses, and the silence, the great silence, which one might think had come down from the sky to calm the earth. But do angels exist? In the past his mother told him long stories in which there were angels with great wings of light, who hovered in the sky above the town, and came down togive help to those who needed it, and she said that you knew when there was an angel present when you felt a draught of wind on your neck, as fast and as light as a puff of air that made you shiver. His brother Édouard laughed at him because he believed these stories, and he said that angels didn't exist, that there was nothing in the sky other than aeroplanes. And what about clouds? But why did clouds prove the existence of angels? David can no longer remember, and it is pointless him trying, for nothing comes back to him.

But now in the morning, it is free, too free, because there is nothing there any more, no one waiting any more. Yet he would like it always to be like this because it is afterwards that it is awful, afterwards, when the day has truly begun, and when the cars, the coaches and the motor-bikes are driving past, and when all the people, with such stony faces, are walking along. Where are they going? What do they want? David prefers to think about angels, about those who fly so high they can no longer even see the earth, only the white carpet of clouds which slides slowly beneath their wings. But it must always be a morning sky, very wide and pure, because that is when the angels must be able to glide for a long time, without the chance of them meeting an aeroplane.

At six o'clock in the morning the street is beautiful and calm. As

refermé la porte de l'appartement, et mis le cordon où est suspendue la clé autour de son cou, et remonté la fermeture à glissière de son blouson de plastique bleu, David se lance dans la rue. Il court entre les voitures arrêtées, il remonte les volées d'escaliers, il s'arrête au centre de la placette, le cœur battant, comme si quelqu'un le suivait. Il n'y a personne, et le jour se lève à peine, éclaircissant le ciel gris, tandis que les maisons sont encore sombres, volets clos, fermées dans le sommeil frileux du matin. Il y a des pigeons, déjà, qui s'envolent devant David dans un grand froissement d'ailes. Ils vont sur les rebords des toits, ils roucoulent. Il n'y a pas encore de grondements de moteurs, pas encore de voix d'hommes.

David marche jusqu'à la porte de l'école, sans même s'en rendre compte. C'est une vilaine bâtisse de ciment gris qui s'est insinuée entre les vieilles maisons de pierre, et David regarde la porte peinte en vert sombre, où les pieds des enfants ont laissé des meurtrissures, vers le bas. Mais il n'est peut-être pas venu par hasard; simplement il veut la regarder encore une fois, la porte, et aussi le mur avec ses graffiti, l'escalier taché de chewing-gum, les vieilles fenêtres crasseuses bouchées par le grillage. Il veut regarder tout, et l'idée que c'est pour la dernière fois fait battre son cœur plus vite, comme si déjà tout était changé, et qu'il était chassé, poursuivi. C'est la dernière fois, la dernière fois, c'est ce qu'il pense, et cela tourne dans sa tête jusqu'au vertige. Il ne l'a dit à personne, ni à sa mère, mais maintenant, c'est sûr, tout est achevé.

Il reste tout de même longtemps là, assis sur les marches du petit escalier qui conduit à la porte, jusqu'à ce que le bruit de l'arroseur le tire de sa rêverie. L'eau jaillit du tuyau en faisant des déchirures et des détonations, ruisselle le long des ruelles. Le jet fait résonner les carrosseries des voitures arrêtées, chasse les ordures le long des caniveaux. David se lève, il s'éloigne de l'école, il commence la traversée de la ville.

Au-delà de la grande avenue, c'est la ville nouvelle, mystérieuse, dangereuse. Il y est allé déjà, avec son frère Édouard, il se souvient de tout, des magasins, des grands immeubles debout devant leurs aires goudronnées, les réverbères plus haut que les arbres, qui font la nuit leur lumière orangée, éblouissante.

soon as he has closed the door of his flat behind him, and put round his neck the string on which the key hangs, and pulled up the zip fastening of his blue plastic jacket, David dashes into the street. He runs between the stationary cars, he climbs up the flights of stairs, he stops in the middle of the little square, his heart beating, as though someone were following him. There is no one, and dawn has hardly broken, lighting up the grey sky, whilst the houses are still dark, shut up in the shivery sleep of the morning, their shutters closed. Some pigeons are already about, flying off in front of him with a loud rustling of wings. They go to the edges of the roofs and coo. There is still no rumbling of cars, nor the sound of men's voices.

David walks up to the school door, without even realizing it. It is an ugly building in grey cement that has crept in between the old stone houses, and David looks at the door, painted dark green, on which the children's feet have left scuff marks, towards the bottom. But he perhaps did not arrive by chance; quite simply, he wants to look at it once more, the door, and also the wall with its graffiti, the staircase stained by chewing-gum, the filthy old windows blocked off with wire mesh. He wants to look at everything, and the thought that it is for the last time makes his heart beat more quickly, as if everything had already changed, and he had been chased away, pursued. It is the last time, the last time, that's what he is thinking, and the idea spins in his head until he becomes dizzy. He has not told anyone, not even his mother, but now, for certain, everything is over.

All the same, he stays there a long time, sitting on the steps of the small staircase which leads to the door, until the sound of the sprinkler wakens him from his reverie. The water is gushing out of the pipe, splitting it open and causing explosions, streaming along the alleyways. The jet makes the bodies of the stationary cars ring out, chases the rubbish along the gutters. David gets up, walks away from the school, begins to cross the town.

Beyond the wide avenue is the new town, mysterious and dangerous. He has already been there, with his brother Édouard, he remembers everything, the shops, the large blocks of flats which stand in front of their tarred areas, the street lamps which are taller than the trees and which at night give off their orangey, dazzling

Ce sont les endroits où l'on ne va pas, dont l'on ne sait rien. Les endroits où l'on se perd.

La ville est grande, si grande qu'on n'en voit jamais la fin. Peut-être qu'on pourrait marcher des jours et des jours le long de la même avenue, et la nuit viendrait, et le soleil se lèverait, et on marcherait toujours le long des murs, on traverserait des rues, des parkings, des esplanades, et on verrait toujours miroiter à l'horizon, comme un mirage, les glaces et les phares des autos.

C'est cela, partir pour ne jamais revenir. Le cœur de David se serre un peu, parce qu'il se souvient des paroles de son frère Édouard, avant qu'il ne parte: «Un jour, je m'en irai, et jamais plus vous ne me reverrez.» Il avait dit cela sans forfanterie, mais avec le regard si plein de sombre désespoir que David était allé se cacher dans l'alcôve pour pleurer. C'est toujours terrible de dire les choses, et puis de les faire.

Aujourd'hui, ça n'est pas un jour comme un autre. La lumière de l'été est venue, pour la première fois, sur les façades des maisons, sur les carrosseries des voitures. Elle fait des étoiles partout, brûlantes pour les yeux, et malgré sa crainte et ses doutes, David se sent tout de même content d'être dans la rue. C'est pour cela qu'il est parti de l'appartement, très tôt, dès que sa mère a refermé la porte pour aller travailler, il est sorti sans même manger le bout de pain beurré qu'elle avait laissé sur la table, il a dévalé les escaliers, et il est sorti, en courant, avec la clé qui battait sur sa poitrine. C'est pour cela, et aussi à cause de son frère Édouard, parce qu'il y a pensé toute la nuit, enfin, une bonne partie de la nuit, avant de dormir.

«Je m'en irai très loin, et je ne reviendrai jamais.» C'est ce que son frère Édouard avait dit, mais il avait attendu presque un an avant de le faire. Sa mère croyait qu'il n'y pensait plus, et tout le monde – enfin, ceux qui l'avaient entendu dire cela – pensait la même chose, mais David, lui, n'avait pas oublié. Il y pensait tous les jours, et la nuit aussi, mais il ne disait rien. D'ailleurs cela n'aurait servi à rien de dire: «Quand est-ce que tu vas partir pour toujours?» parce que son frère Édouard aurait sûrement haussé les épaules sans répondre. Peut-être qu'il n'en savait rien à ce moment-là.

light. These are places you do not go; about which you know nothing. The places where you get lost.

The town is big, so big that you never see the end of it. Perhaps you could walk for days and days along the same avenue, and night would come, and the sun would rise, and you would still be walking alongside the walls, you would be crossing streets, car parks, esplanades, and you would still see shimmering on the horizon like a mirage the windows and the headlights of the cars.

That was it, leave never to return. David felt a pang of anguish because he remembered his brother Édouard's words, before he left: 'One day, I shall go, and you will never see me again.' He had said that without bragging, but with a look on his face that was so full of dark despair that David had gone and hidden in the alcove to cry. It's always terrible saying things and then doing them.

Today is not a day like any other. The summer light has fallen, for the first time, on the fronts of the houses, on the bodies of the cars. It is making stars everywhere, with reflections that burn your eyes, and yet despite his fear and his doubts David feels happy to be in the street. That is why he left the flat, very early, as soon as his mother closed the door to go to work, why he left without even eating the bit of buttered bread that she had left on the table, tore down the stairs, and ran out, with the key beating against his chest. That is why, and also because of his brother Édouard, because he had thought about it all night, well, a good part of the night, before going to sleep.

'I'll go a long, long way away, and I'll never return.' That is what his brother Édouard had said, but he had waited almost a year before doing it. His mother believed that he was not thinking about it any more, and everyone – well, those who had heard him say it – thought the same thing, but, for his part, David had not forgotten. He thought about it every day, and at night as well, but he said nothing. Besides there would have been no point in saying: 'When are you going to leave for good?' because his brother Édouard would certainly have shrugged his shoulders without replying. Perhaps he knew nothing about it at that time.

C'était un jour comme aujourd'hui, David s'en souvient très bien. Il y avait le même soleil dans le ciel bleu, et les rues de la vieille ville étaient propres et vides, comme après la pluie, parce que l'arroseur public venait de passer. Mais c'était très vide et très effrayant, et la lumière qui brillait sur les fenêtres, en haut des maisons, et les roucoulements des pigeons, et les voix des enfants qu'on entendait, qui s'appelaient d'une maison à l'autre, dans le dédale des ruelles encore obscures, et même le calme et le silence du matin étaient terribles, parce que David et sa mère n'avaient pas dormi cette nuit-là, à attendre qu'il revienne, à guetter les coups qu'il frappait à la porte, toujours les mêmes coups: tap-tap-tap, tap-tap. Ensuite, comme c'était un dimanche et que sa mère n'allait pas travailler, il y avait tellement d'angoisse dans le petit appartement que David n'avait pas pu le supporter, et il était sorti tout le jour, marchant à travers les rues, allant de maison en maison, pour chercher un signe, entendre une voix, jusque dans les jardins publics, jusque sur la plage. Les mouettes s'étaient envolées tandis qu'il marchait le long du rivage, se reposant un peu plus loin, piaillant parce qu'elles n'aimaient pas qu'on les dérange.

Mais David ne veut pas trop penser à ce jour-là, parce qu'il sait que l'angoisse va peut-être revenir, et il pense alors à sa mère, assise sur la chaise devant la fenêtre, attendant aussi immobile et lourde qu'une statue. Il s'assoit sur un banc de la placette, il regarde les gens qui commencent à bouger, et les enfants qui courent en criant, avant l'ouverture de l'école.

C'est dur d'être seul quand on est petit. David pense à son frère Édouard, il se souvient de lui maintenant avec netteté, comme s'il était parti avant-hier. Lui avait quatorze ans, il venait d'avoir quatorze ans quand c'est arrivé, tandis que David a à peine neuf ans. C'est trop petit pour partir, c'est peut-être pour cela que son frère Édouard n'a pas voulu de lui. A neuf ans, est-ce qu'on sait courir, est-ce qu'on sait se battre, gagner sa vie, est-ce qu'on sait ne pas se? perdre? Pourtant, un jour ils s'étaient battus dans l'appartement, à propos de quoi? Il ne sait plus, mais ils s'étaient battus pour de vrai, et avant de l'immobiliser avec une clé au cou, son frère Édouard était tombé, c'était David qui l'avait fait tomber en lui faisant un

It was a day like today, David remembered it very well. There was the same sun in the blue sky, and the streets of the old town were clean and empty, like after the rain, because the municipal sprinkler had just been by. But it was very empty and very frightening, and the light which shone on the windows, on the tops of the houses, and the cooing of the pigeons, and the voices of the children that could be heard, calling from one house to another, in the labyrinth of still-dark alleys, and even the calm and the silence of the morning, were frightening, because David and his mother had not slept that night, waiting for him to come back, listening out for the knocks on the door, always the same knocks: tap-tap-tap, tap-tap. Then, as it was a Sunday and his mother was not going to work, there was so much anguish in the little flat that David had not been able to put up with it, and he had been out all day, walking through the streets, going from house to house, to look for a clue, to hear a voice, as far as the parks, as far as the beach. The seagulls had flown up as he walked along the bank, coming to rest a little further away, squawking because they did not like to be disturbed.

But David does not want to think too much about that day, because he knows that the anguish will perhaps return, and he then thinks about his mother, sitting on the chair by the window, waiting, as motionless and heavy as a statue. He sits on a bench in the small square, he looks at the people who are beginning to move around, and the children who run as they shout, before school opens.

It is hard to be alone when you are small. David thinks of his brother Édouard, he remembers him with clarity now, as if he had left the day before yesterday. *He* was fourteen, he had just turned fourteen when it happened, whereas David was barely nine. It is too young to leave, that is perhaps why his brother Édouard did not want him around. At nine, can you run, can you fight, earn your living, do you know how not to get lost? Yet one day they had fought in the flat, but what about? He no longer knew but they really had fought, and before stopping him with a neck-hold, his brother Édouard had fallen, it was David who had made him fall by tripping him,

croc-en-jambe, et son frère avait dit, en soufflant un peu: «Tu sais bien te battre, toi, pour un petit.» David s'en souvient très bien.

Où est-il maintenant? David pense si fort à lui qu'il sent son cœur cogner à grands coups dans sa poitrine. Est-il possible qu'il ne l'entende pas, là où il est, qu'il ne sente pas sur lui le regard qui l'appelle? Mais il est peut-être au bout de la ville, plus loin encore, au-delà des boulevards et des avenues qui font comme des fossés infranchissables, de l'autre côté des falaises blanches des grands immeubles, perdu, abandonné. C'est à cause de l'argent qu'il est parti, parce que sa mère ne voulait rien lui donner, parce qu'elle lui prenait ses gains d'apprenti-mécanicien, et qu'il n'y avait jamais d'argent pour aller au cinéma, pour jouer au football, pour acheter des glaces ou jouer aux billards électriques dans les cafés.

L'argent est sale, David le déteste, et il déteste son frère Édouard d'être parti à cause de cela. L'argent est laid, et David le méprise. L'autre jour, devant son ami Hoceddine, David a jeté une pièce de monnaie dans un trou du trottoir, comme cela, pour le plaisir. Mais Hoceddine lui a dit qu'il était fou, et il a cherché à repêcher la pièce avec une baguette, sans y arriver. Quand il aura de l'argent David pense qu'il le jettera par terre, ou dans la mer, pour que personne ne le trouve. Lui, il n'a besoin de rien. Quand il a faim, dans la rue, il rôde autour des épiceries, et il prend ce qu'il peut, une pomme, ou une tomate, et il se sauve très vite à travers les ruelles. Comme il est petit, il peut entrer dans des tas de cachettes, des soupiraux, des dessous d'escaliers, des réduits de poubelle, des coins de porte. Personne ne peut le prendre. Il se sauve très loin, et il mange le fruit lentement, sans se salir. Il jette les peaux et les graines dans un caniveau. Il aime surtout les tomates, ça a toujours étonné son frère Édouard, c'est même comme ça qu'il l'avait surnommé, autrefois, «Tomate», mais sans méchanceté, peut-être même que dans le fond il l'admirait pour ça, c'était la seule chose qu'il ne pouvait pas faire.

Si, il aimait bien son nom, aussi, ce nom de David. C'était le nom de leur père, avant qu'il soit mort dans un accident de camion, il s'appelait David Mathis, mais lui était si jeune qu'il ne s'en souvenait même plus. Et leur mère ne voulait jamais leur parler de leur père, sauf pour dire quelquefois qu'il était mort sans rien lui laisser, parce

and his brother had said, breathing a little heavily: 'For a little one you don't half know how to fight.' David remembers it very well.

Where is he now? David thinks so hard about him that he can feel his heart pounding in his chest. Is it possible that he cannot hear him, where he is, that he cannot feel on him the look that is calling him? But he is perhaps at the edge of the town, even further, beyond the boulevards and the avenues which are like uncrossable ditches, on the other side of the white cliffs that are the large blocks of flats, lost, abandoned. It was because of money that he left, because his mother would not give him any, because she took his pay as an apprentice mechanic, and because there was never any money to go to the cinema, to play football, to buy ice-creams or to play the pinball machines in the cafés.

Money is dirty, David hates it, and he hates his brother Édouard for leaving because of it. Money is ugly, and David scorns it. The other day, in front of his friend Hoceddine, David threw a coin into a hole in the pavement, for no reason at all, for pleasure. But Hoceddine told him that he was mad, and he tried to fish the coin out with a stick, without success. When he has money David thinks that he will throw it on the ground, or in the sea, so that no one can find it. He doesn't need anything. When he is hungry, in the street, he loiters around the grocery shops, he takes what he can, an apple, or a tomato, and he runs away very quickly through the alleys. Since he is small, he can get into piles of hiding places, basement windows, spaces underneath stairs, dustbin cupboards, behind doors. No one can catch him. He runs a long way away and he eats the fruit slowly, without getting dirty. He throws the skins and the pips into a gutter. He especially likes tomatoes, which always astonished his brother Édouard, and it was even for that reason that he had nicknamed him 'Tomato' in the past, but not maliciously, perhaps even because deep down he admired him for that, it was the only thing that he could not do.

It is true, he also liked his name greatly, this name of David. It was their father's name, before he died in a lorry accident, he was called David Mathis, but he was so young that he could not even remember. And their mother never wanted to talk to them about their father, except to say sometimes that he had died without

qu'elle avait été obligée alors de commencer ce travail de femme
de ménage pour nourrir ses deux enfants. Mais son frère Édouard
devait se souvenir de lui, parce qu'il avait six ou sept ans quand son
père était mort, alors peut-être pour cela, quelquefois, il avait une
drôle de voix, et son regard était troublé, quand il répétait son nom:
«David . . . David . . .»

Quand il avance dans la grande avenue, le bruit des voitures et
des camions est tout d'un coup terrible, insupportable. Le soleil brille
fort dans le ciel, jetant des éclairs sur les carrosseries, éclairant les
hautes façades des immeubles blancs. Il y a des gens qui marchent
sur le trottoir, mais ce ne sont pas des gens pauvres comme dans la
vieille ville, arabes, juifs, étrangers vêtus de vieux vêtements gris et
bleus, ici ce sont des gens que David ne connaît pas, très grands, très
forts. David est content d'être petit, parce que personne ne semble le
voir, personne ne peut remarquer ses pieds nus dans des chaussures
de caoutchouc, ni son pantalon élimé aux genoux, ni surtout son
visage maigre et pâle, ses yeux sombres. Pendant un instant, il veut
retourner en arrière pendant qu'il en est encore temps, et sa main
machinalement serre la clé qui pend autour de son cou.

Mais toujours, quand il a peur de quelque chose, il pense à
l'histoire que sa mère lui a racontée, celle du jeune berger qui avait
tué un géant, d'une seule pierre ronde lancée avec sa fronde, quand
tous les soldats, et même le grand roi étaient terrifiés.[1] David aime
cette histoire, et son frère Édouard l'aime aussi, et c'est pour cela
peut-être qu'il répétait comme cela son nom, comme s'il y avait
quelque chose de surnaturel dans les syllabes du nom. Autrefois,
avec lui, il n'aurait pas eu peur de marcher ici, dans cette rue dont
on ne voit pas la fin. Mais aujourd'hui, ça n'est pas pareil, parce
qu'il sait que son frère Édouard a marché ici, avant de disparaître. Il
le sait au fond de lui-même, mieux que s'il voyait ses traces sur le
ciment du trottoir. Par là, il est venu, puis il a disparu, pour toujours.
David voudrait oublier le sens de ces mots «pour toujours», parce
qu'ils lui font mal, ils rongent l'intérieur de son corps, de son ventre.

Mais il faut faire attention aux gens, aux passants, qui avancent,
avancent aveuglément. Le soleil est haut dans le ciel sans nuage, les
immeubles blancs resplendissent. Jamais David n'avait vu tant de

leaving her anything, because she had been obliged then to begin this work as a cleaning lady in order to feed her two children. But his brother Édouard must remember him because he was six or seven when his father died, so that was perhaps the reason why sometimes he had a funny voice and his face looked troubled when he repeated his name: 'David . . . David . . .'

When he came to the wide avenue, the noise of the cars and the lorries was suddenly awful, unbearable. The sun shone brightly in the sky, casting shafts of light on to the car bodies, lighting up the tall fronts of the white blocks of flats. There were people walking on the pavement, but they were not poor people like in the old town, Arabs, Jews, foreigners dressed in old grey and blue clothes, here were people David did not know, very tall, very strong. David was happy to be small, because no one seemed to see him, no one could notice his bare feet in rubber shoes, nor his trousers that were worn at the knees, especially not his thin, pale face, his dark eyes. For a moment, he wanted to turn round and go back while there was still time, and his hand automatically squeezed the key hanging around his neck.

But, when he is afraid of something, he always thinks about the story that his mother told him, that of the young shepherd who had killed a giant, with a single round stone cast from his sling, when all the soldiers and even the great king were terrified. David likes that story, and his brother Édouard likes it also, and that is perhaps why he repeated his name in that way, as if there were something supernatural in the syllables of the name. In the past, with him, he would not have been afraid to walk here, in this street whose end you could not see. But today it is not the same, because he knows that his brother Édouard walked here, before disappearing. He knows it deep down, better than if he saw his footprints in the cement of the pavement. He came down there, then he disappeared, for ever. David would like to forget the meaning of those words 'for ever', because they hurt him, they gnaw at the inside of his body, of his stomach.

But he must watch out for those people, those passers-by, who come towards him, who come blindly towards him. The sun is high in the cloudless sky, the white blocks of flats are gleaming. David

gens, tous inconnus, et des vitrines, des restaurants, des cafés.
Son frère Édouard est venu par là, parce que c'était l'argent qu'il
voulait, il voulait conquérir l'argent. Dans les rues sombres, dans
l'appartement, dans les couloirs humides, sans lumière, la pauvreté
est comme un drap mouillé sur la peau, ou pire, comme une peau
sale et moite qu'on ne peut enlever. Mais ici, la lumière et le bruit
brûlent la peau, brûlent les yeux, les grondements des moteurs ar-
rachent les souvenirs. David fait des efforts désespérés pour ne pas
oublier tout cela, il veut se souvenir toujours. Son frère Édouard lui
a dit qu'il valait mieux mourir en prison que de continuer à vivre
là, dans l'appartement obscur. Mais quand David a répété cela à
sa mère, elle s'est mise en colère, et elle a menacé de l'enfermer en
maison de correction, très loin, longtemps. Elle a dit qu'il serait un
voleur, un assassin, et d'autres choses encore que David n'a pas bien
comprises, mais son frère Édouard était très pâle, et il écoutait, et il
y avait une lueur dans ses yeux sombres que David n'aimait pas
voir, et aujourd'hui encore, quand il s'en souvient, son cœur se met
à bondir comme s'il avait peur.

«Lâche, sale dégonflé, cafard, salaud», c'est ce qu'a dit son frère
Édouard le lendemain, et il l'a battu de toutes ses forces, en lui cognant
même sur la figure à coups de poing, jusqu'à ce que David pleure. C'est
pour cela qu'il est parti, donc, pour toujours, parce que David avait parlé
à sa mère, avait dit qu'il valait mieux mourir en prison.

Alors David se sent bien fatigué, tout d'un coup. Il regarde en
arrière, et il voit l'étendue de l'avenue qu'il a parcourue, les immeubles, les autos, les camions, tout cela pareil à ce qui est devant
lui. Où aller? Il va à un arrêt d'autobus, il s'assoit sur le petit banc en
plastique. Par terre, il y a des tickets usagés, jetés par les gens. David
en ramasse un, et quand l'autobus arrive, il fait signe, et il monte
dedans, et il poinçonne l'extrémité intacte du ticket. Il va s'asseoir
au fond, si un contrôleur monte, c'est plus facile de descendre avant
qu'il n'arrive. Autrefois, son frère Édouard l'emmenait au stade
comme cela, le dimanche, et avec l'argent de l'autobus, ils
achetaient de la gomme. David préférait acheter un morceau de
pain chaud dans une boulangerie. Mais aujourd'hui, il n'a même pas
une pièce pour acheter du pain. Il pense à la pièce qu'il a jetée dans

had never seen so many people, all strangers, and shop-windows, restaurants, cafés. His brother Édouard came this way, because it was money that he wanted, he wanted to conquer money. In the dark streets, in the flat, in the damp corridors with no lights, poverty is like a damp sheet against the skin, or worse, like a dirty, sweaty skin that you cannot take off. But here the light and the noise burn your skin, burn your eyes, the rumbling of the cars snatches away memories. David makes desperate efforts not to forget it all, he wants to remember always. His brother Édouard said that it was better to die in prison than to carry on living there, in the dark flat. But when David repeated this to his mother, she became angry, and she threatened to shut him away in a reformatory, a long way away, for a long time. She said that he would be a thief, a murderer, and yet other things that David did not fully understand, but his brother Édouard was very pale, and he listened, and there was a light in his dark eyes that David did not like to see, and even today, when he remembers, his heart begins to leap, as though he were afraid.

'Coward, nasty little chicken, sneak, bastard' is what his brother Édouard said the next day, and he beat him with all his might, even punching him in the face, until David cried. That is why he left, for ever, because David had spoken to his mother, had said that it was better to die in prison.

Then David suddenly feels tired. He looks back, and he sees the length of the avenue that he has come down, the blocks of flats, the cars, the lorries, everything is just like what is ahead of him. Where should he go? He goes to a bus stop and sits on the small plastic seat. On the floor are used tickets, thrown there by people. David picks one up, and when the bus arrives, he puts out his arm, and he gets on, and he punches the unused end of the ticket. He goes and sits down at the back, if an inspector gets on it is easier to get off before he reaches him. In the past, his brother Édouard took him to the stadium in this way, on Sundays, and with the bus money they bought gum. David preferred to buy a piece of warm bread from a baker's. But today he does not have a single coin with which to buy bread. He thinks about the coin he threw down the hole in the

le trou du trottoir, peut-être qu'il aurait dû essayer de la repêcher, aujourd'hui?

L'autobus longe le lit du rio sec, là où il y a de grandes esplanades couvertes de voitures immobiles et des terrains vagues sans herbe. Il y a maintenant de grandes murailles debout au bord du fleuve, avec des milliers de fenêtres toutes identiques, où brille la lumière du soleil, comme si elle ne devait jamais s'arrêter. Loin, loin, mais où est la ville? Où est la mer, où sont les ruelles obscures, les escaliers, les toits où roucoulent les pigeons? Là, il semble qu'il n'y ait jamais rien eu d'autre, jamais rien que ces murailles et ces esplanades, et les terrains vagues où l'herbe ne pousse pas.

Quand l'autobus arrive à son terminus, David recommence à marcher sur l'avenue, le long du rio sec. Puis, voyant un escalier, il descend jusqu'au lit du fleuve, et il s'assoit sur les galets. Le soleil de l'après-midi brûle fort, il dessèche tout. Sur le lit du fleuve, parmi les tas de galets, il y a des branches mortes, des débris de caisse, même un vieux matelas aux ressorts rouillés. David se met à marcher sur les galets entre les débris, comme s'il cherchait quelque chose. C'est bien, ici, on n'entend presque plus les voitures et les camions, sauf de temps en temps un crissement aigu de freins, ou bien un long coup de klaxon qui semble aboyer au-delà des murailles des immeubles. C'est un endroit pour les rats et pour les chiens errants, et David n'a pas peur d'eux. Tout de même, il choisit sur la plage une belle pierre, bien polie et ronde, comme le berger de l'histoire qu'il aime, et il la met dans sa poche. Avec la pierre, il se sent plus rassuré.

Il reste longtemps sur le lit du rio sec. Ici, pour la première fois, il se sent bien, loin de la ville, loin des autos et des camions. La lumière du soleil est moins vive déjà, le ciel se voile de brume. De chaque côté du fleuve, les immeubles se dressent, montagnes de ciment aux fenêtres minuscules pareilles à des trous de serpent. Le ciel est vaste, et David pense aux nuages qu'il aimait regarder autrefois, couché sur le dos dans les jardins, ou bien sur les cailloux de la plage. Alors on voyait la forme des anges, le reflet jaune du soleil sur les plumes de leurs ailes. Il n'en parlait à personne, parce qu'il ne faut parler des anges à personne.

Aujourd'hui, maintenant, peut-être qu'ils vont revenir, parce qu'il

pavement, perhaps he should have tried to fish it out, perhaps he'll do it today?

The bus drives along beside the bed of the dry river, where there are broad esplanades covered in stationary cars and wasteland without grass. There are now high walls standing on the bank of the river, with thousands of completely identical windows, in which the light of the sun is shining, as if it would never stop. Far, far away, but where is the town? Where is the sea, where are the dark alleys, the stairs, the roofs on which the pigeons coo? Here it seems that there has never been anything else, nothing other than these walls and these esplanades, and these wastelands where the grass does not grow.

When the bus reaches its terminus, David begins to walk along the avenue, by the dry river. Then, seeing a stairway, he goes down to the river bed, and he sits on the shingle. The afternoon sun is burning hot, it dries everything up. On the river bed, amongst the piles of shingle, there are dead branches, bits of boxes, even an old mattress with rusty springs. David starts to walk on the shingle among the rubbish, as if he were looking for something. It is pleasant here, one can almost not hear the cars and the lorries any more, except from time to time a shrill screech of brakes, or perhaps a long blast on a horn which seems to bark beyond the walls of the blocks of flats. It is a place for rats and for stray dogs, and David is not afraid of them. All the same he picks a large stone off the beach, well polished and round, like the shepherd in the story he likes, and he puts it in his pocket. He feels more at ease with the stone.

He stays for a long time on the bed of the dry river. Here, for the first time, he feels at peace, far from the town, far from the cars and the lorries. The light from the sun is already less bright, the sky is becoming veiled in mist. On either side of the river stand the blocks of flats, cement mountains with tiny windows like snake's eyes. The sky is vast, and David thinks about the clouds that he used to like to watch in the past, lying on his back in the gardens, or even on the pebbles on the beach. Then, you could see the outline of angels, with the yellow reflection of the sun on the feathers on their wings. He did not speak to anyone about it, because you must not talk about angels to anyone.

Today, now, perhaps they are going to come back, because they

le faudra bien. David se couche sur le lit du fleuve, comme autrefois, et il regarde le ciel éblouissant entre ses paupières serrées. Il regarde, il attend, il veut voir passer quelque chose, quelqu'un, fût-ce un oiseau, pour le suivre du regard, essayer de partir avec lui. Mais le ciel est tout à fait vide, pâle et brillant, il étend son vide qui fait mal à l'intérieur du corps.

Il y a si longtemps que David n'a pas ressenti cela: comme un tourbillon qui grandit au fond de lui, qui écarte toutes les limites, comme si l'on était alors un moucheron minuscule voletant devant un phare allumé. David se souvient maintenant du jour où il avait cherché son frère Édouard, à travers toutes les ruelles, sur les places, au fond des cours, même en l'appelant. C'était un dimanche, il faisait froid, parce que c'était encore le plein hiver. Le ciel était gris, et il y avait du vent. Mais en lui il y avait une inquiétude qui grandissait, à n'en plus pouvoir tenir dans son corps, et son cœur battait, parce que sa mère attendait seule à la maison, immobile et froide sur la chaise, les yeux fixés sur la porte. A la plage il l'avait trouvé, avec d'autres garçons de son âge. Ils étaient assis en rond, protégés des regards et du vent froid par le mur de soutènement de la chaussée. Quand David s'était approché, un des garçons, le plus jeune, qui s'appelait Corto, s'était retourné et il avait dit quelque chose, et les autres étaient restés immobiles, mais son frère Édouard était venu vers lui, et il avait dit d'une voix dure: «Qu'est-ce que tu veux?» Et il avait des yeux étranges et brillants, comme de fièvre, qui faisaient peur. Comme David restait sans répondre, il avait ajouté, de sa voix brutale d'étranger: «C'est elle qui t'envoie pour m'espionner? Fous le camp d'ici, rentre à la maison.» Alors Corto était venu, et c'était un garçon étrange qui avait un visage de fille, et un corps long et mince comme celui d'une fille, mais une voix grave pour son âge, et il avait dit: «Laisse-le. Peut-être qu'il veut jouer au ballon avec nous?»[2] Son frère Édouard était resté immobile, comme s'il ne comprenait pas. Corto avait dit à David, cette fois, avec un sourire bizarre: «Viens, petit, on fait une belle partie de ballon.» Alors machinalement, David avait suivi Corto jusque-là où ils étaient assis en cercle sur les cailloux et il avait vu par terre, au milieu, sur un sac en plastique, un tube de dissolution bouché, et il y avait aussi une feuille de papier buvard

will have to. David lies on the river bed, as he did in the past, and he looks at the dazzling sky through his eyelids that are almost completely closed. He watches, he waits, he wants to see something go by, someone, even if it is a bird, to follow it with his gaze, to try to leave with it. But the sky is totally empty, pale and brilliant, it expands its emptiness, which hurts the inside of his body.

It is so long since David felt this: like a whirlwind that is growing deep inside him, which pushes aside all limits, as if one were a tiny midge fluttering in front of a lighted headlamp. David now remembers the day when he looked for his brother Édouard, in and out of all the alleys, in all the squares, in the depths of court-yards, even by calling to him. It was a Sunday, it was cold, because it was still the middle of winter. The sky was grey, and there was a wind. But within him was an ever-increasing worry, unrestrainable, and his heart was beating, because his mother was waiting alone at home, motionless and cold on the chair, her eyes staring at the door. He had found him on the beach, with other boys of his age. They were sitting in a circle, protected from people's gazes and the cold wind by the retaining wall of the road. When David had approached, one of the boys, the youngest, who was called Corto, had turned round and he had said something, and the others had remained still, but his brother Édouard had come towards him, and he had said harshly: 'What do you want?' And his eyes were strange and shining, as though he had a temperature, and they were frightening. As David stood there without replying, he had added in the harsh voice of a stranger: 'Has she sent you to spy on me? Bugger off out of here, go home.' Then Corto had come, he was a strange boy with a girl's face and a long thin body like that of a girl, but with a voice that was deep for his age, and he had said: 'Leave him. Perhaps he wants to play breathalyzer with us?' His brother Édouard had not moved, as if he did not understand. Corto had said to David, this time with a strange smile on his face: 'Come here, littl'un, we're having a great game of breathalyzer.' Then, mechan-ically, David had followed Corto to where they had been sitting in a circle on the pebbles and he had seen on the ground, in the middle, on a plastic bag, a tube of glue with the top on, and there was also a

pliée en deux, que les garçons se passaient de main en main, et à tour de rôle ils mettaient leur figure dans la feuille et ils respiraient en fermant les yeux, et ils toussaient un peu. Alors Corto avait tendu la feuille pliée à David, et il lui avait dit: «Vas-y, respire un bon coup, tu vas voir les étoiles.» Et dans la feuille de buvard il y avait une grande tache de colle visqueuse, et quand David avait reniflé, l'odeur était entrée au fond de lui d'un seul coup, et lui avait tourné la tête, et il s'était mis à trembler, puis à pleurer, à cause du vide qu'il y avait là, sur la plage, près du mur sale, avec Édouard qui n'était pas rentré à la maison depuis le matin.

Ensuite il s'était passé quelque chose d'étrange, David s'en souvient très bien. Son frère Édouard avait mis le bras autour de lui, et il l'avait aidé à se lever, et à marcher sur la plage, et il avait marché avec lui à travers les rues de la vieille ville, et il était entré dans l'appartement, et sa mère n'avait rien osé dire, ni crier, pourtant il était resté dehors tout le jour sans rentrer même déjeuner, mais il l'avait conduit jusqu'au lit, dans l'alcôve, et il l'avait aidé à se coucher, et après il s'était couché à son tour. Mais ce n'était pas pour dormir, parce que David avait vu ses yeux ouverts qui le regardaient jusqu'au moment où il avait sombré dans le sommeil.

Maintenant, c'est comme cela, le tourbillon revient, creuse son vide dans la tête et dans le corps, et l'on bascule comme si on tombait dans un trou profond. C'est le silence et la solitude qui en sont la cause. David regarde autour de lui, l'étendue de galets poussiéreux, les débris qui jonchent le lit du fleuve, et il sent le poids du silence. Le ciel est très clair, un peu jaune à cause du soleil qui se couche. Personne ne vient, par ici, personne jamais. C'est un endroit seulement pour les rats, et pour les mouches plates qui cherchent leur nourriture parmi les détritus que les hommes ont laissés sur le lit du fleuve.

David aussi a faim. Il pense qu'il n'a rien mangé depuis hier soir, rien bu non plus. Il a soif et faim, mais il ne veut pas retourner vers la vieille ville. Il marche sur les plages de galets jusqu'au cours d'eau qui serpente lentement. L'eau est froide et transparente, et David boit longuement, à genoux sur les galets, le visage tout près de l'eau. D'avoir bu comme cela, il se sent un peu mieux, et il a la force de remonter le lit du fleuve, jusqu'à

sheet of blotting paper folded in two, which the boys were handing
round, and one after the other they put their face to the sheet and they
breathed in, closing their eyes, and they coughed a little. Then Corto
had held the sheet out to David, and he had said to him: 'Go on, take
a deep breath, you're going to see the stars.' And in the folded sheet of
blotting paper there was a large blob of slimy glue, and when David
had breathed in, the smell had gone all the way inside him in one go,
and made him dizzy, and he had begun to tremble, then to cry, because
of the emptiness that there was there, on the beach, near the dirty wall,
with Édouard who had not been back home since the morning.

Then something strange had happened. David remembers it very
well. His brother Édouard had put his arm around him, and he had
helped him to get up, and to walk along the beach, and he had
walked with him through the streets of the old town, and he had
gone into the flat, and his mother had not dared to say anything,
not even to shout, yet he had stayed out all day, without even
coming home for lunch, but he had taken him to bed, in the alcove,
and he had helped him to get into bed, and afterwards he too had
gone to bed. But it was not to sleep, because David had seen his
open eyes looking at him until he had drifted off to sleep.

It is just like that now, the whirlwind is coming back, digging its
emptiness into his head and into his body and he is toppling as if he
were falling into a deep hole. It is silence and loneliness that are the
causes. David looks around him, at the stretch of dusty shingle, the
rubbish which is littering the river bed, and he feels the weight of
the silence. The sky is very bright, a little yellow because of the
setting sun. No one ever comes this way, no one ever. It is a place
reserved for the rats, and for the flat flies which seek their food
amongst the refuse that men have left on the river bed.

David is hungry too. He thinks that he has eaten nothing since yesterday evening, drunk nothing either. He is thirsty and hungry, but
he does not want to go back towards the old town. He walks along
the shingle beaches, as far as the stream which winds its slow course.
The water is cold and clear, and David drinks slowly, kneeling on
the shingle, his face almost touching the water. He feels a little
better after drinking like that, and he has the strength to walk

une rampe d'accès un peu en amont. C'est là que les camions viennent décharger leurs bennes, des pierres, des gravats, de la boue.

David quitte les bords du rio sec, il retourne au milieu des maisons, pour chercher à manger. Les immeubles blancs font une sorte de demi-cercle, encadrant une grande place couverte d'autos arrêtées. Au fond de la place, il y a un centre commercial, avec une large porte sombre. Déjà, les lumières brillent autour de la porte, pour faire croire que la nuit est venue.

David aime bien la nuit. Il n'a pas peur d'elle, mais au contraire, il sait qu'il peut se cacher quand elle est là, comme s'il devenait invisible. Dans le supermarché, il y a beaucoup de lumières. Les gens vont et viennent avec leurs petits chariots de métal. David sait comment il doit faire. C'est son ami Lucas qui le lui a dit, la première fois. Il faut choisir des gens avec qui on va entrer, bien choisir des gens qui ont l'air convenable, avec un jeune enfant peut-être. Le mieux, c'est les grands-parents, qui poussent un chariot avec un bébé dedans. Ils marchent lentement, et ils ne font pas attention à ce qui les entoure, alors on peut entrer avec eux, et faire comme si on était avec eux, tantôt devant, tantôt derrière. Les surveillants ne surveillent pas les grands-parents avec des enfants.

David attend un peu, dans un coin du parking. Il voit une grande voiture noire s'arrêter et en sortent un homme et une femme encore jeunes, accompagnés de toute leur famille, cinq enfants. Il y a trois filles et deux garçons, les filles sont grandes et belles, avec de longs cheveux blond foncé qui tombent en cascade sur leurs épaules, sauf la plus petite, qui a quatre ou cinq ans, et qui a des cheveux bruns. Les deux garçons ont entre douze et quinze ans, ils ressemblent à leur père, ils sont grands et minces, la peau bronzée par le soleil, et leurs cheveux sont châtain. Tous ensemble, ils vont vers la porte du Super. La petite fille s'est installée dans un chariot de métal, et c'est l'aînée qui la pousse, en riant aux éclats. La mère l'appelle, elle crie leurs noms: «Christiane! Isa!» Et les garçons courent après elles et arrêtent le chariot.

David les suit, de loin d'abord, puis il entre avec eux à l'intérieur du Super. Il est si près d'eux qu'il les entend parler, il écoute tout ce qu'ils disent. Les enfants vont par groupes de deux, ils se réunissent,

back up the river bed as far as an access ramp a little further upstream. This is where the lorries come to tip their loads, stones, rubble, mud.

David leaves the banks of the dry river, he goes back to be amongst the houses, to look for something to eat. The white blocks of flats form a sort of semi-circle surrounding a large square covered in parked cars. At the far end of the square, there is a shopping centre, with a wide, dark door. The lights are already shining around the door, to make people think that night has come.

David loves the night. He is not afraid of it, on the contrary, he knows that he can hide when it has fallen, as if he were becoming invisible. There are a lot of lights on in the supermarket. The people are coming and going with their little metal trolleys. David knows what he must do. It was his friend Lucas who had told him, the first time. You have to choose people with whom you are going to go in, carefully choose people who look respectable, with a small child perhaps. The best is grandparents who are pushing a trolley with a baby in it. They walk slowly, and they do not pay attention to what is around them, so you can go in with them, and pretend to be with them, sometimes in front, sometimes behind. The store detectives do not watch grandparents with children.

David waits a little, in a corner of the car park. He sees a big black car stop, and out of it get a man and a woman who are still young, accompanied by their whole family, five children. There are three girls and two boys, the girls are tall and beautiful, with long dark blonde hair which cascades on to their shoulders, except for the smallest, who is four or five and who has brown hair. The two boys are between twelve and fifteen, they look like their father, they are tall and thin, their skin tanned by the sun, and their hair is chestnut brown. They walk towards the supermarket door in a group. The little girl has settled in a metal trolley, and it is the eldest girl who is pushing her, laughing loudly. The mother calls her, she shouts their names: 'Christiane! Isa!' And the boys run after them and stop the trolley.

David follows them, at first from afar, then he goes into the super-market with them. He is so near them that he can hear them talking, he listens to everything they say. The children go off in twos,

ils courent, ils reviennent, ils entourent même David, mais sans le voir, comme s'il n'était qu'une ombre. Ils entraînent leurs parents vers la pâtisserie, et David en profite pour prendre un pain qu'il mange sans se presser, tranche après tranche. Les filles sont belles, et David les regarde avec une attention presque douloureuse. La lumière électrique brille sur leurs cheveux blonds, sur leurs anoraks de plastique bleu ou rouge. La plus grande s'appelle Sonia, elle doit avoir seize ans, et c'est elle surtout que David regarde. Elle est si sûre d'elle, elle parle si bien, avec sa voix chantante, en écartant les mèches qui tombent sur ses joues, qui frôlent ses lèvres. David pense à son frère Édouard, à son visage sombre et dur, à ses yeux noirs qui brûlaient de fièvre, il pense à Corto aussi, sur la plage, à son regard trouble, à son teint pâle, aux cernes bruns qui salissaient son visage, il pense au vent froid sur la plage déserte. Les enfants tournent autour de lui, crient, rient, s'interpellent. David écoute avidement leurs noms qui résonnent: «Alain! Isa! Dino! Sonia! . . .» A un moment, les parents se retournent, ils regardent avec étonnement David qui mange ses tranches de pain, comme s'ils allaient lui dire quelque chose. Mais David se détourne, il s'arrête et les laisse partir, puis il recommence à les suivre, mais de loin. En passant devant le rayon des biscuits, il choisit un paquet de galettes au fromage, et il commence à les grignoter. Mais elles sont trop salées et elles lui donnent soif. Alors il repose le paquet entamé et il prend une boîte de biscuits à la figue, qu'il aime bien. La famille, devant lui, entasse beaucoup de choses sur le chariot, des biscuits, de l'eau minérale, du lait, des sacs de pommes de terre, des paquets de pâtes, du savon. Le chariot est si lourd que ce sont les deux garçons à présent qui le poussent, et la petite fille suce son pouce avec l'air de s'ennuyer.

David pense qu'il aimerait bien les suivre comme ça toute sa vie, jusqu'au bout du monde, jusque chez eux. Le soir, ils rentreraient dans une belle maison claire, entourée d'un frais jardin rempli de fleurs et de saules, et ils mangeraient tous autour d'une grande table, comme celles qu'on voit au cinéma, où il y aurait toutes sortes de mets, et des fruits, et des glaces dans des coupes. Et leurs parents parleraient avec eux, et ils raconteraient tous des histoires, de longues histoires qui les feraient rire aux éclats, et ensuite ce serait l'heure de

they meet up again, they run, they come back, they even surround
David, but without noticing him, as if he were just a ghost. They drag
their parents towards the cake counter, and David takes advantage of
this to pick up a loaf of bread that he eats slowly, slice after slice. The
girls are beautiful, and David looks at them with almost painful attention. The electric light shines on their blonde hair, on their blue or
red plastic anoraks. The oldest is called Sonia, she must be sixteen,
and it is her that David looks at the most. She is so sure of herself, she
talks so well, with her singsong voice, as she pushes back the strands of
hair that fall on her cheeks, which brush against her lips. David thinks
about his brother Édouard, about his dark, hard face, about his black
eyes which were burning with fever, he thinks about Corto as well, on
the beach, about his troubled look, about his pale complexion, about
the brown blotches that dirtied his face, he thinks about the cold wind
on the deserted beach. The children are moving around him, shouting,
laughing, calling to each other. David eagerly listens to their names
which are ringing out: 'Alain! Isa! Dino! Sonia! . . .' At one moment,
the parents turn round, they look in astonishment at David, who is
eating his slices of bread, as if they were going to say something to
him. But David turns away, he stops and lets them go on, then he
begins to follow them again, but at a distance. As he goes past the
biscuit counter, he chooses a packet of cheese biscuits, and he begins
to nibble them. But they are too salty and they make him thirsty. So
he puts down the opened packet and he picks up a box of fig biscuits,
which he adores. In front of him, the family is piling up a lot of things
in the trolley, biscuits, mineral water, milk, bags of potatoes, packets
of pasta, soap. The trolley is so heavy that it is the two boys who are
now pushing it, and the little girl is sucking her thumb, looking bored.

David thinks that he would like to follow them like this all his life,
to the end of the world, to their home. In the evening they would
be going back into a beautiful, light house, surrounded by a cool
garden filled with flowers and willows, and they would all be eating
around a large table, like those you see at the cinema, where there
would be all sorts of dishes, and fruits, and ice-creams in tall dishes.
And their parents would talk to them, and they would all tell
stories, long stories, which would make them laugh loudly, and then

se coucher, d'abord la petite Christiane, et ils lui raconteraient une histoire pour l'endormir, chacun son tour, jusqu'à ce que ses yeux se ferment, puis ils iraient se coucher dans leur lit, chacun aurait un lit pour soi, avec des draps ornés de dessins comme on voit, et la chambre serait grande et peinte en bleu pâle. Et avant de dormir, Sonia viendrait en chemise de nuit, avec ses longs cheveux blonds qui roulent sur ses épaules, et elle lui donnerait un baiser, du bout des lèvres, et il sentirait la chaleur de son cou et le parfum de ses cheveux, juste avant d'entrer dans le sommeil. Ça serait juste comme ça, David peut le voir en fermant les yeux.

Maintenant, ils passent tous devant le rayon des fruits, et ils s'arrêtent pour choisir. David revient au milieu d'eux, il veut telle-ment entendre encore leurs voix, sentir leur parfum. Il s'arrête juste à côté de Sonia, et pour elle il choisit une belle pomme rouge, et il la lui tend. Elle le regarde un peu étonnée, puis elle sourit gentiment et elle lui dit merci, mais elle ne la prend pas. Puis la famille s'éloigne de nouveau, et David mange la pomme lentement, les yeux un peu brouillés de larmes, sans comprendre pourquoi il a envie de pleurer. Il les regarde s'éloigner vers l'autre bout du grand magasin, tourner derrière une montagne de bouteilles de bière. Alors, sans se cacher, il sort du Super, en passant entre les caisses, et il va finir sa pomme dehors, en regardant la nuit qui s'est installée sur le parking.

Il reste là longtemps, assis sur une borne de ciment, près de la sortie du parking, à regarder les voitures allumer leurs phares et partir. Les unes après les autres, elles font claquer leurs portes, et puis elles glissent au loin, elles disparaissent, avec leurs feux rouges et leurs clignotants. Malgré le froid de la nuit, David aime bien voir les autos s'en aller, comme cela, avec leurs lumières et les reflets sur leur carrosserie. Mais il faut faire attention aux policiers, et aux gardiens. Ils ont des voitures noires, parfois des vélomoteurs, et ils tournent lentement sur les parkings à la recherche des voleurs. Tout d'un coup, David voit quelqu'un qui le regarde. C'est un homme grand et fort, au visage brutal, qui est sorti du Super par une porte de service et qui a marché sans bruit sur la chaussée, derrière David. Maintenant, il est là, il le regarde, et à la lumière

it would be time to go to bed, first little Christiane, and one after the other, they would tell her a story to make her go to sleep, until her eyes closed, then they would go to lie down in their own beds, each one would have a bed of their own, with sheets decorated with patterns like you see, and the bedroom would be big and painted in pale blue. And before going to sleep, Sonia, in a night-dress, with her long blonde hair tumbling on her shoulders, would appear and she would give him a kiss, with the tip of her lips, and he would feel the warmth of her neck, and smell the scent of her hair, just before drifting off to sleep. It would be exactly like that, David can see it as he closes his eyes.

Now they are going past the fruit counter, and they stop to make their choice. David comes back into their midst, he so much wants to hear their voices again, to smell their scent. He stops just next to Sonia, and for her he chooses a fine red apple, and he holds it out to her. She looks at him in slight astonishment, then she smiles sweetly and she says thank you to him, but she does not take it. Then the family move away again, and David eats the apple slowly, his eyes slightly misted with tears, not understanding why he wants to cry. He watches them move off to the other end of the large shop, turn behind a mountain of beer bottles. Then, without hiding, he goes out of the supermarket, passing between the tills, and he goes and finishes his apple outside, while watching the night which has settled over the car park.

He stays there for a long time, sitting on a cement boundary stone, near the exit to the car park, watching the cars turn on their head-lights and leave. One after the other, their doors are banged, and then they slide into the distance, they disappear, with their red lights and their indicators. In spite of the cold of the night, David enjoys seeing the cars drive away, as they do, with their lights and the reflections on their bodywork. But he must watch out for policemen, and the security men. They have black cars, sometimes mopeds, and they drive slowly around the car parks looking for thieves. Suddenly David sees someone who is watching him. It is a tall, strong man, with a cruel face, who has come out of the supermarket via a service door and who has walked noiselessly along the road, behind David. He has reached him now, he looks at him and his eyes are shining strangely

de la façade du Super ses yeux brillent bizarrement. Mais ce n'est pas un gardien, ni un policier. Il tient dans sa main un sac de pop-corn, et il appuie de temps en temps sa main sur sa bouche, pour avaler le maïs éclaté, sans cesser de regarder du côté de David, avec ses yeux noirs, très brillants. David le regarde de temps à autre du coin de l'œil, et il le voit qui s'approche, il entend le bruit que fait sa grosse main quand elle fouille dans le sac de pop-corn. Il est tout près, maintenant, et le cœur de David se met à battre très fort, parce qu'il se souvient des histoires qu'on raconte, à l'école, des types fous et obsédés qui enlèvent les enfants pour les tuer. En même temps, la peur l'empêche de bouger, et il reste assis sur la borne de ciment, à regarder droit devant lui le parking presque vide où la lumière des réverbères fait de grandes taches jaunes.

«Tu veux du pop-corn?» Quand David entend la voix de l'homme, il a parlé doucement, mais avec quelque chose qui a trem-blé un peu, comme s'il avait peur, lui aussi, David bondit de la borne et il se met à courir aussi vite qu'il peut vers l'entrée du parking, là où il y a encore des voitures arrêtées. Dès qu'il a passé une voiture, il s'arrête, il s'aplatit sur le sol et il rampe sous les voitures, passant de l'une à l'autre, puis il s'immobilise à nouveau, et il regarde autour de lui. L'homme est là, il a couru derrière lui, mais il est trop gros pour se baisser, il marche à grands pas le long des voitures. David voit ses jambes passer, s'éloigner. Il attend encore un peu, et il rampe en sens inverse. Quand il sort de dessous un camion arrêté, il voit la silhou-ette de l'homme, très loin qui s'éloigne en regardant autour de lui.

Maintenant, David a moins peur, mais il n'ose plus marcher dans la nuit. La plate-forme du camion est recouverte d'une bâche, et David défait un côté, et il se glisse sous la bâche. La tôle est froide, couverte de poussière de ciment. Près de l'habitacle, David trouve de vieilles toiles, et il fait son lit avec elles. La faim, la peur, et toute cette journée passée dehors à marcher l'ont fatigué. Il se couche sur les toiles, et il s'endort en écoutant le bruit des moteurs qui passent sur la route, le long du rio sec. Il pense peut-être encore une fois à son frère Édouard, seul comme lui dans la nuit, ce soir.

Quand l'aube se rompt, avant même qu'il fasse jour, David s'éveille. Le froid de la nuit l'a endolori, et aussi le dur plancher de

in the light from the front of the supermarket. But he is not a security man, or a policeman. He has a bag of popcorn in his hand and from time to time he flattens his hand over his mouth to swallow the puffed-up maize, always looking in David's direction, with his black and very shiny eyes. From time to time David looks at him out of the corner of his eye, and he sees him coming nearer, he hears the noise made by his big hand when it delves into the bag of popcorn. He is now quite close, and David's heart begins to beat very loudly, because he remembers the stories that are told at school about mad, obsessed men who kidnap children in order to kill them. At the same time fear prevents him from moving and he remains seated on the cement boundary stone, looking straight ahead of him at the almost empty car park in which the light from the lamp-posts is making large yellow patches.

'Do you want some popcorn?' When David hears the man's voice, he has spoken softly, but with something which trembles a little, as if he too were afraid. David leaps from the boundary stone, and begins to run as fast as he can towards the car park entrance, where there are still some stationary cars. As soon as he gets past one car, he stops, lies flat on the ground and crawls under the cars, moving from one to another, then he stops again and looks around him. The man is still there, he has run after him, but he is too fat to bend down, he is striding past the cars. David sees his legs go by, move away. He waits a little, and crawls in the opposite direction. When he comes out from under a stationary lorry he sees the silhouette of the man a long way off, as he walks away, looking around him.

David is less afraid now, but he no longer dares to walk in the night. The back of the lorry is covered with a tarpaulin, and David undoes one side, and he slides under the tarpaulin. The metal base is cold, covered in cement dust. Near the driver's end, David finds some old canvas, with which he makes a bed. Hunger, fear, and all that day spent walking outside have made him tired. He lies down on the canvas, and he goes to sleep listening to the sound of engines going past on the road, alongside the dry river. He perhaps thinks again about his brother Édouard, alone like him in the night, tonight.

When dawn breaks, even before it is light, David wakes up. The cold of the night has made him sore, as has the hard floor of the

la plate-forme du camion. Le vent fait claquer la bâche, l'écartant et la rabattant en laissant passer l'air froid et humide, et le gris de l'aube.

David descend du camion, il marche à travers le parking. La grand-route est déserte, encore éclairée par les flaques jaunes des lampadaires. Mais David aime bien cette heure, si tôt que tous les habitants de la ville semblent avoir fui loin dans les collines. Peut-être qu'ils ne reviendront jamais, eux non plus?

Sans se presser, il traverse la route et longe le quai. En bas le rio sec est vaste et silencieux. Le lit de galets s'étend à perte de vue en amont et en aval. Au centre, le mince filet d'eau coule inlassablement, encore sombre, couleur de nuit. David descend la rampe d'accès au fleuve, il marche sur les galets. Il a l'impression que le bruit de ses pas doit réveiller des animaux endormis, de grosses mouches plates, des taons, des rats. Quand il arrive près de l'eau, il s'assoit sur ses talons, il regarde le courant qui passe avec force, lançant ses tourbillons, creusant ses remous.

Peu à peu, la lumière augmente, les galets gris commencent à briller, l'eau devient plus légère, transparente. Il y a une sorte de brume qui monte du lit du fleuve, de sorte qu'à présent David ne voit plus les berges, ni les lampadaires, ni les laides maisons aux fenêtres fermées. Il frissonne, et du bout de la main il touche l'eau, la prend dans ses doigts. Il ne sait pourquoi, il pense tout d'un coup à sa mère qui doit l'attendre dans l'appartement obscur, assise sur une chaise devant la porte. Il voulait revenir avec son frère Édouard, maintenant il sait que c'est pour cela qu'il est parti, et il sait aussi qu'il ne le trouvera pas. Il n'avait pas voulu y penser pour ne pas attirer le mauvais sort, mais il croyait que le hasard le guiderait à travers toutes ces rues, ces boulevards, au milieu de tous ces gens qui savent où ils vont, vers l'endroit qu'il ne savait pas. Il n'a rien trouvé, le hasard n'existe pas. Même s'il cherchait cent ans, il ne pourrait pas le trouver. Il sait cela à présent, sans désespoir, mais comme si quelque chose avait changé au fond de lui, et qu'il ne serait plus jamais le même.

Alors il regarde la lumière venir peu à peu sur le lit du fleuve. Le ciel est pur et froid, la lumière est froide aussi, mais elle fait du bien

lorry. The wind is making the tarpaulin flap noisily, lifting it up and blowing it down, letting in the cold, damp air and the grey light of dawn.

David gets out of the lorry and walks across the car park. The main road is deserted, still lit by the yellow pools from the lamp-posts. But David likes this time, so early that all the inhabitants of the town seem to have fled far away into the hills. Perhaps they will never come back either?

Without hurrying, he crosses the road and walks along the quay. Down below the dry river is vast and silent. The shingle bed stretches as far as the eye can see upstream and downstream. In the middle, the thin trickle of water flows indefatigably, still dark, the colour of night. David goes down the access ramp to the river, he walks along the shingle. It seems to him that the sound of his footsteps must be waking up animals that are still asleep, big flat flies, horseflies, rats. When he gets near the water, he sits on his heels, he watches the current flowing strongly, creating eddies, digging out swirls.

The light is getting gradually brighter, the grey shingle is beginning to shine, the water is becoming clearer, transparent. There is a sort of mist which is rising from the river bed, with the result that David can no longer see the banks, nor the lamp-posts, nor the ugly houses with their closed windows. He shivers, and with the tip of his hand he touches the water, grasps it in his fingers. He does not know why but he suddenly thinks of his mother who must be waiting for him in the dark flat, sitting on a chair by the door. He wanted to return with his brother Édouard, now he knows that is why he left, and he also knows that he will not find him. He had not wanted to think about it in order not to attract bad luck, but he believed that fate would guide him through all those streets, those boulevards, to the midst of all those people who know where they are going, towards the place that he did not know. He has found nothing, fate does not exist. Even if he looked for one hundred years, he would not be able to find him. He now knows that, without despair, but as if something had changed within him, and he would never be the same again.

So he watches the light gradually find its way to the river bed. The sky is clear and cold, the light is cold also, but it does David

à David, elle lui donne de la force. La brume de l'aube a disparu. Maintenant on voit à nouveau les immeubles géants, de chaque côté du fleuve. Le soleil éclaire en blanc leurs façades à l'est, fait briller les grandes vitres derrière lesquelles il n'y a personne.

Quand il a faim, David retourne vers le Super. Il n'y a encore presque personne à cette heure, et la musique nasillarde des haut-parleurs semble résonner à l'intérieur d'une immense grotte vide. A l'intérieur du magasin, la lumière des barres de néon est dure et fixe, elle fait briller les choses et les couleurs. David ne se cache plus. Il n'y a pas de familles, ni d'enfants auxquels il puisse se mêler. Il y a seulement des gens affairés, des vendeurs en blouse blanche, les caissières derrière leurs caisses. David mange des fruits, debout devant l'étalage, une pomme jaune, une banane, du raisin noir. Personne ne fait attention à lui. Il se sent tout petit, presque invisible. Seulement à un moment, une jeune fille qui porte la blouse blanche du magasin le regarde manger, et elle a un drôle de sourire sur son visage, comme si elle le reconnaissait. Mais elle continue à ranger les rayons de nourriture, sans rien dire.

C'est en sortant du Super que David a eu envie de prendre de l'argent. C'est venu comme cela, tout d'un coup, peut-être à cause des longues heures passées à attendre, peut-être à cause de la nuit, ou de la solitude sur les galets du rio sec. Soudain, David a compris pourquoi son frère Édouard ne revenait pas, pourquoi on ne pouvait pas le trouver. C'est devant le magasin de chaussures que cela s'est passé. David s'est souvenu du jour où avec sa mère, il est allé au commissariat de police, et ils ont attendu longtemps, longtemps, avant d'entrer dans le bureau de l'inspecteur. Sa mère ne disait rien, mais l'homme posait des questions avec sa voix douce, et de temps en temps il regardait David dans les yeux, et David s'efforçait de soutenir son regard avec le cœur battant la chamade. Peut-être sa mère savait quelque chose, quelque chose de terrible qu'elle ne voulait pas dire, quelque chose qui était arrivé à son frère Édouard. Elle était si pâle, et muette, et le regard de l'homme assis derrière le bureau de métal était brillant comme du jais, et il essayait de savoir, il posait ses questions avec sa voix douce.

C'est pour cela que David s'est arrêté maintenant devant le grand magasin de chaussures, où il y a cette lumière blanche qui brille sur

good, it gives him strength. The dawn mist has disappeared. You can now see the giant blocks of flats again, on either side of the river. The sun is lighting up their eastern façades in white, bringing a shine to the large windows behind which there is no one.

When he is hungry, David goes back towards the supermarket. There is almost no one there at this time, and the whining music from the loudspeakers seems to be echoing inside a huge empty cave. Inside the shop, the light from the neon strips is harsh and unflickering, it makes things and colours shine. David is not hiding any more. There are no families, nor children with whom he can mix. There are only busy people, shop assistants in white overalls, cashiers behind their tills. David eats some fruit, standing at the display, a yellow apple, a banana, black grapes. No one pays any attention to him. He feels quite small, almost invisible. Just for a moment, a girl wearing the white overall of the shop looks at him eating, and she has a funny smile on her face, as if she recognized him. But she carries on lining the shelves with food, without saying anything.

It is on leaving the supermarket that David wants to take some money. It came to him in a flash, all of a sudden, perhaps because of the long hours spent waiting, perhaps because of the night, or his loneliness on the shingle of the dry river. Suddenly, David realized why his brother Édouard was not coming back, why he couldn't be found. It was outside the shoe shop that this happened. David remembered the day when, with his mother, he went to the police station, and they waited a long time, a very long time, before going into the inspector's office. His mother said nothing but the man asked questions in his soft voice and, from time to time, he looked David straight in the eye, and David forced himself to maintain his gaze, whilst his heart pounded. Perhaps his mother knew something, something terrible that she would not utter, something which had happened to his brother Édouard. She was so pale and silent, and the gaze of the man sitting at the desk was as shiny as jet, and he was trying to find out, he was asking his questions in his soft voice.

That is why David now stops outside the big shoe shop, where there is that white light which shines on the red plastic tiles.

les dalles de plastique rouge. Il fait cela presque machinalement, comme s'il refaisait les gestes que quelqu'un d'autre aurait faits avant lui. Lentement, il longe les allées qui vont vers le bout du magasin. Il passe devant les rangées de chaussures sans les voir, mais il sent l'odeur âcre du cuir et du plastique. Les dalles rouges font une lumière enivrante, la musique douce qui descend du plafond l'écœure un peu. Il n'y a personne dans le grand magasin. Les employées sont debout près de la porte, elles parlent, sans regarder le petit garçon qui se dirige vers le fond du magasin.

La musique douce fait des bruits de voix qui recouvrent tout, des:

Ah ouh, ahwa, wahahou . . .

comme des cris d'oiseaux dans la forêt. Mais David ne fait pas attention à ce qu'ils disent, il avance, en retenant son souffle, vers le bout du magasin, là où il y a la caisse. Personne ne le voit, personne ne pense à lui. Il marche sans faire de bruit entre les rayons de chaussures, bottes, tennis, bottines d'enfant, il avance vers la caisse en tenant serrée dans sa main gauche la pierre ronde qu'il a ramassée sur la plage du fleuve, hier soir. Son cœur bat très fort dans sa poitrine, si fort qu'il lui semble que les coups doivent résonner dans tout le magasin. La lumière des barres de néon est aveuglante, les miroirs sur les murs et sur les piliers renvoient des éclairs fixes. Le sol de plastique rouge est immense et désert, les pieds de David glissent dessus comme sur de la glace. Il pense aux gardiens qui tournent dans les magasins, et sur les parkings, dans leurs autos grises, il pense aux gens méchants qui guettent, avec leurs yeux brillants et féroces. Son cœur bat, bat, et la sueur mouille son front, les paumes de ses mains. Là-bas, au bout du magasin, il la voit bien, énorme et éclairée par ses lampes, la caisse est immobile, et il avance vers elle, vers l'endroit où il va enfin pouvoir savoir, rencontrer enfin son frère Édouard, l'endroit brûlant où est caché le message secret. Maintenant, il le comprend, il le sait bien, c'est pour cela qu'il est parti de l'appartement hier matin, avec la clé attachée autour de son cou: pour arriver jusqu'ici, à l'endroit où il va pouvoir commencer à retrouver son frère. Il avance vers la caisse comme si elle le cachait vraiment, et qu'en approchant il allait voir

He does it almost mechanically, as if he were repeating the gestures that someone else might have made before him. Slowly, he goes down the aisles which lead to the far end of the shop. He passes the rows of shoes without seeing them, but he smells the bitter smell of the leather and the plastic. The red slabs give off a heady light, the soft music which is coming down from the ceiling sickens him a little. There is no one in the department store. The employees are standing near the door, they are talking, without looking at the little boy who is making his way towards the far end of the shop.

The soft music makes vocal sounds that mask everything:

Ah ooh, ahooa, ooahahoo,

like bird calls in the forest. But David pays no attention to what they are saying, he moves forward, holding his breath, towards the far end of the shop, where the till is. No one sees him, no one is thinking about him. Soundlessly he walks between the shelves of shoes, boots, trainers, children's bootees, he walks towards the till, clenching tightly in his left hand the round stone that he picked up from the river beach, last night. His heart is beating very loudly in his chest, so loudly that he thinks that the beats must be ringing out throughout the shop. The light from the neon strips is blinding, the mirrors on the walls and the pillars reflect an unflickering light. The red plastic floor is vast and deserted, David's feet slide over it as though on ice. He thinks about the security men who walk round shops and drive around car parks in their grey cars, he thinks about the nasty people who are watching, with their wild, shining eyes. His heart is beating, beating, and sweat dampens his brow, the palms of his hands. Over there, at the far end of the shop, he can see it clearly. Enormous and lit by its lamps, the till is motionless, and he walks towards it, towards the place where he is finally going to be able to know, finally able to meet his brother Édouard, the burning place where the secret message is hidden. Now he understands, he realizes, that is why he left the flat yesterday morning, with the key hanging round his neck: to get here, the place where he is going to be able to begin to find his brother. He walks towards the till as though it really were hiding him, as though by approaching he were

apparaître sa silhouette mince et sombre, son beau visage aux yeux noirs, brillant de fièvre, ses cheveux bouclés emmêlés comme s'il avait marché dans le vent.

Il serre fort la pierre ronde dans sa main, la pierre toute chaude et mouillée de sa sueur. C'est comme cela qu'on fait la guerre aux géants, tout seul dans l'immense vallée déserte, à la lumière aveuglante. On entend au loin les cris des animaux sauvages, les loups, les hyènes, les chacals. Ils gémissent dans le silence du vent. Et la voix du géant résonne, il rit, et il crie à l'enfant qui marche vers lui:

«Viens! Je te donnerai à manger aux oiseaux du ciel et aux bêtes des champs. Viens! . . .» Et son rire fait courir des frissons sur la pierre ronde du lit du fleuve.

Maintenant, David est au fond du grand magasin, devant le comptoir où est installée la caisse. La lumière blanche du plafond se réverbère sur les angles de métal, sur le plastique noir du comptoir, sur le sol rouge sang. David ne regarde rien d'autre que la caisse, il s'avance vers elle, il la touche du bout des doigts, il contourne le comptoir pour être plus près. La musique douce ne cesse pas ses soupirs, ses hululements lointains, et les coups du cœur de David se mêlent aux bruits lents de la musique. C'est une ivresse étrange, comme celle qui emplissait sa tête quand il respirait la feuille de papier buvard imprégnée de l'odeur poivrée de la dissolution. Peut-être que le visage de son frère Édouard est là, tout près maintenant, sombre et hiératique comme le visage d'un indien aux pommettes hautes, en train d'attendre. Qui le tient prisonnier? Qui l'empêche de revenir? Mais le vide tourbillonnant, aveuglant, ne permet pas de comprendre.

David est appuyé contre le comptoir, son visage à la hauteur du tiroir de la caisse. Le tiroir justement est entrouvert, et il glisse lentement sur lui-même, comme si c'était la main d'un autre qui l'ouvrait, qui prenait une liasse de billets et la serrait fort, en la froissant entre ses doigts.

Mais tout d'un coup, le vide cesse, et il n'y a plus que la peur. Quelqu'un est là, à côté de David, un jeune homme un peu gras, au visage presque féminin, encadré de cheveux bruns bouclés. Il tient David par la main, il la serre si fort de ses deux mains que David

going to see his thin, dark form appear, with his black eyes, shining from fever, his curly hair tangled as though he had been walking in the wind.

He squeezes the round stone tightly in his hand, the stone which is quite warm and wet from his sweat. That is how you make war on giants, all alone in the vast, empty valley, in a blinding light. In the distance you can hear the cries of the wild animals, the wolves, the hyenas, the jackals. They groan in the silence of the wind. And the voice of the giant rings out, he laughs, he shouts to the child who is walking towards him: 'Come here! I'll feed you to the birds of the sky and the beasts of the fields. Come here! . . .' And his laugh sends shivers over the round stone from the river bed.

David is now at the far end of the department store, at the counter on which the till is sitting. The white light from the ceiling is reflected on the metal corners, on the black plastic of the counter, on the blood-red floor. David is looking only at the till, he moves towards it, he touches it with his fingertips, he goes round the counter in order to be closer. The soft music continues to emit its sighs, its distant screeching, and David's heartbeats mix with the slow sounds of the music. It is a strange form of drunkenness, like the one which filled his head when he inhaled from the sheet of blotting paper impregnated with the peppery smell of the glue. Perhaps the face of his brother Édouard is here, quite close now, dark and hieratic like the face of an Indian with high cheekbones, waiting. Who is holding him prisoner? Who is preventing him from coming back? But the swirling, blinding emptiness does not allow him to understand.

David is leaning against the counter, his face on a level with the till drawer. The drawer is in fact half-open, and it slides slowly on its own, as if it were the hand of someone else opening it, who was taking a bundle of notes and squeezing it tightly, rustling it between their fingers.

But suddenly, the emptiness stops and only fear remains. Someone is there, next to David, a young man, slightly fat, with an almost feminine face that is framed with curly brown hair. He is holding David by the hand, he is squeezing it so tightly with both his hands that

entend craquer ses jointures, et crie de douleur. Le visage de l'adolescent est tout luisant de sueur, et ses yeux brillent d'une lueur dure, tandis qu'il répète, les dents serrées, mais avec tant de véhémence qu'il postillonne: «Voleur! Voleur! Voleur!» David ne dit rien, il ne se débat même pas. Sa main gauche a laissé tomber par terre le caillou rond du fleuve, qui roule sur le plastique rouge et s'immobilise. «Voleur! Sale voleur!» continue sans se lasser le jeune homme, et maintenant il parle très fort, pour attirer l'attention des vendeuses à l'entrée du magasin.

«Voleur! Voleur! Sale petit voleur!» crie-t-il, et son visage a une telle expression d'excitement et de colère que David n'a plus peur de lui. Simplement, il ferme les yeux, il résiste à la douleur des deux mains du garçon qui broient ses métacarpes[3] et son poignet. Il ne veut pas crier, pas parler, parce que c'est comme cela qu'il doit faire, s'il veut retrouver son frère Édouard. La voix étranglée du jeune homme résonne dans ses oreilles, pleine de menace et de haine: «Sale voleur! Sale petit voleur!» Mais il ne doit pas répondre, pas supplier, ni pleurer, ni dire que ce n'est pas lui qui est venu jusqu'ici, que ce n'est pas l'argent qu'il voulait, mais le visage de son frère Édouard. Il ne doit même plus penser à cela, puisque le géant l'a vaincu, et qu'il ne sera pas roi, et qu'il ne retrouvera pas ce qu'il cherche. Mais il doit se taire, toujours se taire, même quand viendront les gardes et les policiers pour l'emmener en prison. Des femmes sont venues, maintenant, elles sont là autour d'eux, elles parlent, elles téléphonent. L'une d'elles dit: «Lâchez-le, voyons, ce n'est qu'un enfant.» «Et s'il se sauve? C'est un sale petit voleur comme il y en a partout ici, ils attendent qu'on ait le dos tourné pour mettre la main sur la caisse.» «Comment t'appelles-tu? Quel âge as-tu?» «Ce sont leurs parents qui les dressent comme ça, vous savez, ils doivent rapporter l'argent à la maison chaque soir.» «Voleur, espèce de sale petit voleur!»

A la fin, le garçon relâche son étreinte, moins par pitié que parce que ses bras sont fatigués d'avoir tant serré la main de David. Alors David tombe par terre sur le sol rouge sang, il s'affale doucement comme un tas de chiffons, et sa main et son poignet tuméfiés pendent le long de son corps. La douleur le brûle jusque sous l'épaule,

David can hear his joints cracking, and he cries out with pain. The teenager's face is glistening with sweat, and his eyes are shining with a harsh glow, whilst he repeats, his teeth clenched, but with so much vehemence that he is spluttering: 'Thief! Thief! Thief!' David says nothing, he does not even struggle. His left hand has dropped on to the ground the round pebble from the river, which rolls along the red plastic before coming to a halt. 'Thief! Damned thief!' continues the young man without tiring, and now he is talking very loudly in order to attract the attention of the saleswomen at the shop entrance.

'Thief! Thief! Nasty little thief!' he shouts, and there is such an expression of excitement and anger on his face that David is no longer afraid of him. He simply closes his eyes, he withstands the pain inflicted by the boy's two hands, which are crushing his metacarpi and his wrist. He does not want to cry out, or speak, because that is what he must do if he wants to find his brother Édouard. The strained voice of the young man, full of threat and hatred, rings in his ears: 'Damned thief! Damned little thief!' But he must not reply, not beg, nor weep, nor say that it was not him that came here, that it was not the money he was wanting, but the face of his brother Édouard. He must not even think of that any more, since the giant has conquered him, and because he will not be king, and will not find what he is looking for. But he must keep silent, always keep silent, even when the security guards and the police come to take him away to prison. Women have appeared now, they are all around them, they are talking, they are telephoning. One of them is saying: 'Let him go, will you, he's only a child.' 'And what if he runs away? He's a nasty little thief like so many of them round here, they wait till your back is turned so they can dip their hand in the till.' 'What are you called? How old are you?' 'It's their parents who teach them to do this, you know, they've got to take money home every night.' 'Thief, bastard little thief!'

In the end, the boy relaxes his grip, less out of pity than because his arms are tired from having squeezed David's hand so much. Then David falls on the blood-red ground, he collapses gently like a pile of rags, and his swollen hand and wrist hang along his body. The pain is burning up to under his shoulder, but he says nothing, he

mais il ne dit rien, il ne prononce pas une parole, même si les larmes salées coulent sur ses joues et mouillent la commissure de ses lèvres.

Il y a le silence, maintenant, pour quelques instants encore. Plus personne ne parle, et le jeune homme s'est un peu reculé loin de la caisse, comme s'il avait peur, ou honte. David entend toujours les bruits langoureux de la musique lointaine, pareille aux gémissements d'animaux qui se lamentent, il entend le bruit de son cœur qui bat fort, dans ses tempes, dans son cou, dans ses artères à la saignée du coude. La brûlure de sa main est moins forte, il sent entre ses doigts le papier froissé des billets de banque, que personne n'a songé à lui enlever. Avec effort, il se redresse un peu et il jette au loin les billets qui culbutent sur le linoléum comme une vieille boulette. Personne ne bouge pour les ramasser. Devant lui, à travers le brouillard de ses larmes, il voit aussi le visage de sa mère qui attend dans l'appartement obscur, loin au-delà des murs abrupts et des vallées turbulentes de la ville moderne. Il voit cela très vite, en même temps qu'apparaissent, au bout du grand magasin, les uniformes des gardes. Mais cela lui est égal, il n'a plus peur de la solitude, il ne peut plus craindre le monde, ni les regards des gens, parce qu'il connaît maintenant la porte qui conduit vers son frère Édouard, vers sa cachette secrète d'où on ne revient jamais.

does not say a word, even though the salty tears flow down his cheeks and moisten the corner of his mouth.

Silence now reigns for a few moments more. No one else speaks, and the young man has stepped back a little from the till, as if he were afraid, or ashamed. David can still hear the languorous sounds of the distant music, like the groans of animals who are lamenting their fate, he hears the sound of his heart which is beating loudly, in his temples, in his neck, in the arteries in the crook of his elbow. The burning in his hand is less fierce, between his fingers he can feel the crumpled paper of the banknotes, which no one has thought to take from him. It requires an effort but he sits up a little and he throws aside the notes, which topple over on the linoleum like an old pellet. No one moves to pick them up. In front of him, through the fog created by his tears, he can also see the face of his mother, who is waiting in the dark flat, far beyond the sheer walls and the stormy valleys of the modern town. He can see it very quickly, at the same time as the uniforms of the security guards appearing at the other end of the department store. But he couldn't care less, he is no longer afraid of loneliness, he no longer fears the world, or the way people look at him, because he now knows the door which leads towards his brother Édouard, towards his secret hiding-place from which no one ever returns.

The Occupation of the Ground

JEAN ÉCHENOZ

L'Occupation des sols

Comme tout avait brûlé – la mère, les meubles et les photographies
de la mère –, pour Fabre et le fils Paul c'était tout de suite beaucoup d'ouvrage: toute cette cendre et ce deuil, déménager, courir
se refaire dans les grandes surfaces. Fabre trouva trop vite quelque
chose de moins vaste, deux pièces aux fonctions permutables sous
une cheminée de brique dont l'ombre donnait l'heure,[1] et qui
avaient ceci de bien d'être assez proches du quai de Valmy.

Le soir après le dîner, Fabre parlait à Paul de sa mère, sa mère
à lui Paul, parfois dès le dîner. Comme on ne possédait plus de
représentation de Sylvie Fabre, il s'épuisait à vouloir la décrire
toujours plus exactement: au milieu de la cuisine naquirent des
hologrammes que dégonflait la moindre imprécision. Ça ne se
rend pas, soupirait Fabre en posant une main sur sa tête, sur ses
yeux, et le découragement l'endormait. Souvent ce fut à Paul de
déplier le canapé convertible, transformant les choses en chambre
à coucher.

Le dimanche et certains jeudis, ils partaient sur le quai de Valmy
vers la rue Marseille, la rue Dieu, ils allaient voir Sylvie Fabre.
Elle les regardait de haut, tendait vers eux le flacon de parfum
Piver, Forvil, elle souriait dans quinze mètres de robe bleue. Le gril
d'un soupirail trouait sa hanche. Il n'y avait pas d'autre image
d'elle.

L'artiste Flers l'avait représentée sur le flanc d'un immeuble,
juste avant le coin de la rue. L'immeuble était plus maigre et
plus solide, mieux tenu que les vieilles constructions qui se
collaient en grinçant contre lui, terrifiées, par le plan d'occupation
des sols. En manque de marquise, son porche saturé de moulures
portait le nom (Wagner) de l'architecte-sculpteur gravé dans un
cartouche en haut à droite. Et le mur sur lequel, avec toute son
équipe, l'artiste Flers avait peiné pour figurer Sylvie Fabre en pied,

The Occupation of the Ground

Since everything had burnt – mother, furniture, photographs of
mother – there was immediately a lot of work to do for Fabre and
his son, Paul: all that ash, and that mourning, moving house, racing
round the supermarkets to replace everything. Too quickly Fabre
found something less vast, two rooms with interchangeable uses set
beneath a brick chimney whose shadow told the time, and which
had the advantage of being fairly close to the quai de Valmy.

In the evening, after dinner, Fabre used to talk to Paul about his
mother, Paul's mother, sometimes as soon as it was dinner-time. As
they no longer had any picture of Sylvie Fabre, he would tire himself
out in wanting to describe her ever more precisely: in the middle of
the kitchen were born holograms that were deflated by the slightest
inattention to detail. 'It won't come,' sighed Fabre, laying a hand on
his head, over his eyes, and despondency sent him to sleep. It often
fell to Paul to unfold the sofa-bed, thereby transforming the room
into a bedroom.

On Sundays and certain Thursdays they set off on the quai de
Valmy towards the rue Marseille, the rue Dieu, to go and see Sylvie
Fabre. She looked down at them from on high, holding out to them
the bottle of Piver, Forvil perfume, and smiled at them in fifteen
metres of blue dress. The grille of a basement window made a hole
in her hip. There was no other picture of her.

The artist, Flers, had painted her image on the side of a block of flats,
just before you reached the street corner. The block of flats was thinner,
more solid and better maintained than the old buildings that stuck
creakily against it, terrified by the plan for the occupation of the
ground. Without an awning, its doorway, which drowned in mouldings,
bore the name (Wagner) of the architect-sculptor, engraved in a
cartouche in the top right-hand corner. And the wall, on which the artist
Flers had laboured with all his team to paint a full-length portrait of

surplombait un petit espace vert rudimentaire, sorte de square sans accessoires qui ne consistait qu'à former le coin de la rue.

Choisie par Flers, pressée par Fabre, Sylvie avait accepté de poser. Elle n'avait pas aimé cela. C'était trois ans avant la naissance de Paul, pour qui ce mur n'était qu'une tranche de vie antérieure. Regarde un peu ta mère, s'énervait Fabre que ce spectacle mettait en larmes, en rut, selon. Mais il pouvait aussi chercher la scène, se faire franchement hostile à l'endroit de l'effigie contre laquelle, en écho, rebondissaient ses reproches – Paul s'occupant de modérer le père dès qu'un attroupement menaçait de se former.

Plus tard, suffisamment séparé de Fabre pour qu'on ne se parlât même plus, Paul visita sa mère sur un rythme plus souple, deux ou trois fois par mois, compte non tenu des aléas qui font qu'on passe par là. D'une cabine scellée dans le champ visuel de Sylvie Fabre, il avait failli appeler son père lorsqu'on se mit à démolir la vieille chose insalubre qui jouxtait l'immeuble Wagner. Celui-ci demeura seul, dressé comme un phare au bord du canal. Le ravalement de la façade fit naître sur la robe bleue, par effet de contraste, une patine ainsi que des nuances insoupçonnées. C'était une belle robe au décolleté profond, c'était une mère vraiment. On remplaça la vieille chose par un bâtiment dynamique tout carrelé de blanc, bardé de balconnets incurvés, l'autre flanc du Wagner se trouvant heureusement protégé par la pérennité de l'espace vert, qui formait un gazon subsidiaire aux pieds de Sylvie.

Négligence ou manœuvre, on laissait l'espace dépérir. Les choses vertes s'y raréfièrent au profit de résidus bruns jonchant une boue d'où saillirent des ferrailles aux arêtes menaçantes, tendues vers l'usager comme les griffes mêmes du tétanos. L'usager, volontiers, s'offense de ces pratiques. Heurté, l'usager boycotte cet espace rayé du monde chlorophyllien, n'y délègue plus sa descendance, n'y mène plus déféquer l'animal familier. Le trouvant un matin barré d'une palissade, il cautionne cette quarantaine l'œil sec, sans se questionner sur son initiative; son cœur est froid, sa conscience pour soi.

La palissade se dégraderait à terme: parfait support d'affiches et d'inscriptions contradictoires, elle s'était vite rompue à l'usure des

Sylvie Fabre, overlooked a small rudimentary green area, a sort of un-adorned square whose only function was to form the corner of the street.

Chosen by Flers, urged by Fabre, Sylvie had agreed to pose. She had not liked it. It was three years before the birth of Paul, for whom this wall was merely a slice of life before his time. 'Just look at your mother,' said Fabre, all worked up, for this sight drove him to tears or to sexual arousal, depending on his mood. But he could also look for an argument and become frankly hostile towards the effigy, against which his reproaches rebounded in echo – Paul endeavouring to calm his father down as soon as a crowd threatened to gather.

Later, when he was so separated from his father that they did not even speak to each other any more, Paul visited his mother with more varied frequency, two or three times a month, not counting the unplanned occasions when he was just passing that way. He had almost called his father from a booth set firmly in Sylvie Fabre's field of vision when they began to demolish the rather old nasty edifice that adjoined the Wagner block of flats. The latter stood alone, rising like a lighthouse on the edge of the canal. The restoration of the façade created on the blue dress, through the effect of contrast, a sheen as well as unsuspected nuances of shade. It was a beautiful dress with a plunging neckline: she truly was a mother. They replaced the old edifice with a dynamic building, fully tiled in white, clad with curved little balconies, the other side of the Wagner fortunately being protected by the inviolability of the green area, which formed an additional lawn at Sylvie's feet.

By accident or design, the area was allowed to fall into neglect. Green plants became more and more rare, replaced by brown residues littering the mud from which jutted out scrap iron with menacing edges, stretched out towards visitors to the area like the very claws of tetanus. Visitors were readily offended by such practices. Upset, the visitors boycotted this area, which had been erased from the chlorophyllous world, no longer sent their offspring there, no longer took their pets to defecate. Finding it blocked off with a fence one morning, they gave their support to this quar-antine with not a tear in their eyes, without wondering who had taken the initiative; their hearts are empty of emotion, their consciences are private.

The fence would fall into disrepair sooner or later: a perfect place for posters and contradictory writings, it had soon been broken through the

choses, intégrée au laisser-aller. Rassérénés, les chiens venaient
compisser les planches déjà gorgées de colle et d'encre, prompte-
ment corrompues: disjointes, ce que l'on devinait entre elles
faisait détourner le regard. Son parfum levé par-dessus la
charogne, Sylvie Fabre luttait cependant contre son
effacement personnel, bravant l'érosion éolienne de toute
la force de ses deux dimensions. Paul vit parfois d'un œil
inquiet la pierre de taille[2] chasser le bleu, surgir nue, craquant
une maille du vêtement maternel; quoique tout cela restât très
progressif.

Il suffit d'un objet pour enclencher une chaîne, il s'en trouve un
toujours qui scelle ce qui le précède, colore ce qui va suivre – au
pochoir, ainsi, l'avis du permis de construire. Dès lors c'est très
rapide, quelqu'un sans doute ayant vendu son âme avec l'espace, il
y a le trou. Il y eut le trou, tapissé de cette terre fraîche qui est sous
les villes, pas plus stérile qu'une autre; des hommes calmement
casqués de jaune la pelletaient avec méthode, s'aidant de machines,
deux bulldozers puis une grue jaunes. Les planches brisées de la
palissade brûlaient sans flamme dans une excavation, poussant des
spires de colle noire dans l'air. Tendu sur des piquets rouillés, du
ruban rouge et blanc balisait le théâtre. Les fondations enracinées,
toutes les matières premières livrées, on lança la superstructure et
de nouvelles planches neuves traînèrent un peu partout, gainées
d'un grumeau de ciment. Les étages burent Sylvie comme une
marée. Paul aperçut Fabre une fois sur le chantier, l'immeuble
allait atteindre le ventre de sa mère. Une autre fois c'était vers la
poitrine, le veuf parlait avec un contremaître en dépliant des
calques millimétrés. Paul se tint à distance, hors de portée de la
voix énervante.

Au lieu de l'espace vert, ce serait un immeuble à peu près jumeau
du successeur de la vieille chose, avec des bow-windows au lieu de
balconnets. Plus tard tous deux seraient solidaires, gardes du corps
du Wagner préservé, projetant l'intersection de leurs ombres
protectrices sur sa vieille toiture en zinc. Mais à partir des épaules, le
chantier pour un fils devenait insoutenable, Paul cessa de le visiter
lorsque la robe entière eut été murée. Des semaines passèrent

wear and tear of time, becoming part of the comings and goings of life. Completely unruffled, dogs came to pee against the boards that were already swollen with glue and ink, and which quickly rotted: they had fallen apart, and what one could just see between them caused heads to turn away. Her perfume wafting above the decay, Sylvie Fabre none the less struggled against having her body erased, holding out against erosion by the wind with all the strength of her two dimensions. Occasionally and worryingly, Paul saw the freestone chase away the blue, rise naked, breaking a stitch of the maternal clothing; although all of this remained a very slow process.

One object is all that is needed to set off a chain reaction, and there is always one which seals that which precedes it, colours what is to follow – thus the permission to build follows the initial plan. Immediately, everything happens very quickly, someone probably having sold his soul with the area, there is the hole. There was the hole, carpeted with that fresh earth which is beneath towns, no more infertile than any other; calmly, men with yellow helmets dug it methodically, using machines, two yellow bulldozers then a yellow crane. The broken boards of the fence burnt without a flame in a hollow, sending spirals of black glue into the air. Stretched on rusty stakes, red and white tape marked out the stage. With the foundations deeply dug, all the raw materials delivered, they erected the superstructure, and new boards, brand new ones, were littered just about everywhere, covered in lumps of cement. The storeys drank up Sylvie like an advancing tide. Paul once spotted Fabre on the building site when the block of flats was about to reach his mother's stomach. On another occasion it was about chest height, and the widower was talking to a foreman as he unfolded his scale plans. Paul stood at a distance, beyond earshot of that irritating voice.

In place of the green area there would be a block of flats that would be almost identical to the successor to the old edifice, with bow-windows instead of balconies. Later, both would show solidarity, body-guards to the Wagner, which had been preserved, casting the crossover of their protective shadows on to its old zinc roof. But when it reached the shoulders, the building site became unbearable to a son, and Paul stopped visiting when the entire dress had been walled up. Weeks went

avant qu'il revînt quai de Valmy, d'ailleurs accidentellement. L'édifice n'était pas entièrement achevé, des finitions traînaient, avec des sacs de ciment déchirés; mastiquées depuis peu, les vitres étaient encore barrées de blanc d'Espagne pour qu'on ne les confondît pas avec rien. C'était un sépulcre au lieu d'une effigie de Sylvie, on l'approchait d'un autre pas, d'une démarche moins souple.

Après l'entrée, au cœur d'une cour dallée, un terre-plein meuble prédisait le retour de la végétation trahie. Paul considérant cela, une femme qui venait sur le trottoir s'arrêta derrière lui, leva les yeux au ciel et cria Fabre. Paul, dont c'est quand même le nom, se tourna vers elle qui criait Fabre Fabre encore, j'ai du lait. La voix énervante tomba du ciel, d'une haute fenêtre au milieu du ciel: tu simules, Jacqueline. La femme s'éloignait, on ne sait pas qui c'était. Monte, Paul.

Des revers avaient dû sévir pendant leur perte de vue puisqu'il n'y avait plus aucun de ces gros meubles achetés en demi-deuil, lustrés par l'argent de l'assurance. Ce n'était qu'un matelas de mousse poussé contre le mur de droite, un réchaud, des tréteaux avec des plans dessus; déjà les miettes et les moutons se poursuivaient sur le sol inachevé. Mais Fabre se tenait bien vêtu, ne craignait pas l'eau froide. Il avait fait les vitres par lesquelles on distinguait le fond du canal, privé de son liquide pour cause de vidange trisannuelle: trop peu d'armes du crime se trouvaient là, les seuls squelettes étant des armatures de chaises en fer, des carcasses de cyclomoteurs. Sinon cela consistait en jantes et pneus disjoints, pots d'échappement, guidons; la proportion de bouteilles vides semblait normale, en revanche une multitude de chariots d'hypermarchés rivaux déconcertait. Constellé d'escargots stercoraires, tout cela se vautrait dans la vase que de gros tuyaux pompaient mollement sous leurs anneaux gluants, lâchant d'éventuels bruits de siphon.

Fabre s'était présenté le premier au bureau de location, avant même l'intervention des peintres, donnant un regard mort à l'appartement témoin. On ne le dissuada pas franchement d'emménager tout de suite, au quatrième étage côté Wagner, dans un studio situé

by before he returned to the quai de Valmy, and then it was by accident. The building was not entirely completed, finishing touches still needed to be made, and there were still bags of cement torn open; though they had been sealed with putty only recently, the windows were still painted over with whitening so that they would not be confused with nothingness. It was Sylvie's sepulchre, not an effigy of her; one approached it with a different step, with a less supple tread.

Through the entrance, in the middle of a paved courtyard, a terrace of loose earth presaged the return of the greenery that had been betrayed. As Paul contemplated it all, a woman who was coming along the pavement stopped behind him, looked up to the sky and shouted Fabre. Paul, whose surname it is all the same, turned to face the woman, who was shouting Fabre, Fabre again, I've got some milk. The irritating voice fell from the sky, from a window high up in the middle of the sky: you're pretending, Jacqueline. The woman went away, and we do not know who she was. Come up, Paul.

Very many misfortunes must have befallen him since they had stopped seeing each other for there were no longer any of those large pieces of furniture bought in semi-mourning, made so appealing by the insurance money. There was only a foam mattress pushed up to the wall on the right-hand side, a stove, a trestle table with plans on top; crumbs and bits of fluff were already vying for space on the unfinished floor. But Fabre was well dressed, unafraid of cold water. He had cleaned the windows, through which could be seen the bottom of the canal, deprived of its liquid content because of its triennial draining: too few weapons from the crime were in there, the only skeletons being frames of iron chairs, bodies of mopeds. Otherwise, there were wheels and tyres lying apart from each other, exhaust pipes, handlebars; the number of empty bottles seemed par for the course, though it was disturbing to see so many trolleys from rival supermarkets. Studded with skua snails, it all wallowed in the mud gently pumped up by huge pipes under their sticky rings, emitting siphon-like noises.

Fabre had been the first to go to the letting agency, even before the painters had arrived, casting a mournful look over the show flat. It was quite impossible to dissuade him from moving in immediately, to the fourth floor, on the Wagner side of the building, into a studio flat

sous les yeux de Sylvie qui étaient deux lampes sourdes derrière
le mur de droite. Selon ses calculs il dormait contre le sourire,
suspendu à ses lèvres comme dans un hamac; à son fils il démontra
cela sur plans. La voix de Fabre exposait une mission supérieure,
relevant d'une cause auprès de quoi les nerfs du fils pouvaient faire
l'autruche. Paul partit quand même après vingt minutes.

Il rassembla des affaires et revint samedi soir. Le père avait fait
quelques courses: un autre bloc de mousse, quelques outils,
beaucoup de yaourt et de pommes chips, beaucoup de nourriture
légère. Nul ne raconta rien de ces dernières années, rien ne s'évoqua
sous l'ampoule nue; on discourut juste de la nécessité, puis de la
couleur d'un abat-jour. Fabre était un peu plus disert que Paul, avant
de s'endormir il se plaignit doucement, comme pour lui-même, du
système de chauffage par le sol. Regarde un peu le soleil qu'on a,
dit-il aussi le lendemain matin.

Le soleil en effet balaierait tout le studio, comme un projecteur de
poursuite dans un music-hall frontalier. C'était dimanche, dehors les
rumeurs étouffées protestaient à peine, parvenant presque à ce qu'on
les regrettât. Ainsi que tous les jours chômés, les heures des repas ten-
draient à glisser les unes sur les autres, on s'entendit pour quatorze
heures – ensuite on s'y met. Un soleil comme celui-ci, développa
le père de Paul, donne véritablement envie de foutre le camp. Ils
s'exprimèrent également peu sur la difficulté de leur tâche qui
requerrait, c'est vrai, de la patience et du muscle, puis des scrupules
d'égyptologue en dernier lieu. Fabre avait détaillé toutes les étapes
du processus dans une annexe agrafée aux plans. Ils mangèrent donc
vers quatorze heures mais sans grand appétit, leurs mâchoires
broyaient la durée, la mastication n'était qu'horlogère. D'un tel
compte à rebours on peut, avant terme, convoquer à son gré le zéro.
Alors autant s'y mettre, autant gratter tout de suite, pas besoin de se
changer, on a revêtu dès le matin ces larges tenues blanches pailletées
de vieille peinture, on gratte et des stratus de plâtre se suspendent au
soleil, piquetant les fronts, les cafés oubliés. On gratte, on gratte et
puis très vite on respire mal, on sue, il commence à faire terriblement
chaud.

situated beneath Sylvie's eyes, which were two dull lamps behind the right-hand wall. According to his calculations, he slept against her smile, hanging from her lips as though in a hammock; he showed his son this on his plans. Fabre's voice outlined a superior mission, born from an idea in comparison with which his son's nerves might as well bury their head in the sand. Even so, Paul left after twenty minutes.

He packed a few things together and came back on Saturday evening. The father had done some shopping: another block of foam, a few tools, a lot of yoghurt and potato crisps, a lot of light food. Neither said anything about those recent years, nothing was evoked beneath the bare bulb; they simply talked about what was needed, then about the colour of a lampshade. Fabre was a little more loquacious than Paul, before going to sleep he grumbled softly, as though to himself, about the underfloor heating system. Just look at the sun today, he also said the next morning.

Indeed, the sun would sweep the flat, like a roving spotlight in a frontier music-hall. It was Sunday, outside muffled murmurs could scarcely be heard, almost to the point where they were missed. As on every public holiday, meal-times would tend to blend into each other, they agreed upon 2.00 p.m. – then they got down to it. A sun like this, suggested Paul's father, really gives you the desire to get the hell out of here. They also said little to each other about the difficulty of their task, which would require, it is true, patience and muscle, then the scrupulous care of an Egyptologist in the final stages. Fabre had written in detail every stage of the process on a piece of paper stapled to the plans. So, they ate at about 2.00 p.m. but without much appetite, their jaws ground their way through it, their chewing was merely clockwork. With a countdown such as this, one can, should one so wish, reach zero ahead of time. So, they might as well set about it, they might as well start scraping immediately; no need to get changed, first thing in the morning they had put on those sloppy white overalls spattered with old paint; they scrape and layers of plaster are hanging in the sunlight, leaving dots on their foreheads, in the coffee they have forgotten to drink. They scrape, they scrape and then very soon they have difficulty breathing, they sweat and it starts to be very hot.

The Third-rate Film

SYLVIE MASSICOTTE

Le Navet

On plonge dans la pénombre sans dire bonjour. On choisit un
fauteuil comme dans une salle d'attente enveloppée de musak.
Seulement, ça ne gargouille pas dans mon ventre comme chez le
dentiste.

Depuis une semaine, je dis «on», pour tromper la solitude peut-
être. J'ai regardé les affiches et j'ai murmuré: «Pourquoi on n'entre
pas?» Oui, j'ai vraiment murmuré, cela a fait de la buée . . . pour
moi-même.

A la guichetière on a dit le minimum parce qu'on n'avait pas
envie de s'attarder. Cela arrangeait ceux qui faisaient la queue,
derrière. On a su résister au parfum du maïs éclaté parce que ça fait
trop de bruit et qu'on ne supporte pas. En s'approchant lentement
de la salle, on a demandé:

«Est-ce qu'on peut entrer?»

Le garçon a répondu par une question mais on était occupée
à regarder un bouton blanc, bien mûr, sur son menton encore
imberbe. On n'a pas dit ce qu'on était venue voir, alors il s'est
approché pour examiner le billet, puis il a fait signe d'attendre.

On a guetté les grandes portes derrière lesquelles résonnait une
musique émouvante. On a attendu d'apercevoir un premier visage,
chiffonné, agressé à la fois par la foule et les néons. On s'est sou-
venue de l'enfance, de s'être levée pour faire pipi au milieu d'une
soirée où les invités parlaient fort dans trop de lumière.

On a regardé défiler les gens qui sortaient et on s'est demandé
pourquoi on voulait entrer. Mais dès que le portier a cessé de tripo-
ter son bouton et qu'il a fait signe d'avancer, on est partie la première. On a hésité à mettre le billet dans une poche du manteau.
On l'a finalement gardé dans la main pour pouvoir l'enrouler

The Third-rate Film

We plunge into the semi-darkness without saying good-day. We
choose a seat as though we were in a waiting room filled with the
sound of muzak. The difference is that my stomach is not churning
as it does at the dentist's.

For a week now I have been saying 'we', perhaps to give the lie to
loneliness. I've looked at the posters, and I've muttered, 'Why don't
we go in?' Yes, I've really muttered, it has clouded the issue . . . for
myself.

The minimum was said to the ticket girl because we did not
want to hang around. This was good news for those who were
queuing, behind us. We managed to resist the smell of popcorn
because it makes too much noise and we can't bear that. As we
slowly approached the cinema room, we asked:

'Can we go in?'

The boy replied with a question but we were busy looking at a
quite well developed white spot on his still beardless chin. We did
not say what we had come to see, so he came closer to examine the
ticket, then he gestured to us to wait.

We kept watch on the large doors behind which stirring music was
ringing out. We waited to catch sight of the first bemused face,
assailed by both the crowd and the neon lights. We remembered our
childhood, getting up to go for a wee-wee in the middle of an evening
do when the guests were talking loudly and the lights were too bright.

We watched the people filing out and we wondered why we
wanted to go in. But as soon as the doorman stopped fiddling with
his spot and he gestured to us to move forward, we were the first
to move in. We hesitated about putting the ticket in an overcoat
pocket. Eventually we kept it in our hands in order to be able to roll

autour d'un doigt. On a dit pardon. Mais on ne dit pas bonjour quand on entre dans la pénombre.

On se demande pourquoi cet homme déjà assis dans la salle. On a dit pardon pour passer devant lui, dans la rangée étroite, mais on n'ose pas s'installer dans le fauteuil voisin. On laisse l'espace d'une frontière.

L'homme lit un journal et avec la musak, oui, l'impression d'une salle d'attente. Mais ça ne gargouille pas dans son ventre. Il n'y a que le froissement du journal et celui du billet entre mes doigts. Une certaine gêne.

«On dirait qu'il n'y aura pas grand monde, dit-il en tournant une page de son journal.

– On dirait que non.»

L'homme s'est adressé à moi sans me regarder mais il semble à l'aise, parle d'une façon dégagée comme à une femme qu'on ne voit plus au milieu de son salon feutré. Sans se détacher du journal, il demande:

«Et vous?»

Cette fois, il scrute mon regard dans la demi-obscurité.

«Je . . . dirais que non.»

Devant nous s'installent une jeune fille et son copain aux cheveux ébouriffés. L'homme jette un œil au-dessus du journal et ne tarde pas à réagir à cet obstacle dans son champ de vision. Calmement, il plie le journal, ramasse son manteau et quelques objets qu'il avait dispersés autour de lui. Il se soulève avec la force de ses bras pour ensuite se laisser tomber dans le fauteuil voisin, voisin du mien. Plus de frontière.

«Pardonnez-moi, dit-il. Je préfère les chauves!»

Il m'aurait dit «Je préfère les blondes» et j'aurais été rassurée. On regarde l'accoudoir qu'il faudra partager.

«Je vous en prie», fait-il d'un geste galant.

Rétrécie au fond de mon fauteuil, je ne bronche pas.

«La mouche dans une encoignure, souffle-t-il en reprenant son journal.

– Peut-être . . .» dis-je en rougissant dans l'ombre.

Le rire de la fille de devant, plongée dans une bande dessinée. Son copain sourit à peine, distrait au-dessus d'une image qui devrait

it around a finger. We said excuse me. But one does not say good-day when one enters the semi-darkness.

We wonder why that man is already sitting in the cinema. We said excuse me in order to go past him, in the narrow row, but we did not dare sit in the seat next to him. We left enough space for there to be a boundary.

The man is reading a newspaper and with the muzak, yes, it makes it seem like a waiting room. But his stomach is not churning. There is only the rustle of the newspaper and the ticket between my fingers. It is difficult to be wholly at ease.

'It doesn't look like there will be many people here . . .' he said, as he turned a page of his newspaper.

'It doesn't look like it.'

The man spoke to me without looking at me, but he seems at ease and is talking casually, as though to a woman one can no longer see in the middle of her stuffy living room. Without taking his eyes off his newspaper, he asks:

'And what about you?'

This time he examines my gaze in the semi-darkness.

'I . . . wouldn't think so.'

A girl sits down in front of us with her dishevelled boyfriend. The man glimpses over his newspaper and is not slow to react to this obstacle in his field of vision. Calmly, he folds his newspaper, picks up his coat and a few objects that he had scattered around him. He raises himself using the strength in his arms and then drops into the next seat, the one next to mine. There is no boundary any more.

'Excuse me,' he says. 'I prefer bald men!'

If he had said to me, 'I prefer blondes', I would have felt more reassured. We look at the armrest that we shall have to share.

'Be my guest,' he gallantly gestures.

Squeezed into the back of my seat, I dare not move.

'The fly in a corner,' he whispers, as he turns back to his newspaper.

'Perhaps . . .' I said, blushing in the dark.

A laugh from the girl in front, immersed in a cartoon story. Her boyfriend hardly smiles, his attention diverted from a picture that

l'amuser. Elle referme l'album. Mon voisin, son journal. Les rideaux s'ouvrent.

J'essaie de détendre les muscles de mes épaules, d'occuper ma place. La mouche déplie ses ailes. L'homme pose son regard sur moi. Je me dis que le résultat commence à se voir, que je commence à remplir le fauteuil à force de respirer. Sur l'écran: *La mouche dans une encoignure BIENTÔT A L'AFFICHE.*

La proximité de cet homme, alors qu'il y a tant de sièges vacants, me donne l'impression que je l'accompagne. Je me rends compte, tout à coup, qu'il reprise des chaussettes dans le noir. Je le regarde. Il quitte à peine l'écran des yeux, on dirait ma mère devant ses téléromans. L'aiguille glisse de façon naturelle. Un spectacle réconfortant. Mais je suis venue voir un film.

L'héroïne se saoule dans un café presque vide, se dissimulant derrière la fumée de sa cigarette pour déclamer des balivernes. A son insu, un drôle d'homme l'écoute en buvant son whisky, la tête dans les épaules. Pas trop sûr de lui, il dit qu'il s'offre pour la nuit, question d'unir leurs solitudes . . . La femme plisse les yeux, écarte la fumée, cherche à repérer d'où vient la voix chevrotante. En apercevant l'homme, elle s'esclaffe.

– *Voyez-vous ça! Draguée par un infirme! . . . Il manquait plus que ça . . .*
Elle avale d'un trait le reste de son verre et poursuit.

– *Bof, après tout, on s'en fout. Ma mère avait un cul de bison et mon père jouait avec elle! . . .*
Elle se lève en titubant.

A côté de moi, l'homme qui me dévisage. Je lui souris. Une main chaude vient serrer la mienne très fort, puis elle retourne au travail de reprisage.

Le visage convulsionné du handicapé en plein orgasme au-dessus de la protagoniste ivre morte. Je suis dégoûtée. Mon voisin a cessé de repriser. Il range ses chaussettes dans un sac qu'il froisse longuement. Devant nous, au milieu des cheveux en désordre du jeune spectateur, apparaît tout à coup un visage qui émet un «Chut!» exaspéré. Mon voisin lui dit «Pardon» et ajoute, en chuchotant, «Je l'ai fait exprès!»

ought to amuse him. She closes the book. My neighbour, his newspaper. The curtains open.

I try to relax the muscles of my shoulders, to fill my seat. The
fly is unfolding its wings. The man looks at me. I tell myself that the
result is becoming obvious, that I am beginning to fill the seat by
breathing. On the screen appears: *The Fly in a Corner, COMING
SOON.*

The nearness of this man, when there are so many empty seats,
gives me the impression that I have come here with him. I suddenly
realize that he is darning socks in the darkness. I look at him.
He hardly takes his eyes off the screen, just like my mother with her
televised novels. The needle slides just as it should. A comforting
sight. But I have come to see a film.

The heroine is getting drunk in an almost empty café, hiding
behind the smoke of her cigarette to spout her nonsense. Un-
beknown to her, a strange man is listening to her as he drinks his
whisky, his shoulders hunched. Not too sure of himself, he says that
he is offering himself for the night, just so they can bring together
their respective loneliness . . . The woman screws up her eyes,
waves away the smoke, tries to see where the quavering voice is
coming from. On spotting the man she bursts out laughing.

'*Won't you look at that! Pulled by a cripple! . . . That's all I needed . . .*'

She knocks back the remaining contents of her glass and continues:
'*Well, who gives a damn after all. My mother had an arse like a buffalo and
my father played with her! . . .*'

Swaying, she gets up.

Next to me is the man who is staring at me. I smile at him. A
warm hand advances to squeeze mine very firmly, then it returns to
its darning.

The distorted face of the cripple is lost in orgasm on top of the
protagonist, who is dead drunk. I am disgusted. My neighbour has
stopped darning. He is putting his socks away in a bag that he
crumples for a long time. In front of us, framed by the dishevelled
hair of the young spectator, suddenly appears a face which lets out
an exasperated 'Shush!' My neighbour says 'Sorry' and adds in a
whisper, 'I did it on purpose!'

On se regarde. Il a un sourire espiègle et des joues de gamin que je voudrais caresser. J'ai envie de le voir à la lumière.

«On est venus voir un navet», dit-il.

Ma voix répète comme dans un cours de langue: «On est venue voir un navet . . .»

Je boutonne mon manteau et me lève, décidée.

«Allez-y, je vous rejoins», lance-t-il.

Je perds de l'assurance en marchant dans l'obscurité. Je pousse les battants et me retrouve en pleine lumière artificielle, comme dans un petit matin fabriqué où il faut reconstituer les rêves de la nuit.

Immobile entre le boutonneux, près de la porte, et la vendeuse de maïs accoudée à son comptoir désert, je fixe le vide. Je serais passée à travers l'écran que le choc n'aurait pas été plus violent.

«Vous ne vous sentez pas bien, madame?» demande le portier en s'approchant de moi.

De fait, j'ai un peu mal au cœur à la vue de son bouton qu'il a dû faire éclater après le début de la séance.

«Oh . . . ça saigne», dis-je.

Il m'indique les toilettes. Je ne comprends pas. Je guette les portes de la salle de projection d'où mon voisin ne sort toujours pas. J'ai l'impression que c'est peut-être moi, le navet dont il parlait. Il m'a fait sortir pour rien et, à l'intérieur, il se moque bien de moi. Il vient sans doute repriser ici tous les jours, se spécialise dans ce genre d'attrape. J'ai chaud. Je fais un pas. Je me dis «Allez, on s'en va d'ici! On vaut plus que ça.»

On avance. On a oublié ce qui existe dehors. C'est fait pour ça, le cinéma? On se retourne, plan général: la fille au comptoir, le maïs éclaté et le boutonneux au menton ensanglanté. Ma voix parvient jusqu'à eux.

«Vous savez, l'homme qui était là avant tout le monde . . . ?

– L'homme . . .»

Les battants s'écartent doucement. Le portier accourt pour ouvrir plus grand. Mon voisin apparaît, agrippé à une marchette d'aluminium, les hanches proéminentes et les jambes torses. Sur son front,

We look at each other. He has a mischievous smile on his face and boyish cheeks that I would like to stroke. I want to see him in the light.

'We came to see a third-rate film,' he says.

I repeat as though in a language class: 'We came to see a third-rate film . . .'

I button up my coat and get up, determined.

'Off you go, I'll join you,' he interjects.

My resolve wavers as I walk in the darkness. I push open the doors and emerge into bright artificial light, as though into an artificial dawn where one has to recreate the dreams of the night.

Motionless between the pimply youth, near the door, and the popcorn seller leaning on her empty counter, I stare into the emptiness. The shock would not have been more violent if I had walked through the screen.

'Are you not well, madam?' asks the doorman as he comes towards me.

In fact, I feel a bit sick at the sight of his spot, which he must have burst after the beginning of the performance.

'Oh . . . there's blood,' I say.

He points to the toilets. I do not understand. I keep an eye on the doors of the cinema from which my companion has still not come out. I think that I am perhaps the third-rate movie he was talking about. He made me go out for nothing and, back inside, he is having a good laugh at me. He probably comes and darns here every day, specializing in this sort of trick. I am hot. I take a step forward. I say to myself, 'Come on, let's get out of here! We're worth more than that!'

We move forward. We have forgotten what exists outside. Is that why we go to the cinema? We turn round, and in broad outline: the girl at the counter, the popcorn and the pimply youth with the bleeding chin. My voice reaches them.

'You know, the man who was in there before everyone else . . . ?'

'The man . . .'

The doors open softly. The doorman runs up to open them wider. The man next to me appears, clinging on to an aluminium frame, his hips bowing out and his legs twisted. On his brow there is

un pli d'inquiétude se dissipe quand ses yeux clairs me trouvent. La même douceur, sur son visage.

«Vous m'avez attendu», dit-il.

a furrow of worry which disappears when his bright eyes settle on me. The same softness on his face.

'You waited for me,' he says.

The Objet d'Art

JEAN-PAUL DAOUST

L'Objet d'art

A Annie Molin Vasseur

'On n'est jamais guéri tout à fait d'un mal qu'on a aimé.'
CLÉMENT MARCHAND[1]

«A Montréal[2] il fait présentement moins deux degrés. Il y a risque
de neige en soirée. Habillez-vous chaudement. Des vents de . . .».
Elle ferma la radio. Elle passa la main dans ses cheveux noirs
qu'elle avait fait teindre la veille, en bas, dans le hall de la station
Sherbrooke[3] où venait d'ouvrir un nouveau salon de coiffure pour
hommes et pour femmes. Ainsi, elle n'avait pas eu à sortir et affronter une pluie froide. Le coiffeur lui avait aussi coupé et gonflé les
cheveux, lui faisant une sorte d'auréole noire qui nimbait ses yeux
gris d'un «*look* très magazine», jugea-t-elle, ce qui l'amusa. Elle avait
trente ans et elle était magnifique. Elle le savait. Ce qui donnait un
poids encore plus effrayant à sa solitude. Elle alla vers une fenêtre et
se colla le nez à la vitre. Il s'y forma une buée qu'elle essuya du
revers de la main. Puis, elle admira le pont Jacques-Cartier qui
reliait Longueuil à Montréal dans une pose de carte postale.
L'après-midi s'estompait dans un temps maussade. Les lueurs roses
de la ville devaient commencer à être perçues au loin, à la campagne. Elle aimait ce pont qui semblait si léger, étendu entre le ciel
et le fleuve comme un corps heureux. Elle lui tourna le dos et
examina son trois-et-demi, sa suite d'hôtel allongée, qui était dans
un grand désordre. La routine quoi! Elle passa à nouveau la main
dans ses cheveux et retourna au pont et à la ville, vibrant refrain
moderne de métal et de lumières dans la nuit montante. Le crépus-
cule était son heure favorite, où elle pouvait jouir de cette vision
changeante de la ville en train d'arranger son *look* de nuit. Mais,
de se retrouver au milieu de débris de cigarettes et de verres vides,
elle se sentit tout à coup très seule. Elle alluma quelques lampes et

The Objet d'Art

To Annie Molin Vasseur

'We are never completely cured of an evil that we have loved.'
CLÉMENT MARCHAND

'In Montreal it is presently two degrees below zero. There is the possibility of snow this evening. Dress warmly. Winds from . . .' She turned
off the radio. She slid her hand through her black hair which she had
had dyed the day before, down below on the concourse of Sherbrooke
Station where a new hairdressing salon for both men and women had
just opened. That way she had not had to go out and confront the cold
rain. The hairdresser had also cut and given body to her hair, giving
her a sort of black halo effect which made her grey eyes radiant, with
a very 'magazine look', she thought. This amused her. She was thirty
and she was magnificent. She knew it. Which gave an even more terrifying weight to her loneliness. She went towards a window and stuck
her nose against a pane. A mist formed, which she wiped away with
the back of her hand. Then she admired the Jacques-Cartier bridge
which linked Longueuil to Montreal in a postcard posture. The afternoon was becoming hazy in the gloomy weather. The pink lights of the
city would soon become visible in the distance, in the countryside. She
loved this bridge, which seemed so light, stretched between the sky and
the river like a body at peace with itself. She turned away from it and
examined her hotel-like suite, three rooms and a box-room in a row,
which was terribly untidy. So much for routine! She again slid her
hand through her hair and turned to face the bridge and the town, a
vibrant modern refrain of metal and light in the oncoming night. Dusk
was her favourite time, when she could enjoy that changing vision of
the town arranging its night-time 'look'. But she suddenly felt very
alone on finding herself surrounded by cigarette ends and empty glasses.
She turned on a few lamps and saw the post that was lying on the

vit le courrier qui gisait sur la table de cuisine. Elle saisit une
enveloppe contenant une invitation pour un vernissage rue
Saint-Denis, à la galerie Aurore, le soir même. Elle connaissait
l'endroit: un grand logement à l'étage, qui avait été converti en un
espace agréable par la propriétaire, Anne, une de ses amies. On y
présentait l'exposition d'une peintre assez connue qui ramenait du
Tibet ses derniers travaux. «A l'encre de Chine, je suppose.» Mais
cette réflexion ne la fit pas rire. Elle ne riait plus depuis longtemps.
Et ce triste mois de novembre n'arrangeait rien, et cette séparation
d'avec son amant non plus, évidemment. On n'efface pas douze ans
de vie commune comme de la buée sur une vitre. Et, à Montréal,
quand les feuilles d'automne ont plié bagage et sont parties avec
toutes les couleurs du monde il ne reste plus que du gris qui piétine
à attendre l'invasion barbare de la neige à qui la pollution réglera
son compte. Alors, ce vernissage pouvait être une échappatoire
honorable pour sortir de l'appartement en débâcle. Elle tourna le
dos au désordre et se réinstalla aux fenêtres pour se perdre dans le
paysage urbain. Elle avait eu la chance inouïe de trouver cet espace,
au quatorzième étage, qui faisait le coin sud-ouest de l'immeuble
et lui offrait une vue privilégiée sur le fleuve et le centre-ville
et même sur le mont Royal[4] qui, à cette heure-ci, commençait à se
tapir dans l'ombre glacée de la croix qui s'allumait. Et elle
pouvait descendre directement dans le métro sans avoir à sortir,
ce qui était, dans ce rude climat, une bénédiction. Et, au deuxième,
une piscine chauffée d'une grandeur olympique pouvait facilement
donner l'illusion d'être ailleurs. Elle occupait cet appartement depuis
cinq mois. Depuis . . . Elle ne voulait plus y penser. Une peine
d'amour, on n'en guérit jamais. On s'en remet. C'est tout. Elle
était en convalescence. Et l'année sabbatique tombait pile.
L'Université de Montréal, où elle donnait des cours en histoire de
l'art, la reverrait l'an prochain, en septembre. Mais tout ça semblait
loin et elle en était soulagée. Ce soir, elle avait envie de sortir, de
se frotter aux lumières de la ville; ce vernissage était le bienvenu. Elle
relut le carton d'invitation. L'artiste avait retravaillé, dans son atelier
du Vieux-Montréal, des dessins et des objets conçus au Tibet. Elle
prit un verre et le remplit de vin rouge, puis s'arrêta devant la

kitchen table. She seized an envelope containing an invitation to a private view in the rue Saint-Denis, at the Aurore gallery, that very evening. She knew the spot: a large flat on the first floor, which had been converted into a pleasant space by the owner, Anne, one of her friends. There was an exhibition there of a fairly well-known painter who had brought back her most recent work from Tibet. 'In China ink, I suppose.' But this thought did not make her laugh. It had been a long time since she had laughed. And this gloomy month of November did not make anything better, and nor did splitting up with her lover either, obviously. You cannot erase twelve years of living together like the mist on a window pane. And in Montreal, when the autumn leaves have packed their bags and gone with all the colours in the world, all that is left is a grey that marks time, waiting for the barbaric invasion of the snow which the pollution will soon sort out. So, this private view could be an honourable escape from her flat, which was in such a mess. She turned her back on the disorder and returned to the windows to lose herself in the urban landscape. She had been uniquely lucky to find this flat, on the fourteenth floor, on the south-west corner of the apartment block, with a privileged view over the river and the town centre, and even over the Mont Royal, which, at this time of the evening, was beginning to disappear in the chilled shadow created by the cross that was lighting up. She could go straight down into the metro, without the need to go outside, which was a blessing in this harsh climate. And, on the second floor, a heated, Olympic-size swimming pool could easily give one the illusion of being elsewhere. She had lived in this flat for five months. Since . . . She did not want to think about it any more. One is never cured of a problem of the heart. One recovers. That is all. She was in a period of convalescence. And her sabbatical year had come at just the right time. She would return to the University of Montreal, where she gave lectures on the history of art, next year, in September. But all of that seemed far into the future and she was relieved about that. This evening, she felt like going out and rubbing shoulders with the lights of the town; this private view was most welcome. She reread the invitation card. In her studio in Old Montreal, the artist had reworked drawings and objects done in Tibet. She picked up a glass and filled it with red wine, then stood

ville qui enfilait sa robe de star et elle sourit pour la première fois depuis longtemps. Ce soir, la vie donnait l'impression d'être belle. Elle porta un toast à son reflet, dans la vitre, qui semblait flotter sur les étoiles de la ville et, fermant les yeux, elle but une longue gorgée. Elle eut l'impression de voir les bulles rouges tomber dans sa gorge. Quand elle les réouvrit, le vin avait presque disparu. Elle alla s'en chercher d'autre. La soirée, après tout, ne faisait que commencer. Comme d'habitude.

En entrant dans la galerie d'art, elle aperçut plusieurs personnes entassées dans la pièce du devant, communément appelée autrefois le salon double. Elle bifurqua vers le corridor et ouvrit la porte de la salle de bains où, par chance, il n'y avait personne. Pendant que les rumeurs de la cohue cognaient contre la porte, elle retoucha son maquillage, se peigna en dégageant son front pour qu'on voie bien la lumière surprenante de ses yeux. Une fois satisfaite, elle sortit, prête à affronter le monde. Elle prit soin de saisir une coupe de vin rouge au passage et salua les connaissances, les ami(e)s. L'exposition n'était pas mal, mais sans plus. Le vin était bon. Le vin la consolait. La calmait. Elle en avait de plus en plus besoin. Elle se sentait loin, très loin de tous ces gens dont, pour plusieurs, elle connaissait les anecdotes qui font les vies. Loin comme ces dessins accrochés au mur, peints en un lointain pays. Pays qu'elle avait pourtant visité elle aussi. En allant vers l'arrière, c'est-à-dire vers la cuisine, il fallait traverser une grande pièce, qui en des temps plus anciens avait sans doute servi de salle à manger. L'exposition continuait là aussi, mais différemment. Sur les murs, d'autres dessins, mais par terre, de grands blocs de plexiglas contenant différentes sculptures étaient déposés et c'est là qu'elle le vit.

Une forme repliée sur elle-même, aux reflets noirs et lumineux comme si une énergie violette émanait d'elle, et ouverte comme si elle ne craignait pas de laisser voir la surprenante force enfouie dans ses rondeurs imperturbables qui la nourrissait, où au centre un bijou (une améthyste?) palpitait comme un œil de cyclope.

Elle en fut fascinée. Il s'imposa d'emblée à elle. Et elle chercha quel mot pouvait bien définir cet objet-là. Il portait un titre simpliste,

looking out on the town, which was slipping into its filmstar's gown, and smiled for the first time in a long time. This evening, life gave the impression of being beautiful. She raised her glass to her reflection in the window, which seemed to be floating among the stars of the town, and, closing her eyes, she took a long drink of wine. She had the impression of seeing red bubbles falling down her throat. When she opened her eyes again the wine had almost all gone. She went to get some more. After all, the evening was only just beginning. As usual.

On entering the art gallery, she spotted several people crowded together in the front room, commonly called the double living room in the past. She turned off towards the corridor and opened the door to the bathroom, which was fortunately empty. As the hubbub from the crowd echoed against the door she touched up her make-up, combed her hair to reveal her forehead so that the amazing light in her eyes could be easily seen. Once she was satisfied, she went out, ready to confront society. She made sure to take a glass of red wine on the way, and greeted the people she knew, her friends. The exhibition was not bad, but nothing more than that. The wine was good. The wine consoled her. Calmed her. She relied on it more and more. She felt removed, very removed from all those people about whom, in several cases, she knew what had gone on to make up their lives. As removed as those drawings hanging on the wall, painted in a far-away country. A country which she too had, however, visited. As she went towards the back, that is to say towards the kitchen, she had to walk through a large room which, in days long gone by, had probably been used as a dining room. The exhibition continued there as well, but it was different. There were more drawings on the walls, but on the floor had been placed large blocks of plexiglas containing different sculptures, and that is where she saw it.

A shape that was folded over on itself, with black and shiny reflections as if a purple energy emanated from it, and open as if it were not afraid to reveal the surprising strength from which it fed hidden in its imperturbable curves, and in the centre a jewel (an amethyst?) was pulsating like the eye of a cyclops.

She was fascinated by it. Immediately, she felt compelled by it. And she searched for the word that could adequately define that object. It

voire moqueur: «objet d'art». Et suivaient, sorte de sous-titre en
caractères plus petits, ces mots intrigants: vidéo de roman. Il était là,
prisonnier de cette cage, comme un insecte étrange, une relique de
l'ère paléozoïque.[5] Un film d'images incongrues défila dans sa tête.
Elle n'en revenait tout simplement pas. Elle restait là, comme accro-
chée à sa coupe, et le scrutait. Elle avait une envie irrésistible de le
toucher, de le voir se lover dans le creux de sa main, de l'effleurer de
sa joue.

Il n'y avait pas encore, à côté de lui, de point rouge. Et pour
cause: le prix était exorbitant! L'objet, elle en était sûre, était conçu
pour elle. Mais jamais elle n'aurait les fonds nécessaires pour se le
payer, à moins d'oublier le voyage dans le Sud, mais cela était hors
de question. Elle se trouvait confrontée, pensa-t-elle, à des problèmes
de riche. Mais justement, elle ne l'était pas assez. Elle avait beau
imaginer mille scénarios, l'objet restait hors de portée. Alors, en proie
à une angoisse qu'elle jugea ridicule, elle veilla sur lui en retournant
mille fois dans son cerveau des scénarios de conquête, c'est-à-dire que
les mêmes chiffres brillaient dans des stratagèmes tous plus impossibles
les uns que les autres. Elle restait là, à boire son vin qu'un serveur
attentif remplissait avec un sourire de requin d'eau douce. Elle ne le
voyait même pas. Seul l'objet comptait. Un objet pompeusement
nommé «objet d'art».

Autour d'elle et de l'objet, les gens circulaient, bavardaient. Et
plus ça riait et jacassait, plus il lui semblait impérieux de le soustraire
à toute cette clinquante vulgarité. Elle se savait atteinte d'une folie
subite, comme si elle avait été envoûtée par un sortilège. Elle
observait les gens et n'en revenait pas de tant d'inconscience. Ce
monde d'artistes, de critiques, d'écrivains était là à folâtrer comme si
l'exposition faisait partie de l'apéro, des courses, des affaires courantes
. . . Alors qu'elle restait profondément troublée, comme si elle était
pour la première fois de sa vie, confrontée au sacré. Il fallait
absolument qu'elle le possède! Car elle en était tombée follement
amoureuse. Oui, «amoureuse» était le mot juste. Et lui, il restait là,
dans son écrin, à l'évaluer, à la narguer, à la séduire.

Quand elle vit la propriétaire s'approcher avec au bout du doigt
une tache rouge, elle eut un malaise. Comme si elle voyait la mort

bore a simplistic, not to say mocking, title: *Objet d'Art*. Beneath, as a sort of subtitle in smaller letters, these intriguing words: 'Video of a Novel'. It was here, a prisoner in this cage, like a strange insect, a relic of the Palaeozoic era. A stream of incongruous images went through her head. She simply could not get over it. She stood there, as if glued to her wine-glass, and examined it. She had an irresistible desire to touch it, to see it coil up in the palm of her hand, to brush it gently against her cheek.

There was not yet a red dot next to it. And there was a good reason: the price was exorbitant! She was sure that the object had been made for her. Yet she would never have enough money to buy it for herself unless she forgot about the trip to the South, but that was out of the question. She was confronted, she thought, by problems of wealth. But the simple fact was that she did not have enough. It was pointless to imagine countless scenarios: the object was beyond her means. So, racked by a sense of anguish that she considered ridiculous, she watched over it, turning over in her mind a thousand scenes of victory, that is to say that the same figures shone in her plans, each more impossible than the last. She stood there, drinking her wine, which an attentive waiter kept on refilling, smiling like a freshwater shark. She did not even see him. Only the object mattered. An object with the pompous title of *Objet d'Art*.

People were moving around her and the object, chatting. And the more they laughed and chattered, the more it seemed to her imperative to shield it from this tawdry vulgarity. She knew she was over come by a sudden attack of madness, as if she had been put under a magic spell. She looked at the people and could not get over so great a lack of awareness. This world of artists, critics, writers was there, frolicking, as if the exhibition were part of the aperitif, the shopping and the gossip . . . Whereas she was deeply troubled, as if for the first time in her life she had come face to face with holiness. She absolutely had to have it! For she had fallen madly in love with it. Yes, love was precisely the right word. And it remained there, in its case, assessing her, deriding her, seducing her.

When she saw the owner coming towards her with a red dot on the end of her finger, she felt dizzy. As if she was witnessing the

arriver. Elle se sentit au bord d'un grand malheur et seul l'objet, elle le savait maintenant, pouvait la sauver. Mais Anne lui adressa un sourire chaleureux et colla l'étiquette au bas d'un dessin insignifiant. Maintenant, elle comprenait: il lui fallait l'objet coûte que coûte. Et elle sombra dans sa contemplation. Le vernissage était une réussite. Et quiconque aurait porté la moindre attention à cette femme n'aurait vu qu'une séduisante jeune personne en train d'observer, d'étudier certains objets, là, dans une boîte transparente. Il n'aurait pu deviner qu'elle était ensorcelée. Mais elle, elle piaffait. Elle ne pouvait se libérer du joug de l'objet. Elle avait beau se traiter de folle, elle n'avait jamais vu quelque chose d'aussi beau, d'aussi inquiétant. Elle en était séduite jusqu'à l'âme. Elle le voyait dans ses moindres détails, dans ses moindres nuances, jusque dans les ombres de ses replis, de ses entrailles, jusque dans ses reflets les plus subtils, et cet œil, qui la regardait comme une étoile brûlante, jonchait, juste pour elle, l'horrible plexiglas. Il fallait qu'elle l'achète. C'était devenu une question de vie ou de mort. C'était aussi simple, aussi terrible que ça. Mais le prix! Elle avait peine à se décider.

Le serveur remplit son verre et lui adressa la parole: «Il fait chaud, n'est-ce pas?» Elle le regarda. D'abord elle ne le vit pas, puis elle aperçut des dents se préciser, blanches et droites, en un sourire de publicité pour pâte dentifrice. Elle essaya d'en faire autant. «Vous vous sentez bien?» Elle hocha la tête en signe d'affirmation. Du fond de l'enfance remonta alors cette image de l'ange rose, dans la crèche, qui remercie les fidèles quand les sous tombent dans la fente de son cou. Elle eut un fou rire, ce qui encouragea le jeune serveur à poursuivre: «Il y a tellement de monde, n'est-ce pas?» De sa main gauche, elle lui toucha le coude. Il frissonna. Elle ne s'en aperçut pas et réussit à lui marmonner qu'elle voulait voir Anne, immédiatement. Il répliqua – et elle put alors voir une langue se tordre en un humide point rouge prêt à se coller sur son front: «La propriétaire?» Elle hocha la tête à nouveau. Cérémonieusement, il s'inclina comme un valet dans un film muet et disparut. Mais tout ce monde n'en finissait pas d'aller et de venir. Elle fixa l'objet et se sentit mieux. Elle avait enfin pris sa décision.

Quand Anne se pointa, l'index à nouveau tatoué d'un cercle

arrival of death. She felt as if she were on the edge of a great misfortune and only the object, she now knew, could save her. But Anne smiled warmly at her and stuck the label at the bottom of an insignificant drawing. Now she understood: she had to have the object, whatever it cost. And she sank into deep thought. The private view was a success. And if anyone had paid the slightest attention to this woman they would only have seen an attractive young person contemplating, studying certain objects, there, in a transparent box. They could not have guessed that she was bewitched. But she was beside herself with impatience. She could not free herself from the yoke placed on her by the object. It was pointless calling herself mad, she had never seen anything so beautiful, so alarming. Seduction had pierced her to her very soul. She could see it in its smallest detail, its most subtle nuances, even the shadows in its folds, its entrails, down to the most subtle of its reflections, and that eye, which looked at her like a burning star, shattered, just for her, the awful plexiglas. It was imperative that she buy it. The matter had become one of life or death. It was as simple, as terrifying as that. But the price! She found it hard to make up her mind.

The waiter filled her glass and said: 'It's hot, isn't it?' She looked at him. At first she did not see him, then she perceived teeth coming into focus, white and straight, in a smile that could have been an advertisement for toothpaste. She tried to do the same. 'Do you feel all right?' She nodded to say yes. Then, from the depths of her childhood, rose that image of the pink angel, in the crib, who thanks the faithful when the coins fall through the slot in his neck. She got the giggles, which encouraged the young waiter to carry on: 'There are so many people here, aren't there?' She touched his elbow with her left hand. He shivered. She did not notice and managed to mutter to him that she wanted to see Anne, immediately. He replied – and she could then see a tongue twist into a damp red point ready to stick itself to her forehead: 'The owner?' She nodded again. With great ceremony he bowed like a servant in a silent movie and disappeared. But all those people were still coming and going. She stared at the object and felt better. She had finally made up her mind.

When Anne turned up, her index finger again tattooed with a red

rouge, elle paniqua. Mais Anne l'apposa au bas d'un autre dessin, quelconque. Puis Anne vint vers elle. Elle était toute menue et son visage était comme séparé en deux. En haut, les yeux étaient tristes: en bas, le sourire était radieux. Alors on ne savait jamais si Anne était heureuse ou malheureuse. Ce qui faisait qu'on gardait toujours une certaine distance, un certain malaise quand on ne la connaissait pas vraiment. Elles échangèrent des banalités d'usage puis elle lui désigna l'objet. Anne rentra ses lèvres, contrariée. Un silence singulier s'ensuivit, que la foule autour mettait en exergue. Puis Anne, de sa voix rauque lui dit: «Bien entendu, tu ne peux pas savoir que c'est la première fois que l'artiste consent à le mettre en vente?» Bouleversée, elle regarda Anne. «Tu vois, elle n'a jamais voulu s'en défaire. Elle dit que c'est son porte-bonheur. Mais comme elle veut retourner au Tibet, cette fois pour très longtemps, elle a besoin d'amasser le plus d'argent possible. Mais je te l'avoue bien sincèrement, elle espérait que personne ne l'achèterait.» «Mais, je le veux.» Cette réplique, dite sèchement, cingla Anne qui leva la main gauche comme pour conjurer un mauvais sort. Pendant de longues secondes le silence engonça leur regard, puis finalement Anne s'en ella en lui disant «Puisque tu y tiens, *alea jacta est.*»[6] La phrase sembla menaçante. En tremblant, elle déposa sa coupe au-dessus de l'objet, sur le carré de plexiglas, puis fouilla dans son sac de cuir noir qu'elle portait en bandoulière. Elle avait mis une robe à col roulé, en laine noire, d'où s'échappaient de longues jambes finement aiguisées par des souliers pointus, noirs eux aussi, aux talons d'une hauteur vertigineuse. Elle trouva son carnet de chèques de la Caisse Populaire Saint-Louis-de-France. Elle vit le nom et l'adresse clignoter. Les mots semblaient s'éloigner puis se rapprocher, rapetisser et grandir, comme si le nom du saint passait successivement à travers ses yeux et à travers une loupe. Elle s'appuya légèrement et entendit un craquement: l'assemblage de plastique s'écroulait dans un tintamarre effrayant et elle roulait au milieu des débris, tenant, entre ses mains ensanglantées, l'objet tant convoité. Elle se remit d'aplomb. Elle avait peine à respirer. Elle secoua la tête comme pour chasser ces hallucinations. Anne réapparut et lui demanda:

dot, she panicked. But Anne put it at the bottom of some drawing or other. Then Anne came towards her. She was quite slender and her face looked as though it were divided into two. Above, her eyes were sad; down below her smile was radiant. So one never knew whether Anne was happy or unhappy. Which meant that people always remained at a certain distance, always had a sense of disquiet when they did not really know her. They exchanged customary trivialities then she pointed to the object. Anne smiled wryly, ill at ease. There followed a strange silence, made all the more acute by the surrounding crowd. Then Anne said in her husky voice: 'Of course, it is not possible for you to know that this is the first time that the artist has agreed to put it up for sale?' Taken aback, she looked at Anne. 'You see, she has never wanted to part with it. She says that it's her good-luck charm. But since she wants to return to Tibet, this time for a very long time, she needs to get all the money that she possibly can. But, I'll be perfectly honest with you, she was hoping that no one would buy it.' 'But I want it.' This reply, pronounced so curtly, took Anne completely by surprise and she raised her left hand as though to ward off bad luck. For seconds that seemed to last for ever, the silence meant that they could only look uneasily at each other, then at last Anne went off, saying: 'Since you're so keen on it, *alea jacta est*.' The phrase seemed threatening. Trembling, she put her wine-glass down on top of the object, on the cube of plexiglas, then searched in her black leather bag, which she wore across her shoulder. She had put on a roll-neck dress made of black wool, out of which emerged her long legs, made extremely shapely by her pointed shoes, which were also black and had terrifyingly high heels. She found her cheque book, issued by the Caisse Populaire Saint-Louis-de-France. The name and address seemed to flicker. The words seemed to move away then come close, grow smaller and bigger, as if the name of the saint were constantly passing before her eyes and through a magnifying glass. She leant gently and heard a crack: the plastic construction was collapsing with a terrifying din and she was rolling amid the debris, holding, in her hands covered in blood, the object that she so desired. She regained her composure. She was finding it hard to breathe. She shook her head as though to drive away these hallucinations. Anne reappeared and

«Ça va?» Elle fit signe que oui. En guise d'excuse, elle désigna la foule tout autour. Mais Anne ne semblait pas convaincue. Elle réussit à trouver un stylo et remplit le chèque, en bonne et due forme, comme une automate. Elle émit une profonde respiration qui inquiéta Anne. «Ça peut attendre tu sais.» Elle la torpilla aussitôt d'un regard où se mêlaient la surprise et la peur. Anne, sidérée, refit ce geste de la main gauche qui semblait signifier cette fois: «Comme tu voudras!» Alors, Anne prit le chèque, la remercia et, le temps de le dire, marqua d'un point sanglant le *i* du vidéo, et disparut, happée par la foule bruyante. Elle était enfin seule avec lui, maintenant «son objet d'art». Enfin à elle! Si seulement elle avait eu le temps d'y toucher, mais Anne avait agi avec tellement de dextérité, de vitesse . . . «en cachette», songea-t-elle. Elle prit son verre. Comme par magie le serveur était là, toutes canines sorties. Elle lui sourit, cette fois pour vrai, soulagée. Il vola vers elle pour remplir sa coupe. Il était fasciné par sa beauté, par ses yeux de cette couleur incroyable. Mais ne se souciant absolument pas de lui, elle retourna à sa conversation privée avec l'objet, entrecoupée de moult toasts intimes. Elle but. Et elle but.

Quand elle s'aperçut que la foule s'était éclaircie elle envoya, en catimini, un baiser à l'objet qui sembla lui faire un clin d'œil retentissant. Elle sursauta. Elle vida son verre. Elle n'eut aucune peine à se rendre jusqu'au portique où l'attendait le serveur. Il l'aida à enfiler son ample manteau de drap noir acheté à la boutique Parachute de Soho à New York. Il lui dit des insanités qu'elle avait entendues des milliers de fois. Anne la remercia à nouveau et lui dit que l'artiste aimerait la voir. Mais elle rétorqua qu'elle était trop fatiguée et qu'elle lui parlerait une autre fois. Elle aurait aimé amener l'objet avec elle, mais elle connaissait les règles du jeu: une fois l'exposition terminée, elle pourrait le récupérer, pas avant. Mais comme elle l'aurait voulu tout de suite! Elle garda ce désir secret. A contrecœur, elle descendit les marches. Anne, songeuse, la regarda partir. Une fois dehors, le vent froid la gifla brutalement. A côté, l'Express était bondé, comme à l'accoutumée. Elle y entra, et put prendre par miracle la place d'un client qui réglait son addition. Elle commanda du vin rouge, une bavette

asked: 'Are you all right?' She nodded in assent. As an excuse she pointed to the crowd around her. But Anne did not look convinced. She managed to find a pen and, like an automaton, wrote out the cheque, exactly as required. She let out a deep breath, which worried Anne. 'That can wait, you know.' She immediately fired a look at her in which were mixed surprise and fear. Anne, beside herself with surprise, repeated that gesture with the left hand which this time seemed to mean: 'As you wish.' Then Anne took the cheque, thanked her and, in the time that it took to say it, marked with a blood-red circle the 'i' of 'Video', and disappeared, swallowed up by the noisy crowd. At last she was alone with it, and now it was her 'objet d'art'. At last, it was hers! If only she had had the time to touch it, but Anne had acted with such dexterity, such speed . . . 'in secret', she thought. She picked up her glass. As though by magic, the waiter appeared, all his canines on view. She smiled at him, this time for real, relieved. He rushed over to fill her glass. He was fascinated by her beauty, by the incredible colour of her eyes. But paying him no attention whatsoever, she returned to her private conversation with the object, interspersed with many a private toast. She drank. And she drank.

When she noticed that the crowd had thinned out, she furtively blew a kiss to the object, which seemed to wink at her in a way that had a great effect on her. She jumped. She drained her glass. She had no difficulty in reaching the portico where the waiter was waiting for her. He helped her to slip into her loose-fitting black woollen coat bought in the Parachute de Soho shop in New York. He uttered some inane phrases, which she had heard thousands of times before. Anne thanked her again and said that the artist would love to meet her. But she retorted that she was too tired and that she would speak to her another time. She would have liked to take the object away with her, but she knew the rules of the game: once the exhibition was over, she would be able to collect it, not before. But how she would have loved to have it immediately! She kept her desire a secret. Reluctantly, she went down the stairs. Dreamily, Anne watched her leave. Once outside, the cold wind lashed her face. Next door, the Express was heaving, as usual. She went in and was miraculously able to get the seat of a customer who was paying his bill. She ordered red wine, a medium-

cuite à point et les frites qu'elle adorait. Elle mangea et but avec
appétit. Tout allait comme dans le meilleur des mondes. Elle venait
de sacrifier son voyage dans les Antilles pour un objet qui peut-être
n'en valait pas la peine. «*So what!*», se répéta-t-elle. Elle avait bien
sacrifié douze ans de sa vie, immolé sa jeunesse, pour quelqu'un qui
n'en valait pas la peine, alors où était le drame? Elle but. Elle refit
deux fois son maquillage dans les toilettes. Ses yeux chatoyaient dans
le miroir comme des lunes sur le Nil. Elle se savait de plus en plus
soûle et, en même temps, de plus en plus lucide. Elle se dédoublait,
s'analysait et s'étonnait d'elle-même. Dehors, la poudrerie commençait.

Elle paya avec sa carte American Express et sortit. Le vent maintenant fouettait la nuit sans pudeur. Elle traversa la rue et s'engouffra
un peu plus haut dans un bar qu'elle aimait bien et dont un de ses
amis, Julien, avait trouvé le nom: le Passeport. C'était archiplein. Les
décibels secouaient la place. Elle laissa son manteau au vestiaire, et
se dirigea vers le bar du fond. Colette, sa barmaid préférée, l'accueil-
lit en levant les bras en l'air et en lui disant qu'elle paraissait en
superforme. Elle lui demanda, comme d'ordinaire, du rouge. Colette
lui suggéra du vin nouveau, ce qui lui parut une excellente idée. Elle
but et le reste de l'univers se perdit peu à peu dans un flou aux
couleurs délavées que transperçait par intermittence l'œil violet de
«l'objet d'art». Quand elle se sentait trop dériver, elle allait sur la
piste de danse et virevoltait comme une plume arrachée sous les
étoiles artificielles. Elle passa ainsi le reste de la soirée à boire et à
danser. Puis, Colette l'invita à aller dans un endroit où l'on servait
illégalement de l'alcool après les heures de fermeture, mais elle
refusa. Elle voulait rester seule pour mieux rêver à lui, à «l'objet
d'art».

Elle ressortit pour se retrouver sur le trottoir métamorphosé en
une peau de zèbre tourmentée et glaciale ou aucun taxi n'attendait.
Elle releva le col de son manteau pour défier la tempête. Elle n'avait
pas d'autre choix. Elle retraversa la rue et passa devant la galerie
Aurore. Toutes les fenêtres étaient noires. Mais elle savait que derrière, au fond d'un sarcophage vitreux, un œil mystérieux brillait.
L'Express était fermé. Seules quelques pâles lumières veillaient sur

rare undercut and chips, which she adored. She ate and drank with relish. Everything was turning out as perfectly as possible. She had just sacrificed her trip to the West Indies for an object which was perhaps not worth it. '*So what!*' she repeated to herself. Had she not sacrificed twelve years of her life, sacrificed her youth, for someone who was not worth it, so why make such a big deal of it? She drank. She did her make-up twice in the toilets. Her eyes glistened in the mirror like moons over the Nile. She knew she was getting more and more drunk and, at the same time, more and more lucid. She was developing a split personality, analysing and becoming astonished at herself. Outside, the blizzard was picking up.

She paid with her American Express card and left. The wind was now whipping the night indecently. She crossed the street and then, a little further up, she dived into a bar that she liked a lot and the name of which, Le Passeport, had been found by one of her friends, Julien. It was full to bursting. The sound was so loud it shook the place. She left her coat in the cloakroom, and went towards the bar at the back. Colette, her favourite barmaid, welcomed her by raising her arms in the air and saying that she looked to be in tremendous shape. As usual, she asked for red wine. Colette suggested new wine to her, which seemed an excellent idea. She drank and the rest of the world gradually disappeared in a fuzziness of faded colours, pierced now and then by the violet eye of the 'objet d'art'. When she felt that she was drifting too much, she went on the dance floor and pirouetted like a plucked feather beneath artificial stars. And thus she spent the rest of the evening, drinking and dancing. Then, Colette invited her to go to a place where they illegally served alcohol after closing time, but she declined. She wanted to remain alone in order to dream more clearly about it, the objet d'art.

She went outside and found the pavement metamorphosed into a tortured, icy zebra skin and no taxi in sight. She raised the collar of her coat in order to combat the storm. She had no choice. She crossed the street again and walked past the Aurore gallery. No light shone from any of the windows. But she knew that behind them, deep in a glass sarcophagus, a mysterious eye shone. The Express was closed. Only a few pale lights watched over the ghosts of the

les fantômes de la soirée. En face, l'entrée du nouveau Théâtre d'Aujourd'hui[7] avait l'air d'un aquarium vide. Mais le vent froid et la poudrerie l'empêchèrent de s'arrêter. Elle ferma les yeux et songea que maintenant elle avait son talisman. Rendue devant le fleuriste Marcel Proulx, elle s'agrippa à un petit arbre squelettique, gracieuseté de la ville de Montréal. La vitrine du fleuriste, où s'étalaient des fleurs magnifiques aux coloris séduisants, lui rappela méchamment qu'elle venait de sacrifier son voyage vers leurs contrées chéries, et chaque pétale d'un hibiscus écarlate sembla lui adresser un reproche sanguinolent. Puis, au coin de la rue Roy, elle vit poindre un taxi au bout de la rue Berri. Mais il tourna à droite, passa entre l'église Saint-Louis-de-France et la Caisse Populaire où aboutirait dans quelques heures un chèque faramineux signé de son nom, et il s'éclipsa au bout de Roy où, sur une petite place déprimante, gisent des chaises dont personne ne sait que faire. Le taxi allait sans doute emprunter la rue Saint-André pour répondre à l'appel d'une personne impatiente de partir en voyage, et dont l'avion décolle au petit matin pour un pays ensoleillé. Elle se vit comme Alice au pays des merveilles à la croisée des chemins: ou tourner à gauche et affronter le vent diabolique qui, comme dans une chasse-galerie, chialait et jurait, empalé au clocher de l'église, ou continuer tout droit et essayer par la suite de se faufiler devant la maison dite «des sourds et muets» où était mort Louis Fréchette,[8] le poète de *La légende d'un peuple*. Elle opta pour ce dernier trajet. La neige lui coulait dans le cou et son foulard mouillé ne servait plus à grand-chose. Ses souliers à talons hauts sortaient d'un cauchemar intégral. Le froid lui serrait les chevilles et menaçait de la clouer à même les interstices du trottoir qu'elle devinait à travers ses larmes. Quand elle était petite et qu'elle jouait à la marelle, elle gagnait à coup sûr le paradis, mais maintenant, son ange gardien l'avait abandonnée dans cet enfer blanc où elle dérivait comme une aile brisée. Elle maudit ce pays au climat barbare et seule l'encouragea l'idée de jouir de ce spectacle, une fois installée dans la chaleur de l'appartement, même si de puissantes bourrasques l'assaillaient de toutes parts. Rendue devant le café Cherrier, déserté lui aussi, elle put respirer. En face, les arbres du

evening. Opposite, the entrance to the new Théâtre d'Aujourd'hui looked like an empty aquarium. But the cold wind and the blizzard prevented her from stopping. She closed her eyes and thought that she now had her talisman. Outside the Marcel Proulx florist's she clung on to a small, skeletal tree, a gift of the town of Montreal. The florist's window, in which were displayed magnificent, seductively coloured flowers, cruelly reminded her that she had just sacrificed her journey to their beloved countries, and every petal of a scarlet hibiscus seemed to make a blood-red reproach to her. Then, at the corner of rue Roy, she made out a taxi at the end of rue Berri. But it turned right, went between the Saint-Louis-de-France church and the Caisse Populaire where, in a few hours' time, would arrive an astronomically large cheque signed with her name, and it disappeared from sight at the end of Roy where, in a depressing little square, lie some chairs that no one knows what to do with. The taxi was probably going to turn into rue Saint-André to answer the call of someone who was impatient to set off on a journey, and whose aeroplane would take off in the very early morning for a sunny country. She felt like Alice in Wonderland, at the crossroads: either she turned left and faced the diabolical wind, which, as though in a shooting gallery, was weeping and swearing, impaled on the church steeple, or she went on straight ahead and tried, as a result, to inch her way past the house said to be 'of the deaf and dumb' where Louis Fréchette had died, the poet who had written *La légende d'un peuple*. She plumped for the second way. The snow was running down her neck and her wet scarf was virtually useless. Her high-heeled shoes were the stuff of a complete nightmare. The cold gripped her ankles and threatened to nail her right into the cracks of the pavement that she could make out through her tears. When she had been little, playing hopscotch, she had always been certain that she would go to heaven, but now her guardian angel had abandoned her in this white hell through which she was drifting like a broken wing. She cursed this country with its barbaric climate, and her only encouragement was to think about enjoying this spectacle, once she was nestling in the warmth of her apartment, even if violent squalls of wind beset her from every direction. Outside the café Cherrier, also closed, she was able to catch her breath. Opposite, the trees on

carré⁹ Saint-Louis gémissaient comme des fantômes d'opéra. Médusée, elle s'arrêta pour écouter ces plaintes saisissantes, puis elle repartit de plus belle. Encore une centaine de mètres et ça y était. Elle aurait voulu piquer vers le building recouvert de tôles grises, le plus laid de la ville, où siégeait l'Institut d'hôtellerie, échoué là bêtement comme un sosie minable du Darth Vader de *La guerre des étoiles*, mais elle savait qu'à cette heure-là les portes du métro étaient verrouillées. Donc, il n'y avait pas moyen de prendre le tunnel qui reliait les sorties ouest et est de la station Sherbrooke pour ainsi profiter de ce bras souterrain et entrer directement dans son building. Elle s'enhardit à franchir le triple tronçon de l'artère Berri. Sous le viaduc, le vent lui fonça dessus en hurlant comme un maniaque et la rattrapa. Il l'étouffait lentement comme une pieuvre cruelle sortie des abysses de la ville. Mais de se savoir si près de chez elle lui redonna des forces. Elle se jeta littéralement en avant. Elle perdit conscience du temps et finit par se retrouver sous la marquise de son immeuble injustement baptisé place du Cercle. Elle s'engouffra dans le portique en faux marbre beige et se cala contre la porte. L'odyssée venait enfin de se terminer. En tremblotant, elle tira les clefs de son sac et réussit à ouvrir l'autre porte d'entrée. Ses doigts gelés semblaient un refuge pour toutes les aiguilles du monde. L'ascenseur l'attendait. Elle parvint à appuyer sur le chiffre quatorze. Comme au ralenti la cage se referma. Elle arriva au bon étage et prit une autre clef pour déverrouiller la porte du 1404. Elle fut accueillie par le magnifique spectacle de la tempête qui se déroulait sur l'écran des fenêtres. Elle resta un moment éberluée de comprendre qu'elle venait de traverser cette tourmente-là. Elle se laissa tomber dans un fauteuil. Puis elle commença à retirer ses vêtements. Elle se brossa vigoureusement les dents, se démaquilla en catastrophe. Le vent brassait les fenêtres. Les lumières de la ville vacillaient comme des phares en folie. «La première tempête de neige, à Montréal, est toujours fascinante», murmura-t-elle avant de sombrer dans le lac calme de ses draps roses. Mais elle rêva à d'immenses sculptures de glace, noircies par des tourbillons de fumée qui entouraient un cratère rougeoyant au centre duquel palpitait un iris violet qui l'aspira.

Saint-Louis square groaned like opera ghosts. Dumbfounded, she stopped to listen to these arresting moans, then she set off again, at a faster pace. Another hundred metres and it would all be over. She would have liked to make for the building covered in grey sheet metal, the ugliest in the town, where sat the Institut d'Hôtellerie, foolishly grounded there like a pathetic double of Darth Vader from *Star Wars*, but she knew that at that hour the doors to the metro were bolted. So there was no way she could go down the tunnel which linked the west and east exits of Sherbrooke Station in order to take advantage of that underground passage and get straight into her building. She steeled herself to cross the three-lane section of the Berri thoroughfare. Under the viaduct, the wind rushed at her, screaming like a maniac, and caught her. Slowly, she was being stifled as though by a cruel octopus that had come out of the deepest regions of the town. But, knowing herself to be so close to home gave her renewed strength. She literally threw herself forward. She lost all awareness of time and eventually found herself beneath the awning at the entrance to her apartment block, unjustifiably called Circle Square. She hurtled through the portico made from imitation beige marble and leant, with relief, against the door. At last, the odyssey had come to an end. Trembling, she took her keys out of her bag and managed to open the other door. Her frozen fingers seemed to be a haven for all the pins in the world. The lift was there, waiting. She succeeded in pressing the figure fourteen. The door closed as if in slow motion. She got to her floor and took out another key to unbolt the door to 1404. She was greeted by the magnificent spectacle of the storm which was unfurling on the screen that were the windows. She stood for a moment, astounded by the realization that she had just walked through that gale. She dropped into an armchair. Then she began to take off her clothes. Vigorously, she brushed her teeth and took off her make-up, which had run everywhere. The wind was beating on the windows. The lights in the town were flickering, like headlamps gone mad. 'The first snow-storm in Montreal is always fascinating,' she muttered to herself before sinking into the calm waters of her pink sheets. But she dreamt of immense ice-sculptures, darkened by whirls of smoke surrounding a crater that glowed red and in the centre of which flickered a violet iris which sucked her in.

Elle se réveilla en fin d'avant-midi,[10] mal en point, la tête lourde, le cœur sur pilotis. Elle avala deux aspirines et se recoucha. Par les fenêtres, elle était agressée par un ciel d'un bleu vif, saupoudré d'une légère neige que le vent ballottait dans des torrents d'air glacial, pendant que les buildings de la ville perçaient le ciel de leurs scalpels miroitants. En tremblant elle alluma une cigarette et, en même temps, la radio. C'était l'heure des informations régionales, à Radio-Canada. Quand l'annonceur parla d'un sinistre sur le Plateau Mont-Royal ayant nécessité à l'aube trois alertes, elle cessa de fumer. Il donna l'adresse du triplex qui abritait deux logements occupés et une galerie d'art. Personne n'avait perdu la vie mais les dommages étaient considérables. La possibilité d'un incendie criminel n'était pas écartée. Le bulletin de la météo suivait: «Un ciel dégagé pour aujourd'hui et cette nuit, mais du temps froid. Il fait présentement moins deux degrés à Dorval. Ce qui est un peu en-dessous de la normale . . . Au signal sonore, il sera midi.» Même la radio fermée, ce son lancinant continua d'allonger dans sa tête une ligne noire comme une épitaphe sans mots. Elle pleurait.

She woke up in the late morning, feeling unwell, with a heavy head and her heart pounding. She swallowed two aspirins and went back to bed. Through the windows she felt attacked by a bright blue sky, sprinkled with some light snow that the wind was tossing in the currents of icy air, whilst the buildings in the town pierced the sky with their shimmering scalpels. Trembling, she lit a cigarette and, at the same time, turned on the radio. It was time for the regional news on Radio-Canada. When the announcer talked about a fire on the Plateau Mont-Royal having brought about three alerts at dawn, she stopped smoking. He gave the address of the three-storey apartment block that contained two occupied flats and an art gallery. No lives had been lost but the damage had been considerable. The possibility of arson had not been eliminated. The weather forecast followed: 'A clear sky today and tonight, but cold. It is presently two degrees below zero in Dorval. Which is slightly below the average for this time of year . . . At the beep it will be midday.' Even with the radio off, that piercing sound continued to draw a black line in her head, like an epitaph without words. She wept.

The Hunters' Café

DANIEL BOULANGER

Le Café des Chasseurs

Montfavert avait transformé sa cuisine en atelier de menuiserie et vivait dans son tricycle d'infirme de guerre. Il ne se déplaçait plus qu'au rez-de-chaussée de sa maison qui donnait sur le cours Jules-Taupin. L'étage et le grenier lui servaient de paradis. Il y pensait toujours et ne pouvait pas s'y rendre. Quand il avait tourné les bois d'un mobilier de poupée dont la vente relayait l'argent de sa pension d'invalidité et qu'il avait donné à manger aux araignées qu'il élevait dans un buffet à portes de verre, dont il éclairait l'intérieur avec une rampe de néon, il changeait de siège et partait faire son tour de ville dans un fauteuil à moteur. On l'entendait à toutes les cornes de la rose des vents[1] et l'on était heureux qu'il ne circulât jamais la nuit; il aurait réveillé jusqu'aux pierres.[2] Ce bruit quasi journalier ne le faisait guère aimer, bien que sa conversation fût des plus enrichissantes. Il connaissait tous les conflits de l'histoire, et il suffisait de le héler pour qu'il arrêtât le vacarme de son engin et vous donnât la date d'une contre-offensive dans le Jutland[3] ou la Cyrénaïque,[4] effectifs et noms des chefs. On le voyait vivre le fait d'armes jusqu'à changer de couleur, et il arrivait que l'on apprît la cause réelle de cette douleur qu'on le suppliait de nous pardonner d'avoir fait naître.

— Pas du tout, répondait-il. C'est au contraire un plaisir. Vous me voyez branlant à cause d'Angèle. Elle est morte la nuit dernière.

— Désolé.

— Elle allait avoir deux ans. Une araignée qui répondait à tous mes appels, qui accourait à mon approche, qui dansait, monsieur! Bien ferme et souple sur ses pattes en étoile, elle se laissait rebondir comme une balle.

— Vous en avez d'autres! disait-on pour le consoler.

— Quel être en remplace un autre? Enfin!

The Hunters' Café

Montfavert had transformed his kitchen into a carpenter's workshop and lived in his war invalid's tricycle. He moved only around the ground floor of his house, which looked on to Jules-Taupin Walk. The first floor and the attic were his paradise. He was always thinking about them and could not get up there. When he had turned the wood to make doll's-house furniture, the proceeds from which supplemented his invalidity pension, and when he had fed the spiders that he was breeding in a sideboard with glass doors, the inside of which he lit with a neon strip light, he changed seats and set off to go round the town in a motorized wheelchair. His horn could be heard everywhere and people were glad that he never went about at night; he would have woken even the dead. This almost daily noise scarcely made him liked, although talking to him was a most enriching experience. He knew all the battles in history, and you merely had to call out to him for him to stop the din made by his machine and tell you the date of a counter-offensive in Jutland or in Cyrenaica, troop numbers and the names of the leaders. He lived the feat of arms to the point where he could be seen changing colour, and it even came about that you learnt the true source of this pain, which you begged him to forgive you for having caused.

'Not at all,' he replied. 'On the contrary, it's a pleasure. You see me shaking because of Angèle. She died last night.'

'I'm so sorry.'

'She would have been two. A spider which answered whenever I called, which ran up to greet me, which danced, I'll say. Solid and supple on her star-shaped feet, she let herself be bounced like a ball.'

'You've got others!' people said to console him.

'What creature can replace another? Please!'

On le laissait remettre les gaz et rouler vers le Café des Chasseurs où il avait ses quartiers de délassement. Là, sans quitter ses roues, il s'installait à la table des amis pour des jeux de hasard qui faisaient place à des conversations sur l'armée, ses souvenirs, ses transformations, son avenir, à des lectures de bulletins d'anciens combattants ou de revues de polémologues. Montfavert était abonné à diverses publications, sans compter brochures et encyclopédies dont le spécimen lui était arrivé avec une lettre de souscription. Il ne se passait d'ailleurs pas de semaine qu'il ne cédât à la vente par correspondance, et sa mémoire était confortée par ces rangées d'histoires de tout genre qui mettaient ses finances à sec. Un jour, il arriva aux Chasseurs dans un grand désarroi.

– Montfavert! Tu en fais une tête!

– Je suis jaloux, dit-il simplement et vexé. Je vous ai souvent parlé d'un vieux camarade: Agricole Palaneuve! Nous avons fait les mêmes hôpitaux! Mais c'est bien un Parisien! Il n'y en a que pour Paris! Paris, toujours! Ange ne m'a même pas fait signe! Comme si j'étais enterré dans ce trou!

– De quoi s'agit-il?

– D'un haut fait!

– Alors, de quoi te plains-tu?

Montfavert sortit un fascicule d'une des sacoches du tricycle.

– Une nouvelle publication. Le premier numéro. Très cher, trop cher! Enfin, le papier est glacé. Et au beau milieu je tombe sur Palaneuve! Suis-je toujours son ami? Je vous fais juge.

– On t'écoute.

– Ça s'intitule: «L'outrage».

Le cabaretier apportait du vin blanc.

– Un alsace[5] de derrière les fagots,[6] dit-il joyeusement. Une nouvelle source. Vous n'allez plus la quitter!

– Non, coupa Montfavert en repoussant la bouteille, pas aujourd'hui. Du rouge, s'il te plaît.

La tablée s'étonna, mais la main du paralytique restait impérieuse. Le rouge arriva et il commença:

L'outrage

He was allowed to turn his engine back on and drive to the Hunters' Café, where he had his quarters for relaxation. There, without getting out of his wheelchair, he settled down at the regulars' table to play games of chance that would give way to conversations about the army, his memories, his transformations, his future, his reading of old combatants' newsletters or war magazines. Montfavert had subscriptions to various publications, not including brochures and encyclopaedias of which he had received the specimen copy and the accompanying subscription letter. Moreover, not a week went by without him giving in to a mail order, and his memory was comforted by those rows of stories of every sort which bled his finances dry. One day he arrived at the Hunters' in a state of utter confusion.

'Montfavert! You look in a real state!'

'I'm jealous,' he merely said, 'and annoyed. I've often talked to you about an old comrade: Agricole Palaneuve! We were in the same hospitals! But he's a Parisian through and through! Only Paris counts! Always Paris! Ange did not even give me a hint! As if I was buried in this hole!'

'What are you talking about?'

'Of a historic deed!'

'So, what are you complaining about?'

Montfavert took a magazine out of one of the bags of his tricycle.

'A new publication. The first edition. Very expensive, too expensive. Still, the paper is glazed. And right in the middle I come across Palaneuve! Am I still his friend? I'll let you be the judge of that.'

'We're listening.'

'It's called "The Outrage".'

The landlord brought some white wine.

'An extra-special Alsace,' he said gleefully. 'From a new supplier. You'll never drink anything else!'

'No,' interrupted Montfavert, pushing the bottle away, 'not today. A bottle of red, please.'

Everyone around the table was amazed, but the hand of the paralysed man remained authoritative. The red wine arrived, and he began:

The outrage

Quand il lut qu'un Scandinave s'était fait cuire un œuf sur la flamme du Soldat Inconnu,[7] Agricole Palaneuve laissa glisser le journal, ferma les yeux dans sa chaise roulante, et ses mains blanchirent de douleur à tant serrer les accoudoirs. Il y avait belle lurette qu'il avait versé sa dernière larme, là-bas, au fond de sa guerre, et si d'autres malheurs avaient fondu depuis sur le pays, aucun acte n'approchait en vilenie du sacrilège que l'on venait de relater, en pleine paix, à la veille de défiler pour la commémoration de l'Armistice. Il décrocha son appareil téléphonique pour appeler le Ministre qui le pensionnait. Des préposés se le passèrent de bureau en bureau, mais il ne put obtenir le secrétaire général qu'il connaissait suffisamment pour lui dire son indignation au nom de tous ceux qui n'avaient osé l'appeler, mais les employés qui étaient tous au courant, passant leur matinée à lire la presse, ne paraissaient guère s'émouvoir. Agricole avait même cru percevoir dans l'écouteur quelques ricanements «Il n'y a plus rien de bon à attendre, gémit-il, plus rien ni de loin ni de près.» Il se trouvait sous le jet d'une Providence qui se soulage et il se rappela les fourmis qu'il aimait arroser au hasard des promenades et des besoins, autrefois. «Tout se tient», songeait-il et il ajouta: «Puisqu'ils ne veulent pas m'entendre, ils vont me voir!»

La concierge de son immeuble vint le sortir de son cinquième étage et le poussa dans l'ascenseur. Agricole Palaneuve se retrouva dans la rue et fit démarrer le petit moteur de son fauteuil. Les rues les plus passantes, les carrefours ne l'effrayaient pas, conscient du danger qu'il faisait naître chez les automobilistes et malgré sa désespérance comptant toujours qu'il inspirait de la pitié et donc des attentions. Les quolibets, les injures ne manquaient cependant pas de pleuvoir sur lui et les conseils du genre: «Reste avec ta nounou!», «Plante-toi au soleil, ça repoussera!» Ah, certes, il pouvait parler de la méchanceté, de la goujaterie humaines! Il retenait certaines malveillances, les duretés les mieux venues pour les rapporter aux amis qui se trouvent dans le même état que lui et il les comparait à celles qu'eux-mêmes avaient entendues. Il leur arrivait d'en prendre des fous rires. Leurs réunions se passaient toujours au Champ-de-Mars[8]

When he read that a Scandinavian had cooked himself an egg over the flame dedicated to the Unknown Soldier, Agricole Palaneuve let his newspaper slide to the ground, closed his eyes as he sat in his wheelchair, and his hands went white from pain, so hard was he squeezing the armrests. It was a very long time since he had shed his last tear, over there, in the depths of his war, and if other misfortunes since then had befallen the country, no deed came close in baseness to the act of sacrilege that had just been told, in peace-time, the day before the procession to commemorate the Armistice. He picked up his telephone to call the minister who gave him his pension. He was passed from office to office by officials, but he could not get hold of the secretary-general, whom he knew sufficiently well to describe his indignation to in the name of all those who had not dared to call, but the employees, who all knew what had happened, for they spent the morning reading the newspapers, scarcely seemed to be moved. Agricole had even thought that he had made out someone sniggering at the other end of the line. 'There's nothing worth waiting for any more,' he sighed, 'nothing either in the long or the short term.' He found himself under the flow of water from a Providence relieving itself and he recalled the ants on which, in days gone by, he liked to urinate as he chanced to walk by and as the need arose. 'It's all fitting into place,' he thought, and he added: 'Since they do not want to hear me, they're going to see me!'

The caretaker of his block of flats came to take him out of his fifth-floor flat and pushed him into the lift. Agricole Palaneuve found himself in the street once more and started the little motor on his wheelchair. The busiest streets, the crossroads, did not frighten him any more, for he was aware of the danger he posed to car drivers, and in spite of his despair he always counted on inspiring pity, and thus attention. Jeers and insults never failed, however, to rain down upon him, together with advice of this sort: 'Stay with your nanny!', 'Plonk yourself in the sun and it will grow back!' Ah, he could indeed talk about human nastiness and boorishness! He retained certain expressions of spite, the most apt obscenities, in order to relate them to friends in the same condition as him, and he compared them with those that they too had heard. They even got the giggles about them. Their meetings always took place on the Champ-de-Mars and,

et par temps de pluie dans l'un des cafés proches de École Militaire.[9] On les poussait au-delà de l'arrière-salle des billards dans une sorte de pergola[10] aux murs aveugles où le public n'allait guère et d'où ils pouvaient suivre les poules que les joueurs disputaient ou les programmes de la télévision sur l'écran réservé au personnel. Les serveurs prenaient là leurs repas aux heures creuses du matin et de l'après-midi. Il s'y retrouvait parfois quatre ou cinq petites voitures, mais Agricole Palaneuve pouvait toujours compter sur celle de Jacques Mouchelin qui ne quittait guère l'endroit, habitait le quartier, n'activait ses roues qu'avec les mains et que les amis surnommaient le Casanier.[11] Agricole, ce jour-là, avait décidé de leur soumettre le problème, d'envisager une riposte au geste blasphématoire du Scandinave et de commencer par signer ensemble une lettre au Ministre pour lui montrer qu'ils n'entendaient pas que l'outrage restât impuni. La vue d'un match de tennis joué par des handicapés en petite voiture les conforta. Cela se passait en Amérique et le vainqueur du tournoi à la fin du reportage parut leur lancer sa raquette, éclatant de joie à l'image des joueurs qui courent sur leurs deux jambes. Un souffle de liberté passa sous la pergola et le haut mur aveugle qui la fermait renvoya leurs bravos.

Agricole posta la lettre. Les jours passaient sans réponse quand elle arriva, deux semaines après. A la pergola les amis écoutèrent Palaneuve qui la lut de sa belle voix. Le Ministre laissait percer son émotion, sa compréhension, mais faisait entendre que le mieux était d'oublier une insanité. On avait souvenir, ajoutait-il, de gestes plus ignobles en cet endroit sacré, ce qui n'était pas une raison, certes, de prendre la Flamme pour un réchaud de cuisine. Le Scandinave était un Danois. Après une forte amende, il avait été rejeté au-delà de la frontière. La lettre se terminait par une exhortation à la vigilance, «bien qu'en ce domaine comme dans les autres nul être et nul temple ne puissent être à l'abri d'une souillure. Le malade mental est à tous les coins de rue».

– Il ne s'agit pas d'une rue, dit Casanier, mais de la plus belle avenue du monde.

– Certes! dirent les autres.

when it rained, in the nearby cafés of the École Militaire. They were
pushed beyond the back room where billiards were played into a sort
of windowless pergola, where the general public scarcely went and
from where they could follow the games that the players were playing
or watch television programmes on the screen reserved for the staff.
The waiters took their meals in there at the quiet times of the morning
and the afternoon. There were sometimes four or five invalid carriages,
but Agricole Palaneuve could always count on finding Jacques Mouchelin's, for he rarely left the room, lived in the area, turned his wheels
only with his hands and was nicknamed Casanier by his friends. That
day, Agricole had decided to put the problem to them, to think up a
response to the blasphemous gesture of the Scandinavian and to begin
by all signing a letter to the minister in order to show him that they did
not intend that the outrage should go unpunished. They were comforted by the sight of a game of tennis played by disabled people in
small wheelchairs. It was taking place in America and, at the end of
the broadcast, the winner of the tournament seemed to throw his
racket to them, bursting with joy just like players who run about on
two legs. A breath of freedom passed through the pergola and the high
windowless wall which enclosed it echoed their cheers.

Agricole posted the letter. Days went by without a reply, until
it arrived two weeks later. In the pergola the friends listened to
Palaneuve, who read it out in his fine voice. The minister allowed
himself to be moved, expressed his understanding, but made it
clear that it was best to forget an act of madness. Everyone could
remember, he added, more unworthy acts in this sacred place,
which was not, of course, a reason to use the Flame as a kitchen
stove. The Scandinavian was Danish. After a heavy fine he had
been sent back across the border. The letter ended with a call for
vigilance 'although in this respect as in others, no being and no
temple could be protected from such a filthy deed. The mentally ill
are at every street corner.'

'It is not a question of a street,' said Casanier, 'but of the most
beautiful avenue in the world.'

'Quite right,' said the others.

– Qu'ils doublent le nombre des gardiens! lança Agricole. Ce n'est jamais de l'argent perdu quand il s'agit d'honneur.

On entendait le heurt voisin des boules de billard, la rumeur assourdie des salles, si semblable au vacarme des poulaillers.

– J'ai une idée, dit Agricole que les autres regardaient depuis un moment. Nous allons t'offrir un moteur et tu mettras ta part, Casanier.

– Je n'en ai pas besoin! s'écria le manuel.

– C'est indispensable, dit Palaneuve, tu regretterais de ne pas en avoir et donc de ne pas en être! Bien que tu sois le seul à faire bande à part, en un sens.

– Je suis ici, s'écria Casanier, bien plus souvent que vous! C'est toujours moi qui vous attends!

– Cette fois nous serons à l'heure, tous les six, et ensemble, et sur le même rang et d'autres encore! J'ajoute que nous aurons tous un moteur, pour avant et pour après.

– Avant, après quoi? demandaient les autres.

– Mes amis . . .

Et il leur exposa le projet qui devait faire réfléchir le cuisinier de l'Inconnu et ranimer l'affaire que tous étouffaient, du Ministre au dernier passant. Sous la pergola courait[12] en liseron sur toutes choses et sur les six infirmes le silence particulier des comploteurs fleuri du pavillon pâle et multiple des questions que l'on n'ose poser et qui attendent pour tomber le souffle du plus courageux. Le Casanier se lança:

– Nous ne sommes pas en nombre suffisant?

– Nous allons battre le ban et l'arrière-ban des nôtres, dit Agricole, convoquer sans explication pour affaire importante les concernant. C'est moi qui leur parlerai. Nous sommes lundi. Je veux tous nous voir dans deux jours et nous arrêterons la manœuvre.

Bien qu'il n'eût jamais dépassé le grade de sergent, Agricole Palaneuve parlait sans réplique, en généralissime, et les autres le reconnaissaient comme le plus décidé et le plus adroit d'entre eux. Agricole ressentait tout cela et de ce fait sentait

'They should double the number of guards!' shouted Agricole. 'Money is never wasted when it is a matter of honour.'

They could hear the click of the billiard balls in the nearby room, the muffled noise from the other rooms, so very like the din that comes out of hen-houses.

'I've an idea,' said Agricole, whom the others had been looking at for quite some time. 'We're going to get you an engine and you're going to do your bit, Le Casanier.'

'I don't need one,' exclaimed the man, who moved his chair by hand.

'It's vital,' said Palaneuve. 'You would regret not having one and thus not being in with us! Even though you're a lone wolf, in a sense.'

'I'm here much more often than you!' exclaimed Le Casanier. 'It's always me who waits for you!'

'This time, all six of us will be on time, and together, and in the same row, and with others as well! Let me add that we shall all have an engine, for before and afterwards.'

'Before and after what?' asked the others.

'My friends . . .'

And he laid before them the plan that was to make the one who had done his cooking over the Unknown Soldier think, and to revive the affair that everyone was suppressing, from the minister to the last passer-by. Beneath the pergola, convolvulus-like, the peculiar silence of the plotters spread over everything and over the six invalids, and the many questions that no one dared utter, and which waited to be asked for the breath of the bravest amongst them, fluttered above them like as many pale flags. Casanier began:

'Surely, there aren't enough of us?'

'We're going to gather every last one of us together,' said Agricole, 'and assemble them, without explanation, for this important matter which concerns them. I will speak to them. Today is Monday. I want us all to be here in two days and we'll draw up our plan of attack.'

Although he had never been promoted above the rank of sergeant, Agricole Palaneuve spoke with complete authority, like a generalissimo, and the others accepted that he was the most resolute and the most adept of their number. Agricole took all this on board

la victoire au bout de ses ordres. Il rentra chez lui et le Casanier, exceptionnellement, lui fit un bout de route, suppléant au moteur qui lui manquait encore et dont il sentait maintenant la nécessité par une poigne d'acier. Tenant d'une main son guidon, il avait saisi de l'autre l'accoudoir d'Agricole et se laissa remorquer sur la longueur de l'arrondissement.[13] Il lâcha Palaneuve à regret et le regarda s'éloigner, qui reprenait sa grande vitesse et doublait les plus rapides des piétons.

Si l'on demandait à nos semblables ce qu'ils aimeraient sauver d'un désastre absolu, ce serait pour la plupart une image ou une lettre, la photographie de ce qui leur est le plus cher ou la déclaration que leur a faite leur plus haut amour. La signature peut varier à l'infini, d'un enfant à une mère, d'une épouse à un chef. Agricole ne prenait ses décisions et ses songes qu'en face d'un mot signé par le général de Gaulle.[14] Il l'avait mis sous verre, encadré d'une baguette en peau de cheval et suspendu au-dessus de sa table de nuit.

Il regarda la signature prestigieuse et sourit: le Général serait d'accord avec l'événement dont Agricole l'entretenait en remuant les lèvres, laissant échapper un mot, ici et là, comme pour s'excuser du côté farceur que d'aucuns pourraient y voir, mais il redevint grave et eut une nuit d'un sommeil profond, comme il n'en avait connu autrefois qu'à la veille des attaques, faisant pour ainsi dire le vide de lui-même et l'apprêt d'un homme neuf et disponible.

Ce fut un vendredi qu'Agricole et les siens rappelèrent l'attention du monde sur le dévouement de ceux qui sont morts pour que les autres vivent. Il ne songeait pas que laver la tache d'un affront c'est encore le rappeler et que vouer Un Tel aux gémonies c'est le remettre au premier rang. Le Scandinave allait connaître une nouvelle flambée, si l'on peut se permettre cette image. L'oubli si préférable n'est pas difficile, il est impossible.

Les Anciens[15] d'un régiment s'étaient groupés ce jour-là, selon l'habitude de cette quotidienne cérémonie, vers le haut des Champs-Élysées,[16] occupant le trottoir avant de défiler sur la chaussée, drapeaux en tête, vers l'Étoile et l'Inconnu qu'ils allaient fleurir. C'était toujours un difficile problème, une aggravation de

and hence scented victory with his every command. He returned
home and, for once, Casanier went part of the way with him,
substituting for the engine which he still did not have, and for which
he now felt the need, a grip of steel. His steering bar in one hand, he
had seized Agricole's armrest with the other and allowed himself to be
towed through the *arrondissement*. It was with regret that he let go of
Palaneuve and watched him drive off into the distance, building up
to maximum speed and overtaking even the quickest pedestrians.

If we asked our fellow men what they would like to save from a
total disaster, most would reply that it would be a picture or a letter,
the photograph of the person most dear to them or the declaration of
affection made by their most loved one. The signature might be
infinitely variable in appearance, from that of a child to that of a
mother, from that of a wife to that of a leader. Agricole did not make
his decisions or create his dreams without having before him a note
signed by General de Gaulle. He had put it under glass, framed it
with a strip of horse hide, and hung it above his bedside table.

He looked at the prestigious signature and smiled: the General
would approve of the event that Agricole was telling him about as
he moved his lips, letting out a word now and then, as though to
apologize for the farcical side of it that some might see, but he became
serious again and slept deeply for all of one night, as he had previously
done only on the eve of attacks, emptying himself, as it were, and
getting ready a new and alert man.

It was a Friday when Agricole and his companions brought the
attention of the world back to the devotion of those who had died
so that others might live. He did not think that washing away the
stain of an insult is to remind people of it and that holding someone
like that up to public obloquy is to rank him highly. The Scandinavian
was going to get roasted again, if such an image is permissible. The
oblivion that is preferable is not just difficult, it is impossible.

Following the custom of this daily ceremony, the Old Soldiers from
a regiment had gathered that day towards the top of the Champs-
Élysées, filling the pavement before parading on the road, flags at the
head of the column, towards the Étoile and the tomb of the Unknown
Soldier, on whose grave they were to put flowers. A difficult problem

la circulation toujours dense à cette heure et en ce lieu, malgré le nombre accru des gardiens de la paix, souples et efficaces, dans le carrousel des voitures. Les hommes décorés, coiffés de bérets et de calots, tapaient la semelle et se donnaient des nouvelles, venues de tous les coins de France. Malgré le froid, les traces de neige, le givre sur les arbres nus, une bonne humeur régnait, car l'on parlait de la vie, des naissances et des agrandissements, des fredaines de ceux qui les avaient quittés depuis la dernière ranimation de la Flamme et du plaisir simple, fondamental, d'être ensemble, toujours fidèles au poste. La cérémonie en devenait secondaire et l'on songeait par petits groupes au repas de souvenirs arrosé qui suivrait avant de regagner chacun son coin. Tout à coup on entendit une rumeur qui venait du rond-point, dans le bas, un concert de klaxons qui gagnait l'avenue et couvrait tout Paris d'un pelage de loup[17] dans le soir qui tombait.

Agricole Palaneuve et la vingtaine d'infirmes qu'il avait réunis venaient de quitter le bas-côté de l'avenue qu'ils avaient gagnée avec leurs moteurs de tous les coins de la capitale et, les gaz coupés, poussant à la main leur roue, avançant à deux bras l'un de l'autre sur une seule file horizontale, ils bouchaient la moitié montante[18] des Champs-Élysées. Devant eux le flot compact des voitures s'éloignait tandis que derrière, dans l'impossibilité de doubler les paralytiques, les véhicules commençaient à s'agglutiner, à caler, à reprendre difficilement à deux kilomètres-heure, à mugir, à donner de l'avertisseur sur tous les tons, rythmes et rages. Le vacarme prenait la densité, la force de la mer en furie et, comme la mer, le bruit avait des retombées subites, des reprises, un nouvel élan formidable et perdu. Maintenant, devant la ligne des fauteuils roulants, l'avenue était presque dégagée. Les lampadaires s'allumaient. Les Anciens, là-haut, s'aventuraient sur la chaussée pour regarder la manifestation, et des promeneurs commençaient à descendre vers Palaneuve, surpris de marcher en sens inverse sur la voie libre, sans le moindre sifflet d'un sergent de ville, sans rappel à l'ordre. Le bas de l'avenue était noir de carrosseries à touche-touche et l'on devinait que la masse augmentait. Des voitures de police arrivèrent des rues adjacentes et de la

was always posed by an increase of the ever-dense traffic at that time and in that spot, in spite of the greater number of policemen, quick-thinking and efficient, in the merry-go-round of the cars. The men, wearing their medals, berets and forage caps, were stamping their feet and exchanging news, for they had come from all over France. In spite of the cold, the traces of snow, the frost on the bare trees, everyone was in good humour for they were talking about life, about births and marriages, about the pranks of those who had left them since the last gathering at the Flame, about the simple, basic pleasure of being together, still manning the fort. The ceremony assumed a secondary importance and in small groups they thought about the reunion dinners, well supplied with wine, which would follow before they all went home. Suddenly, a hubbub could be heard coming from the roundabout, lower down, a chorus of horns which was reaching the avenue and stealthily covering all Paris in the advancing evening.

Agricole Palaneuve and the twenty or so invalids that he had gathered together had just left the lower end of the avenue that they had reached with their motors from all corners of the capital. Their engines turned off, propelling the wheels by hand, two arms' lengths separating them, and advancing in a single horizontal line, they were blocking off the half of the Champs-Élysées which rises. Before them the dense flow of cars was moving off into the distance whereas behind, unable to overtake the invalids, the vehicles were beginning to form a solid mass, to stall, to set off again with difficulty at two kilometres an hour, to roar, to sound their horns in every pitch, rhythm and fury. The din assumed the density, the strength, of a storm-tossed sea and, like the sea, the noise suddenly stopped, started again, with new, terrible, wild vigour. Now, in front of the line of wheelchairs, the avenue was almost clear. Street lamps were coming on. The Old Soldiers, at the top of the avenue, ventured out on to the road to look at the demonstration, and people out for a stroll were beginning to come down towards Palaneuve, surprised to be walking in the wrong direction on the clear road, without the hint of a whistle from a policeman, without being called back into line. The lower end of the avenue was black from cars that were bumper to bumper and one suspected that the mass was increasing. Police cars arrived from adjoining streets and

partie descendante où les véhicules n'obéissaient plus aux feux de circulation, la curiosité des conducteurs l'emportant sur leur presse habituelle. Agricole, le Casanier, les autres peinaient avec délice, le visage pâle jusqu'à l'os. Certains se demandaient s'ils tiendraient le coup jusqu'à la Flamme, mais ils roulaient, le poitrail couvert de décorations, le calot en éperon. Ils arrivaient au milieu de leur peine, à mi-chemin du triomphe, leur souffle les enveloppant de buée, lorsque Agricole Palaneuve, sentant faiblir les muscles de sa troupe et non point sa ferveur, s'avisant aussi que les piétons allaient par bonhomie, amusement, gentillesse ou farce leur barrer la route et l'élan, lança l'ordre que ses compagnons attendaient.

– Moteur!

Ils remirent les gaz. Le concert des klaxons un instant surpris reprit de plus belle et les suivit tel que jamais Agricole ne l'eût espéré. Ce n'était plus des quolibets, du moins le pensait-il, mais une aide. Qu'importe le motif! Tous ces gueulards étaient les décorateurs du théâtre qu'il régissait. Ils ajoutaient maintenant les lanternes et les phares. A la hauteur des Anciens, les porte-drapeaux se faufilèrent entre eux et les voitures. Agricole demanda aux siens de ralentir. Le service d'ordre sur la place de l'Étoile les attendait. Les seules voitures qui roulaient se faufilaient à la périphérie. Les responsables des gardiens et des Anciens prenaient cette manifestation imprévue pour organisée sans qu'ils en aient eu vent et donnaient aux fauteuils roulants l'aisance qu'il leur fallait. Au beau milieu de la place, à cent pas de l'Inconnu, Agricole arrêta sa machine et sa troupe fit cercle autour de lui. Un banc de Japonais, des reporters amateurs photographiaient à tout clac, couraient entre les étendards. Les klaxons devenaient hystériques. La ville hurlait.

– Et alors? cria un brigadier.

– Avancez! lança un autre.

Les agents de la circulation entouraient maintenant les infirmes, mais Agricole Palaneuve ne bronchait pas. Il tira

from the downward side of the avenue, on which cars were no longer obeying the traffic lights since their normal hurry was taking second place to the curiosity of their drivers. Agricole, Casanier and the others toiled with delight, their pale faces taut to the bone. Some wondered if they would make it as far as the Flame, but they pushed on, their chests covered in medals, their forage caps square on their heads. They had reached the halfway point of their toil, halfway to triumph, their breath enveloping them in mist, when Agricole Palaneuve, feeling the muscles, but not the ardour, of his troops to be weakening, noticing also that the pedestrians, be it from goodheartedness, amusement, kindliness or as a joke, were blocking their route and their momentum, yelled out the order that his companions were waiting for:

'Engines on!'

They re-started their engines. Surprised for a moment, the chorus of horns started again even louder and followed behind them in a way that Agricole could never have hoped for. They were no longer jeering, they were a help, at least that is what he thought. What did the motive matter! All those loud-mouths were the set-designers in the play that he was directing. Now they were adding their sidelights and their headlights. When they came level with the Old Soldiers, the flag-bearers threaded their way between them and the cars. Agricole asked his men to slow down. The police were waiting for them on the place de l'Étoile. The only cars that were moving were threading their way along the edge. The officials amongst the guards and the Old Soldiers assumed that this unexpected demonstration had been organized without them getting wind of it and gave the wheelchairs all the assistance they needed. In the very centre of the square, a hundred feet from the Unknown Soldier, Agricole stopped his engine and his squad made a circle around him. A bank of Japanese people, amateur reporters, were clicking madly away at their cameras, running between the flags. The car horns were becoming hysterical. The city was screaming.

'Now what?' cried a brigadier.

'Advance!' shouted someone else.

The traffic police were now beginning to surround the invalids, but Agricole Palaneuve did not flinch. Solemnly, he pulled an

solennellement d'une sacoche de sa machine un œuf et le laissa tomber sur le pavé.

Le responsable des Anciens s'approcha de Casanier:

– Qu'est-ce que c'est? demanda-t-il. De quel régiment êtes-vous?

– Allez devant, dit Agricole, maintenant on vous suit.

La musique militaire massée sous l'Arc attaquait *Le Chant du départ*.[19] On les attendait tous. Les avertisseurs s'éteignirent. Dans le grondement de la circulation reprise un clairon lança un cri d'une tristesse infinie comme venu d'un autre temps. Le Casanier penché vers Palaneuve lui pressa la main.

– Nous lirons tout cela demain dans le journal, dit Agricole, et tant pis pour ceux qui ne croient à rien!

De leurs petites voitures ils regardaient la flamme vouée au bleu que la nuit cuivrait. Pour Agricole la porte du Ciel devait être ainsi, en forme de lance et transparente. Il serra les accoudoirs de son fauteuil car il sentait monter des larmes.

– Casanier, dit-il comme le clairon s'évanouissait, dispersion! Chacun sa route comme prévu et tous à la pergola! Vos lampes en brassard! J'ai fait mettre au frais du vin d'Alsace.

Le Café des Chasseurs était devenu silencieux. Les consommateurs qui s'étaient groupés regagnèrent leurs tables en rapportant leurs chaises.

– Alors, dit Montfavert d'une voix tragique, Palaneuve n'aurait pas pu me faire signe?

– Certes! dit une voix faible. Un ami est d'abord un homme qui pense à vous, mais peut-être a-t-il voulu t'épargner le déplacement?

Montfavert tapa sur les accoudoirs de sa machine.

– Je peux traverser la France avec ça!

– Oui, c'est un coup rude! L'outrage est aussi pour toi. Évidemment, tu laisses tomber cette publication?

– J'ai envoyé mon chèque de souscription ce matin, répliqua Montfavert, dès l'ouverture de la poste. Pour moi l'amitié, c'est aussi d'oublier tout un côté de l'ami.

egg from a bag on his wheelchair and dropped it on
the road.

The official from the Old Soldiers went up to Le Casanier:

'What's going on?' he asked. 'What regiment are you from?'

'Go on ahead,' said Agricole. 'We'll follow you.'

The massed military band waiting under the Arc struck up 'Le
Chant du départ'. Everyone was waiting for them. Horns were turned
off. In the growl of the traffic, which had started to move again, a bugle
sounded a cry of infinite sadness which seemed to come from another
age. Casanier, leaning towards Palaneuve, squeezed his hand.

'We'll read about it all in the paper tomorrow,' said Agricole,
'and hard luck on those who do not believe in anything!'

From their tiny carriages they looked at the flame dedicated to the
blue that the night was turning to copper. In Agricole's mind the gateway
to heaven must be like this, in the shape of a lance and transparent. He
gripped the armrests on his wheelchair for he could feel tears rising.

'Casanier,' he said as the bugle faded away, 'dismiss! Everyone
goes back as we planned, everyone to the pergola! Lamps fixed to
your arms! I've had the wine from Alsace chilled.'

The Hunters' Café had fallen silent. The customers who had
formed a group went back to their tables, carrying their
chairs.

'So,' said Montfavert, with a note of tragedy in his voice,
'couldn't Palaneuve have got in touch?'

'Of course he could,' said a faint voice. 'A friend is primarily a man
who thinks of you, but perhaps he wanted to spare you the journey?'

Montfavert tapped the armrests of his wheelchair.

'I can go from one side of France to the other in this!'

'Yes, it's a bit much. This was also an insult to you. Of course,
you'll stop taking that magazine?'

'I sent the cheque for my subscription this morning,' replied
Montfavert, 'as soon as the post office opened. In my view
friendship is also about forgetting a whole aspect of a friend.'

Accursed Notebooks
(an extract from *La Déconvenue*)

LOUISE COTNOIR

Les Cahiers maudits

Elle déchire une dernière page avant de quitter le bar de l'hôtel Lutecia. Je ne comprends pas pourquoi elle s'acharne ainsi, tous les soirs, à les remplir, à les relire avant de les détruire *systématiquement*. Et le cahier s'appauvrit chaque fois, s'amincit jusqu'à ce qu'elle en sorte un tout neuf de son cartable, pour de nouveau le remplir et le vider, avec méthode, de tous ses feuillets! Cette entreprise absurde me déconcerte; j'en cherche en vain la raison. Avec intensité et désespoir, elle recommence ce travail précis. Comme s'il s'agissait pour elle d'échapper au malheur, au vide. Quand il pleut, elle boit pour réchauffer ses doigts tremblants.

Elle ne parle à personne durant des jours, des mois. Un bloc de silence pendant qu'elle noircit les feuilles irrévocablement vouées à la destruction. Elle se raconte sans doute une vie rêvée, se donne une densité, se figure réelle. Ou peut-être retaille-t-elle le monde jusqu'à ce qu'il lui devienne supportable? Chose certaine, elle soustrait sans cesse, s'impatiente devant les déficits. Elle parle dans sa tête.

Tout cela, je l'imagine. Je ne sais rien de cette femme, sinon son entêtement à venir hanter ce bar. Je l'aperçois, chaque fois penchée sur ses diaboliques cahiers comme sur une nuque en partance, comme pour y poser un baiser. Je vois l'angle de sa tête quand elle s'incline, presque heureuse. Son corps famélique n'est pas sans évoquer celui des déportés revenant des camps. Ses joues creuses m'indiquent qu'elle ne sait pas avoir faim. Elle sirote longuement cet éternel ballon de rouge qu'elle écarte parfois, un obstacle au texte qu'elle s'acharne à fabriquer et qu'elle anéantit à chaque fois.

Accursed Notebooks

She tears out a final page before leaving the bar of the Lutecia Hotel. I do not understand why she fills them so furiously every evening, then rereads them with equal fury, before *systematically* destroying them. And every time the notebook wastes away, grows thinner, until she pulls a brand new one from her briefcase, just to fill it and methodically empty it of all its leaves! This absurd venture worries me; I seek the reason in vain. She recommences this meticulous task with intensity and despair. As if it were for her a question of escaping from misfortune, from emptiness. When it rains, she drinks to warm her trembling fingers.

She does not speak to anyone for days, or even months. A period of silence whilst she blackens the pages that are irrevocably destined for destruction. No doubt, she is telling herself about a life that only exists in dream, is giving herself solidity, is imagining herself to be real. Or is she perhaps reshaping the world until it becomes bearable for her? One thing is certain, she is constantly hiding, growing impatient at her shortcomings. She is talking to herself.

I can only imagine all of this. I know nothing about this woman, apart from her stubborn insistence on coming and haunting this bar. Each time I can see her bent over those diabolical notebooks like someone leaning over the back of a neck that is about to move away, as though to plant a kiss on it. I can see the angle of her head, when she bends over; she is almost happy. It is impossible not to see in her scrawny body those of the prisoners returning from internment camps. Her hollow cheeks tell me that she does not know how to be hungry. She takes for ever to sip at that long-lasting glass of red wine, which she occasionally pushes to one side, as though it were an impediment to the text that she is furiously trying to create and which she destroys every time.

«Les mots pour hurler, pour être entendue.» Cette quête d'une parole vive, compensatoire, prend la forme d'une musique inaudible. C'est pourquoi elle reprend sans cesse la phrase pleine de nœuds, de blessures irréparables. Des images trop vives, d'un irréel dévorant, envahissent son crâne. Elle n'entend rien du vacarme autour. Le souffle freiné, immobile et glacé, son corps flotte, en suspens.

Elle veille à ne pas oublier, une sorte d'ordalie qui demande l'impossible. Le recueillement de ses gestes prend la forme d'une prière sous ses doigts nerveux. Les phrases se formulent à la vitesse accélérée de la vision. Écrire semble un rituel. «Je voudrais laisser une trace matérielle et touchante.» Le récit insensé qui la mobilise dépasse la détresse de ses origines. Une passion démesurée ranime les voix disparues.

L'inconcevable de cette répétition du désastre se matérialise quand elle peut enfin déchiqueter une à une les pages du manuscrit. Elle atteint alors le détachement. C'est du moins ce que je pense lire sur son visage devenu tout à coup serein, presque extatique.

La femme exerce sur moi une telle fascination que je me sur-prends à venir régulièrement au bar de cet hôtel, prise à mon tour par l'acharnement qu'elle met à inscrire les figures, les fêlures. Je cherche avec elle une issue à ce labyrinthe où nous nous égarons chaque soir: elle dans ses cahiers maudits, moi dans ma tête rêveuse.

«Le deuil impossible.» Les nerfs se tendent, l'espace du cerveau se laisse envahir par un défilé de visages fugaces, je m'arrête. Dans ce monologue confus qu'elle se tient, ce discours sans cohérence, elle veut fixer une dernière scène, un regard effacé. C'est à ce travail d'exhumation qu'elle se livre comme s'il y allait de sa propre vie. Elle ne voudrait pas mourir anonyme. Elle refuse de se joindre aux *fausses bonnes consciences*, à la dimension collective du mot *Shoah*.[1] Elle ne sait pas s'adapter, ne sait pas renoncer.

Je crains de la voir disparaître, de la voir s'anéantir. Je me rappelle avoir lu un roman . . . des femmes, comme elle, venaient tous les jours d'après-guerre consulter le grand babillard de l'hôtel, venaient attendre, ici même, pendant des heures, le retour de leurs disparus . . . toutes leurs énergies concentrées sur le désir de photographier la perte, de faire peut-être enfin leur deuil . . .

'Words to scream, so that she might be heard.' This search for a living, compensatory language takes the form of inaudible music. That is why she constantly restarts the sentence full of knots and unhealable wounds. Images that are too vivid, of an all-consuming unreality, invade her mind. She can hear nothing of the din that surrounds her. Her breathing checked, still and icy, her body floats, in suspense.

She ensures that she does not forget, a sort of ordeal which asks the impossible. The concentration in her movements takes the form of prayer beneath her twitchy fingers. The sentences are created at the accelerated speed of her vision. Writing seems to be a ritual. 'I would like to leave a material and evocative reminder.' The demented account that motivates her goes beyond the distress of its origins. An excessive passion gives life to voices that have disappeared.

The unimaginable in this rehearsal of disaster materializes when she can finally tear out the pages of the manuscript one by one. She then achieves detachment. At least, that is what I think I can read on her face, which suddenly becomes serene, almost ecstatic.

The woman fascinates me so much that I surprise myself by coming regularly to this hotel bar, so overwhelmed am I by the relentless determination with which she etches figures, cracks. I am with her in seeking an exit to this labyrinth through which we wander every evening: she in her accursed notebooks, I in my dreamy head.

'Mourning is impossible.' My nerves become taut, the space in my mind allows itself to be invaded by a procession of half-glimpsed faces. I stop. In this confused monologue she is delivering to herself, this incoherent speech, she wants to define a final scene, a gaze that has disappeared. It is in this task of exhumation that she engages herself, as if her own life were at stake. She would not like to die anonymous. She refuses to be one of those *false good consciences*, on the collective scale of the word *Shoah*. She cannot adapt, she cannot give up.

I am afraid that I will see her disappear, see her destroyed. I remember reading a novel . . . women, like her, in the period after the war, came every day to read the big hotel newspaper, came to wait in this very spot, for hours on end, for the return of those who had disappeared . . . all their energy concentrated on their desire to photograph the loss, perhaps finally to mourn . . .

La gare de l'Est . . . les trains . . . J'ai vu cette femme, parmi
tant d'autres, y déambuler aussi . . . Une sorte de pèlerinage.
Ses pas savent le désert de l'absence et, pourtant, ne renoncent
pas à chercher le miracle. *Une foi de charbonnier.*[2] Entre la gare
de l'Est et l'hôtel Lutecia, elle refait le trajet interminable. Je ne lui
sais que cette activité itérative, chaque jour, avec dans la tête le
mot *départ*. Sur l'immense panneau lumineux, les noms restent
les mêmes: Dachau, Auschwitz, Buchenwald.[3] Cette évidence
paraît la conforter. Elle esquisse un sourire diffus. «Tout ne peut
donc pas s'effacer.» Cette unique certitude la rapproche de toutes
ces femmes qui, avant elle, venaient fébriles vers ce mémorial
singulier.

Les trains arrivaient, avec l'attente déçue. Mais ils revenaient.
L'espoir ne connaissait pas de limites. Ainsi, le sens inversé de la
mort faisait rêver ces femmes abandonnées par le sort. Il devenait
peut-être pensable *d'en revenir*. La gare de l'Est prenait des airs de
contestation, de refus. La salle des pas perdus trouvait un sens réel,
une utilité concrète. Les rails pouvaient défaire le chemin, ramener
de la mort à la vie . . . Leur doublement pour une fois servait à
quelque chose. La gare de l'Est s'octroyait un nouveau sens, devenait symbole, témoin de ce qui n'aurait jamais dû arriver, de ce qui
ne pouvait pas s'imaginer: les survivants . . . Le chagrin s'y trans-
formait en spectacle, il pouvait se mettre à distance, s'apaiser. Il s'écri-
vait comme une lettre d'amour à l'absent, comme si l'on avait
quelque chose à se faire pardonner. Peut-être l'erreur d'une Histoire
qui nous regarde.

Cette femme se tient debout, seule sur ce quai qui ressemble
maintenant à une allée de cimetière. Un matin de novembre, elle
dépose un bouquet de myosotis sur les rails. Elle pense *ne m'oubliez
pas*, mais elle entend *Vergissmeinnicht*.[4] Le geste laisse les voyageurs
indifférents. Elle tient mal sur ses jambes, reste longtemps sur le
quai. En attente de quelqu'un qui ne vient pas, pas encore, pas
aujourd'hui.

Dans l'odeur tenace des acacias, d'où émergent les énergies que la
mort ne peut détruire, je fixe de nouveau cette femme qui écrit ce
qui n'a de nom dans aucune langue. C'est alors que je remarque,

The Gare de l'Est . . . the trains . . . I saw this woman there, amongst so many others, walking up and down . . . A sort of pilgrimage. Her footsteps know the emptiness of absence and yet do not give up looking for the miracle. *Blind faith*. She makes the same interminable journey between the Gare de l'Est and the hotel Lutecia. All I know about her is this repeated activity, every day, with the word *departure* on her mind. The names are the same on the vast, illuminated noticeboard: Dachau, Auschwitz, Buchenwald. This obviousness seems to comfort her. The faintest of smiles passes over her face. 'So not everything can be wiped out.' This unique certainty brings her close to all those women who, before her, came feverishly to this strange memorial.

The trains arrived, and with them the disappointment of their expectation. But the trains kept on coming. Hope knew no limits. And thus, the inverted meaning of death caused these women, abandoned by fate, to dream. It perhaps became possible to imagine coming back from there. The Gare de l'Est assumed an atmosphere of challenge, of refusal. The waiting hall found a real meaning, a definable usefulness. The rails could undo the path that had been trodden, bring back from death to life . . . For once, the fact that there were two of them served a purpose. The Gare de l'Est was given a new meaning, became a symbol, a witness to what should never have happened, to what could not be imagined: the survivors . . . Grief became a spectacle there, it could distance itself, subside. It was as though a love-letter were being written to the missing one, as if one had something for which to seek forgiveness. Perhaps the error of a History that concerns us all.

This woman is standing, alone on that platform which now resembles the pathway in a cemetery. One November morning she places a bouquet of forget-me-nots on the rails. She thinks *do not forget me*, but she hears *Vergissmeinnicht*. The gesture passes unnoticed by the travellers. She is unsteady on her feet, and remains on the platform for a long time. Waiting for someone who is not coming back, not yet, not today.

Amid the lingering scent of the acacias, from which come sources of energy that death cannot destroy, I stare once more at this woman who is writing that which has no name in any language. It

pour la première fois, ce qui me semble des taches d'encre à son poignet. J'ai les mains fiévreuses, j'ai envie de vomir. L'inexplicable prend la forme de ce corps brisé qui se penche, chaque soir, sur des cahiers pour y trouver une façon d'aimer, malgré tout. L'écriture reprend la vie à son point mort, à l'instant de l'élan arrêté. «Toute ma famille en cendres.» La fumée bleue monte en spirale au-dessus des charniers, une cigarette se consume lentement au fond du cendrier déjà débordant de mégots.

La femme ramasse les feuillets noircis, les empile. Elle les prend un à un et les déchire . . . une sorte de rituel pour apaiser les morts . . . une incantation affectueuse pour les relier au présent. Quand il n'y a plus rien à comprendre, plus rien à faire, reste le travail des mots en deuil. La perspective de l'aube, comment alors l'envisager?

Elle ne remarque pas ma présence insistante, s'entête à retrouver la lumière au-dessus des arbres rachitiques du baraquement . . . Elle torture sa mémoire pour qu'elle lui rende, noir sur blanc, le sourire de sa mère, ce matin d'automne 1943. Elle arrive parfois à dessiner son profil maigre, la robe-sac, commune, presque une fosse. Elle serre encore les doigts glacés du petit frère, il a à peine dix ans, et il ne sait pas rire. Ses ongles s'enfoncent dans sa paume jusqu'au sang, jusqu'à ce qu'on les arrache l'un à l'autre, et que seul s'installe, au fond de ses oreilles, au creux de son ventre, le cri.

Elle lève la tête et la plume, incapable d'aller au-delà de cette souffrance. L'effondrement de l'image la laisse sans larmes. «C'est un livre d'ombres.» Il n'y a pas de cimetière, de pierre commémorative, pas de fleurs, pas un carré de terre pour accueillir ces morts-là.

Restent les cahiers que je lui vole sans ménagement et que j'emporte avec moi. Elle ne bouge pas, ne crie pas, ne pleure pas. Habituée depuis si longtemps au rapt, aux départs sans explication, sans retour. Elle ouvre un cahier tout neuf et reprend l'histoire sans cesse inachevée et recommencée . . . Comme si rien n'avait eu lieu.

is then that, for the first time, I notice what appear to be ink stains on her wrist. My hands are feverish, I want to vomit. The inexplicable takes the shape of this broken body which leans, every evening, over notebooks to find in them a way to love, in spite of everything. Writing restarts life when it is at a standstill, its momentum checked. 'All my family in ashes.' The blue smoke spirals up above the mass graves, a cigarette burns itself out at the bottom of an ashtray already overflowing with fag-ends.

The woman picks up the darkened leaves of paper, piles them up. She takes them one by one and tears them up . . . a sort of ritual to appease the dead . . . a cherished incantation to link them to the present. When there is nothing left to understand, nothing left to do, there only remains the work of words in mourning. How then is it possible to envisage the prospect of dawn?

She does not notice my insistent presence, she persists in finding the light above the spindly trees of the camp again . . . She is torturing her memory in order that it gives her back, in black and white, her mother's smile, that autumn morning in 1943. She sometimes manages to draw her thin profile, her sack-dress, almost a common grave. She again squeezes the icy fingers of her little brother, he is barely ten and does not know how to laugh. Her fingernails sink into the palm of her hand until it starts to bleed, until they are torn from each other one by one, and until, deep in her ears, in the pit of her stomach, begins that cry.

She looks up and raises the nib of her pen, incapable of going beyond this suffering. The disappearance of the image leaves her without tears. 'It is a book of ghosts.' There is no cemetery, no commemorative stone, no flowers, not a patch of earth to welcome those dead people.

All that remains are the notebooks that I steal from her without any sense of respect and that I take away with me. She does not move, does not shout, does not cry: she has been used for so long to theft, to unexplained departures from which there is no return. She opens a brand-new notebook and resumes the story that is constantly left unfinished and begun again . . . As if nothing had happened.

Héloïse

SYLVIE GERMAIN

Héloïse[1]

«Si ton nom a sept lettres, sept branches brûlent ton nom.»
EDMOND JABÈS[2]

Héloïse n'avait jamais quitté ses quelques arpents de terre brous-
sailleuse entourés de pommiers, de frênes et de trembles aux
branchages tordus par le vent. Elle avait atteint un très grand âge
au long duquel elle n'avait connu d'autres aventures que celles,
muettes, des bancs de nuages en haute transhumance, celles, si
vives, des volées d'oiseaux en migration, et celles, tout en frissons
et bruissements, des arbres en feuillaison, en floraison et en
défeuillaison.

Le gris ardoise qui longtemps avait été le sien s'était fané, il avait
pris un ton d'un blanc cendreux. Tout son être semblait s'être ainsi
étamé de cendre et de poussière, et sa voix particulièrement.

Le cri qui lui tenait lieu tout à la fois de parole, de chant, de
plainte et de murmure, avait perdu toute vigueur; il ne se languissait
plus désormais qu'en furtifs râles tout grenus de tristesse. Il se levait
soudain, mais ne s'élançait pas; c'était un cri sans modulation et
sans force, un sanglot assourdi.

Celle qui avait acheté cette ânesse plus de vingt ans auparavant
l'avait ainsi nommée parce que le nom d'Héloïse la tourmentait
depuis l'enfance. Elle-même s'appelait Marthe, mais elle n'avait
jamais aimé son prénom qu'elle trouvait trop dur, et du jour où,
encore petite fille, elle avait découvert cet autre nom, si léger, si
fluide, elle n'avait eu de cesse de le désirer pour elle-même. Pendant
des années elle s'était entêtée à réclamer ce nom à ses parents, les
suppliant de le lui offrir à Noël ou à son anniversaire en guise de
cadeau. Elle reçut des jouets, des livres d'images, des poupées – que
bien sûr elle appelait toutes Héloïse –, mais jamais ce prénom dont
la douceur la faisait tant rêver. Lorsqu'elle se fiança, Marthe

Héloïse

'If your name has seven letters, seven branches burn your name.'
EDMOND JABÈS

Héloïse had never been away from her few acres of land covered in undergrowth, surrounded by apple trees, ash trees and aspens with branches that had been twisted by the wind. She had reached a grand old age and throughout her life she had known no adventures other than those that were silent, banks of clouds in full migration, those that were so full of life, flocks of birds on their way to summer nesting grounds, and those full of shivers and rustling, trees coming into leaf, coming into blossom and then losing their leaves again.

Her hair, slate-grey, had for a long time had faded, and had become an ash-white colour. Her whole being seemed to have been silvered with ash and dust, and especially her voice.

Her cry, which replaced at one and the same time speech, song, moan and murmur, had completely lost its vigour; all that remained henceforward were barely audible groans flecked right through with sadness. It rose suddenly, but never screamed out; it was a cry with no variety of tone, with no strength, a muffled sob.

The woman who had bought this she-donkey more than twenty years before had given her this name because the name of Héloïse had plagued her since childhood. Her name was in fact Marthe, but she had never liked her first name, which she considered too harsh, and from the day when, still a little girl, she had discovered this other name, so light, so fluid, she had never ceased to want it for her own. For years she had stubbornly begged for this name from her parents, beseeching them to give it to her as a present at Christmas or for her birthday. She received toys, picture-books, dolls – which naturally she all called Héloïse – but never that name whose softness made her dream so much. When she became engaged, Marthe

demanda à celui qui allait devenir son époux de l'appeler
Héloïse; celui-ci, garçon bourru et taciturne, jugea absurde ce
caprice et n'y répondit pas. Marthe reporta alors sa lancinante
passion sur la fille qu'elle espérait mettre au monde; par avance
elle plaçait la fillette sous le beau vocable d'Héloïse, comme sous
la protection d'une sainte, et elle langeait, berçait l'enfant dans
la luminosité de ce mot tout fleuri de voyelles. Mais elle n'eut
jamais d'enfant, son propre corps lui refusa l'ultime chance
d'incarner enfin le prénom bien-aimé. Et celui-ci demeura enfoui
dans le silence, splendeur toujours plus triste et désolante d'être
laissée en déshérence. Et c'est ainsi qu'une jeune ânesse que
Marthe acquit un jour hérita de ce nom mélodieux magnifié
par des femmes de légende.

   Le simple fait de l'avoir ainsi nommé fit que Marthe porta à
l'animal un attachement extrême; elle traitait l'ânesse avec plus
de délicatesse que s'il se fût agi d'une levrette de race pure ou
même d'une licorne. Elle lui parlait comme à une enfant – celle
qu'elle n'était plus mais qui rêvait toujours en elle, et celle
qu'elle n'avait pas eue mais qui pourtant dormait en elle. Elle
lui parlait comme à l'amante qu'elle n'était pas, mais qui
passionnément veillait en elle. Elle lui parlait infiniment, par
mots, par gestes et par regards, comme on s'adresse à un ange
qui va, invisible et merveilleux, à nos côtés. Et elle poursuivait
avec d'autant plus de tendresse ce dialogue d'amour que sa vie
était plombée de solitude. Guillaume, son mari, homme taiseux,
ne disait pas dix mots par jour. Il était bien de cette terre et de
ce ciel où il était venu au monde, aride et sombre. Il était aussi
avare de mots que cette terre de pierrailles l'était de fleurs et de
lumière.

Une nuit, un violent orage éclata. Marthe, réveillée en sursaut,
pensa aussitôt à l'ânesse restée dehors. Elle sauta hors de son
lit et courut en toute hâte sans même prendre le temps de se
chausser et de passer un manteau sur sa chemise de nuit.
Guillaume perçut vaguement à travers son sommeil l'orage

asked the man who was going to become her husband to call her Héloïse; he, a surly, taciturn young man, considered this whim to be absurd and paid it no attention. So Marthe directed her obsessive passion to the girl to whom she hoped to give birth; in anticipation she bestowed upon the little girl the fine name of Héloïse, as though placing her under the protection of a saint, and she changed the nappies of the child, rocked her, in the glow of this word, which blossomed with vowels. But she never did have a child, her own body refused her the last chance finally to give flesh to the beloved name. And it remained buried in silence, a splendour that was ever more sad and distressing for having been left with no heir. And so it was that a young she-donkey that Marthe acquired one day inherited this melodious name made great by women of legend.

The mere fact that Marthe had given her this name meant that she became extremely attached to the animal; she treated the she-donkey with more tenderness than she would have done had she been a pure-bred greyhound or even a unicorn. She spoke to her as though to a child – the one she no longer was but who still dreamt within her, and the one she had not had but who none the less slept within her. She spoke to her as though to the lover that she was not, but who passionately kept watch within her. She spoke to her endlessly, with words, with gestures, and with looks, as one addresses an angel who, unseen and mysteriously, walks beside us. And she continued this lovers' dialogue with even greater tenderness because her life was weighed down with loneliness. Guillaume, her husband, a silent man, did not utter ten words a day. He really was a product of that earth and that sky where he had been born, parched and sombre. He was as avaricious with words as that stony earth was with flowers and light.

One night a violent storm broke. Marthe, woken with a start, immediately thought about the she-donkey, which was still outside. She leapt out of bed and ran as fast as she could, without even pausing to put on her shoes or slip a coat over her night-dress. Through the veil of sleep Guillaume was vaguely aware of the storm that was

qui tonnait et des pas qui dévalaient des marches, mais il ne se réveilla pas.

Marthe avait à peine ouvert la porte du perron que le vent la lui arracha des mains et la fit claquer contre le mur en la disloquant à moitié. La pluie était si drue qu'elle rebondissait en jets sur le sol qu'elle frappait, et l'eau semblait sourdre autant du ciel que de la terre. Marthe s'élança dans la cour; ses pieds nus glissaient dans la boue et la pluie lui cinglait le visage. Entre les arbres de l'enclos dont les branches semblaient tournoyer, elle aperçut Héloïse qui tremblait de tout son corps sous les rafales de vent glacé et de pluie brasillante. L'ânesse en cet instant lui apparut, dans la blancheur incandescente des éclairs et les tourbillons de feuillages arrachés, tel un animal fabuleux, avec ses hautes oreilles dressées droit vers le ciel ainsi que des ailes d'ange immobile. Le beau nom d'Héloïse resplendissait dans la boue, tout ruisselant et sonore de lumière, ailé pour un envol dans le ciel en éclats, dans la nuit en remous. Le corps d'Héloïse, transfiguré par l'orage, évoquait la monture d'un cavalier d'Apocalypse.[3] Marthe tendit les bras vers l'ânesse aux yeux exorbités d'effroi, comme pour la retenir sur cette terre qu'elle semblait prête à quitter d'un grand coup d'aile, et elle l'appela d'une voix affolée de tendresse. «Hél . . .», mais la foudre lui coupa la parole, le nom resta inachevé. Elle s'écroula d'une masse, la face contre le sol, bras écartés. Alors l'ânesse, tendant son cou sous la pluie, poussa un cri si long et transperçant qu'il refoula au loin tous les bruits de l'orage.

Ce fut ce cri qui réveilla Guillaume. D'un bond il se leva, sans même avoir eu le temps de reprendre conscience. Son esprit était encore tout ombré de sommeil. «Marthe», dit-il, comme s'il cherchait un repère. «Marthe», répéta-t-il dans l'obscurité de la chambre. Il regarda le lit, tâtonna les oreillers et grommela. Il enfila son pantalon et sortit de la chambre. Sur le palier il appela à nouveau sa femme. Mais le nom de Marthe allait se perdre dans le silence de la maison, et les seuls échos qui lui revenaient étaient le cri obsédant de l'ânesse et le violent battement d'une porte heurtant un mur. Il descendit; il vit le seuil béant, le carrelage luisant de flaques à reflets

thundering and the footsteps that were racing down the stairs, but he did not wake up.

Marthe had scarcely opened the door on to the stone steps outside when the wind tore it from her grasp and crashed it against the wall, all but tearing it from its hinges. The rain was falling so hard that it rebounded in spurts from the ground that it struck, and the water seemed to spring as much from the earth as from the sky. Marthe raced into the yard; her bare feet slid in the mud and the rain lashed at her face. Between the trees in the paddock, whose branches seemed to be swirling round, she spotted Héloïse, trembling from head to toe beneath the blasts of the icy wind and the burning rain. At that moment, the she-donkey appeared to her, in the incandescent whiteness of the lightning and the whirl of torn foliage, like a mythical animal, with her long ears pointed straight towards the sky like the wings of a motionless angel. The beautiful name of Héloïse was resplendent in the mud, streaming and vibrant with light, winged for a flight into the exploding sky, into the turbulent night. The body of Héloïse, transfigured by the storm, conjured up the mount of a horseman of the Apocalypse. Marthe stretched out her hands to the she-donkey, whose eyes were wide with terror, as though to hold her down on this earth that she seemed ready to leave with a great beat of her wings, and she called to her in a voice terror-stricken with tenderness. 'Hél . . .', but the lightning cut her short and the name remained unfinished. She collapsed in a heap, her face to the ground, her arms splayed. Then the she-donkey, stretching her neck in the rain, let out such a long and piercing cry that it drove back into the distance all the noises of the storm.

It was this cry that woke Guillaume. He leapt up, without even taking the time to come round. His mind was still clouded with sleep. 'Marthe,' he said, as though looking for an indication of where she was. 'Marthe,' he repeated in the darkness of the bedroom. He looked at the bed, felt at the pillows and muttered. He slipped on his trousers and went out of the room. On the landing he called out again to his wife. But Marthe's name was lost in the silence of the house, and the only echoes that came back to him were the haunting cry of the she-donkey and the loud banging of a door as it beat against the wall. He went downstairs; he saw the gaping door, silver reflections shining

argentés et, par-delà la trouée du seuil, une grande tache blanche qui semblait ondoyer sur place dans la boue. L'ânesse répétait son cri avec obstination. Déjà l'orage s'éloignait, des lueurs bleuâtres éclaboussaient le ciel par-delà les collines, la foudre craquait de loin en loin. Guillaume se tenait toujours sur le seuil, immobile comme s'il venait d'être à son tour pétrifié. Il regardait la tache blanche s'estomper lentement dans l'obscurité de la nuit ressoudée. Enfin il s'avança, un peu titubant, vers cette forme blême et ondulante.

La chevelure brune de Marthe déversée tout autour de sa tête se confondait avec la boue, certaines longues mèches ressemblaient à des racines d'arbuste calciné. Le vent gonflait sa chemise qui claquait avec un bruit saccadé, découvrant haut ses jambes. Guillaume s'agenouilla auprès du corps de Marthe; ses mains engourdies de stupeur s'égaraient en gestes hésitants au-dessus de la chevelure boueuse, des épaules raidies, des jambes nues, nacrées de pluie, sans oser se poser.

Un geste enfin s'arracha de ses mains; il saisit dans sa paume un des talons de Marthe dont la rondeur rehaussait la cambrure du pied. Cette rondeur lovée au creux de sa main éveilla en lui une connaissance nouvelle du corps de Marthe. Une connaissance faite d'étonnement et d'infinie tendresse. Il tenait ce talon rond et ferme comme un sein de jeune fille, il le souleva jusqu'à ses lèvres, l'embrassa; il confondait la chaleur de ses propres lèvres avec celle, déjà éteinte pourtant, du pied si joliment cambré. Les pas qui tout à l'heure avaient traversé son sommeil s'en revenaient danser contre sa bouche, résonner dans son corps, courir tout autour de son cœur. Les pas de Marthe en allée dans la nuit cognaient dans sa poitrine et lui foulaient le sang au même rythme que celui de la porte brisée heurtant le mur, que celui de l'ânesse pleurant son cri.

La bourrique! Guillaume soudain desserra son étreinte; tout le sang qu'il avait cru sentir battre dans le corps de Marthe reflua vers son cœur esseulé. Les pas de Marthe s'enlisèrent dans ce sang de douleur, et un sang de colère entra en crue du fond de ses entrailles. Guillaume se releva, marcha droit vers l'ânesse

from pools of water on the tiles, and through the open doorway a large white mark that seemed to ripple in one place in the mud. The she-donkey was stubbornly letting out her cry over and over again. Already the storm was moving away, spatters of bluish light glowed over the hills, the lightning was cracking further and further away. Guillaume was still standing in the doorway, motionless as if he too had just been paralysed with fear. He watched the white mark fade slowly into the darkness of the reconstituted night. At last, he moved forward, swaying slightly, towards that pallid, rippling shape.

Marthe's brown hair sprayed all around her head was as one with the mud, some of her long locks were like the roots of a charred shrub. The wind inflated her night-dress, which flapped, drumming out a staccato sound, revealing the very tops of her legs. Guillaume knelt down next to Marthe's body; his hands, numbed by disbelief, moved aimlessly with hesitant gestures over her muddy hair, her stiffened shoulders, her bare legs shining like mother-of-pearl from the rain, without daring to come to rest.

Finally, he forced his hands into action; he grasped in the palm of his hand one of Marthe's heels, the roundness of which enhanced the arch of her foot. This coiled roundness in the palm of his hand awoke in him a new awareness of Marthe's body. An awareness born from astonishment and from infinite tenderness. He held this heel, round and firm like a girl's breast, he raised it to his lips, kissed it; he mistook the warmth of his own lips for that of her foot, so attractively curved and from which the warmth had, however, disappeared. The footsteps that had so very recently crossed through his sleep returned to dance against his mouth, to echo in his body, to run all round his heart. Marthe's footsteps as she went off into the night banged in his chest and made his heart pound at the same rhythm as the broken door knocking against the wall, at the same rhythm as the she-donkey with her mournful cry.

The donkey! Guillaume suddenly released his embrace; all the blood that he had thought he could feel beating in Marthe's body flowed back towards his heart bereft of hope. Marthe's footsteps were sucked down into this blood of grief, and a blood of anger flooded up from his deepest entrails. Guillaume stood up, walked straight towards the she-

dont le cri opiniâtre enflammait sa colère. Il se posta face à
la bête et la frappa aux yeux d'un revers brutal de la main.
Héloïse se cabra et poussa un cri autre, plus bref, plus perçant.
Guillaume la saisit par la crinière et la roua de coups de pied,
de genou, dans le ventre et les pattes. Il luttait en si grande
haine avec l'ânesse qu'il lui était presque enlacé. Il la fit
même tomber et continua son combat dans la boue. Il ne
ressentait pas les coups qu'il recevait de l'animal se débattant,
il ne sentait que ceux qu'il lui donnait. L'ânesse réussit enfin
à se redresser et s'enfuit loin de Guillaume. Lui demeura un
long moment accroupi dans la boue, à bout de souffle et de
fureur.

Les années passèrent. Guillaume vivait plus que jamais en reclus
depuis la mort de Marthe, et la solitude où il s'emmurait avait
quelque chose d'âpre, de jaloux. Les jours, les nuits s'amonce-
laient comme des déchets de fer rejetés par la mer sur un rivage
désert. Le temps n'était plus qu'une lente concrétion de vide.

Il ne parlait à personne, pas même à lui, fût-ce en de vagues
monologues intérieurs. Ce n'était plus tant qu'il était avare de mots,
c'était qu'il était devenu absolument pauvre de mots. Il proférait
plus que de sourds borborygmes, des grognements mauvais à
l'adresse d'Héloïse. Il finit par perdre le sens du langage; il ne savait
plus faire de phrases, et sa pensée se racornit sur sa propre
souffrance comme l'ongle griffu d'un vieillard se recourbe et entre
dans la chair. Mais sa souffrance, à défaut d'être nommée, exprimée,
avait pris corps. Un corps chétif aux os saillants, aux flancs et pattes
tout écorchés. Celui d'Héloïse.

Le soir de l'orage il avait voulu tuer l'ânesse, mais il ne l'avait que
blessée. Il lui avait laissé la vie sauve – sauve pour la misère, la faim,
la frayeur. Il vouait à l'animal une haine en perpétuelle alerte de mal-
veillance. Il gardait la bête captive dans l'enclos en friche, attachée
en permanence à un piquet par une corde qui lui meurtrissait le cou.
Il la brutalisait, lui faisait endurer la soif et la faim, la privait
d'ombre en été et d'abri en hiver. La bête cependant s'entêtait à sur-
vivre; les années s'écoulaient, elle vieillissait, toujours plus maigre et

donkey, whose stubborn cry was inflaming his anger. He came to a halt facing the animal and struck her brutally in the eyes with the back of his hand. Héloïse reared up and let out another cry, shorter and more piercing. Guillaume seized her by the mane and rained blows upon her, with his foot, with his knee, in the stomach and on the legs. So great was the hatred with which he struggled with the animal that they were almost entwined. He even made her fall and continued the fight in the mud. He could not feel the blows that he received from the struggling animal, he could only feel those that he was giving her. The she-donkey finally managed to stand up and fled far from Guillaume. For his part he remained for a long time crouched in the mud, breathless, his fury abated.

The years went by. Guillaume lived a more reclusive life than ever since the death of Marthe, and the loneliness in which he immured himself held something bitter, something jealous. The days, the nights, piled up like iron waste cast up by the sea on to a deserted shore. Time was no more than a slow coalescence of emptiness.

He talked to no one, not even to himself, not even in vague unspoken monologues. It was no longer so much the case that he was mean with words, it was more that he had become totally devoid of words. Now all he uttered were dull rumbles, unpleasant grunts when he addressed Héloïse. He eventually lost the meaning of language; he could no longer compose sentences, and his thoughts hardened about his own suffering as the claw-like fingernail of an old man bends and pierces his flesh. But his suffering, which he could neither name nor express, had become corporal. A sickly body with protruding bones, flanks and legs that had been flayed. Héloïse's.

The evening of the storm he had wanted to kill the she-donkey, but he had merely wounded her. He had allowed her to live – to live in wretchedness, in hunger, in terror. He felt towards the animal a hatred that was constantly on the watch for maliciousness. He kept the animal prisoner in the fallow paddock, permanently tied to a stake with a rope that cut into her neck. He ill-treated her, made her endure thirst and hunger, deprived her of shade in summer and of shelter in winter. Yet the animal was determined to survive; the years went by, she grew old,

plus pelée, les yeux couverts d'une taie grise, mais elle ne mourait pas. Cet acharnement à durer, cette endurance au malheur, cette résistance à la mort, exacerbaient la rage de Guillaume pour l'increvable bourricot.

Il aurait pu l'achever mais, malgré l'envie de l'abattre qui s'emparait souvent de lui, il l'épargnait. Le spectacle de cette lente agonie lui procurait une obscure jouissance, comme s'il y distillait le poison de sa haine, y sublimait sa vengeance. Mais surtout, il y avait le cri d'Héloïse, son cri tout assourdi, éraillé, infiniment plaintif. Guillaume ne pouvait le supporter et, dans le même temps, il ne pouvait se passer de l'entendre. Il lui fallait l'entendre; tout le jour, et le soir, et jusque dans la nuit aux heures d'insomnie, il tendait l'oreille pour l'écouter.

Car il l'écoutait, avec avidité. Il l'écoutait à la folie, ce braiment essoufflé qui frayait d'étranges voies dans l'invisible et la mémoire, qui faisait grelotter le silence, et évoquait la voix errante de ceux qui ont perdu visage, perdu séjour sur la terre des vivants. C'était un cri d'humain et de bête mêlé, mêlé et déchiré. C'était le cri de sa propre solitude, de sa propre détresse, poussé au-dehors de lui. C'était le cri de tous, de tout, de personne. Celui des vivants et des morts en appelant les uns aux autres. C'était le cri du monde, du monde désert, abandonné. Un cri nu, archaïque, monté des confins du temps, et qui dévastait tout sens, la mémoire et l'espoir, et retournait le cœur sur son néant. Le cri de Dieu peut-être; de Dieu doutant de lui-même à travers la douleur démesurée des hommes.

Ce cri hantait Guillaume, il le liait à l'ânesse plus violemment que la corde rugueuse n'attachait l'animal à son piquet fiché dans la pierraille. Et il n'avait aucune défense contre ce cri. Son corps, dès qu'il l'entendait, était aussitôt saisi de frissons, cela lui nouait la gorge et les entrailles, lui mordait la chair comme une fièvre et s'enfonçait jusqu'à son cœur avec un goût de larme et de poussière.

Cet hiver-là le froid fut particulièrement intense. Il faisait craquer la terre, les branches, éclater les gouttières, geler les rivières et mourir les oiseaux. Les nuits étaient étincelantes; le ciel se laquait d'un

becoming ever thinner and balder, her eyes covered with a grey film, but she did not die. This fierce determination to last, this endurance of misfortune, this resistance to death, intensified Guillaume's fury towards the tireless donkey.

He could have finished her off but, in spite of the desire to kill her that often overcame him, he spared it. The sight of that slow death afforded him an indefinable joy, as if he were distilling the poison of his hatred, sublimating his revenge. But above all else there was Héloïse's cry, her quite muffled, rasping cry, immeasurably doleful. Guillaume could not bear it and, at the same time, he could not go without hearing it. He had to hear it; all day, and all evening, and even at night, when sleep eluded him, he pricked his ears to listen to it.

For he listened to it avidly. He listened to it madly, that breathless braying which made strange inroads into the invisible and the memory, which made the silence shiver, and evoked the wandering voices of those whose faces have gone, whose stay is over in the land of the living. It was a cry that was human and animal combined, combined and torn. It was the cry of his own loneliness, of his own distress, a cry uttered outside him. It was the cry of everyone, of everything, of no one. It was the cry of the living and the dead calling to each other. It was the cry of the world, of the empty, abandoned world. A naked, archaic cry, which had risen from the outer limits of time, and which ravaged all senses, memory and hope, turning the heart back in on its nothingness. The cry of God perhaps; of God doubting Himself through the limitless suffering of mankind.

This cry haunted Guillaume, for it bound him to the she-donkey with more violence than the coarse rope tied the animal to her stake driven into the scree. And he had no means of defending himself against this cry. As soon as he heard it, his body was immediately seized by a shivering fit, it knotted his throat and his entrails, bit into his flesh like a fever and plunged into his heart with a taste of tears and dust.

That winter the cold was particularly biting. It caused the earth and tree branches to crack, gutters to shatter, rivers to freeze and birds to die. The nights were sparkling; the sky shone with the

noir très pur où luisaient les étoiles comme de splendides grains de mica, et les arbres écorcés par le gel tordaient leurs branches blêmes, en deuil des oiseaux, vers ces grains scintillants. Mais à l'aube une brume blanchâtre s'exhalait de la terre et s'enroulait aux arbres, fleurissant les haies de laiteux chrysanthèmes que le vent effeuillait bientôt.

Ce fut par un tel matin qu'Héloïse tut son cri. En rentrant dans l'enclos Guillaume aperçut l'ânesse figée auprès de son piquet, le corps à demi voilé de brouillard. Elle avait quelque chose d'étonnamment fragile, humble et hautain à la fois. Il s'avança vers elle, elle ne bougea pas, ne détourna même pas la tête.

Sa tête, elle la tenait bien haute et droite, hors de la brume qui floconnait jusqu'à son cou; ses yeux grands ouverts avaient une expression encore plus douce et vide que de coutume. Des yeux tant roués de nuit et brûlés de chagrin que leur absence de regard ouvrait sur un regard second. Son front, le creux de ses oreilles, ses cils brillaient de givre. Les minuscules cristaux de glace qui incrustaient ses paupières entouraient ses yeux d'un cerne lumineux. Guillaume n'osait toucher l'ânesse. Il tourna lentement autour d'elle, dissipant de ses mains hésitantes le brouillard accroché à ses flancs comme on écarte un voilage de lin, comme on soulève un voile de mariée. Il tournait, brassant la brume avec des gestes de nageur glissant au ralenti dans l'eau qui toujours se referme sur lui. Il effleurait presque l'ânesse maintenant, laquelle, caparaçonnée[4] de glace, avec son ventre et ses oreilles hérissés de fines stalactites, sa crinière et queue parsemées de cristaux, ses yeux couleur d'argent mati fixant un regard lunaire dans le vide, lui parut fantomatique. Il frôla du bout des doigts le chanfrein de l'ânesse, puis posa en tremblant ses deux mains sur sa tête, les fit glisser le long du cou tendu, et, lentement, tout doucement, il la caressa. La glace craquait et fondait sous ses paumes et le corps d'Héloïse commençait imperceptiblement à ruisseler. Les gouttes glissaient sur ses flancs en un froid et muet pleurement. Et lui se tenait penché vers elle, envahi d'un émoi sans mesure. Ses mains n'étaient plus siennes, elles semblaient s'être détachées de son corps, mues par un désir inconnu. Elles s'affairaient avec délicatesse autour de l'animal ainsi que des mains de femme

purest of blacks in which the stars glistened like magnificent grains
of mica, and the trees stripped of their bark by the frost twisted
their pallid branches, in mourning for the birds, towards these twink-
ling grains. But at dawn a whitish mist rose from the earth and coiled
around the trees, bringing the hedgerows into bloom with milky
chrysanthemums that the wind quickly stripped away.

It was on such a morning that Héloïse silenced her cry. On entering the paddock Guillaume noticed the she-donkey rigid by her stake,
her body semi-veiled in mist. There was something about her that
was astonishingly fragile, humble and yet haughty at the same time.
He went towards her, she did not move, did not even look round.

Her head was held high and straight, out of the mist that rose like
snowflakes up to her neck; her eyes, wide open, looked even gentler
and emptier than normal. Eyes so beaten by night and burnt with
grief that their sightlessness seemed like a kind of trance. Her
forehead, the skin inside her ears, her eyelashes shone with frost.
The tiny ice crystals that encrusted her eyelids surrounded her eyes
with a luminous ring. Guillaume did not dare touch the she-donkey.
He walked slowly around her, waving away with his hesitant hands
the mist that had stuck to her flanks as one brushes away a veiling
of flax, as one lifts a bride's veil. He turned, causing the mist to
eddy with the movements of a swimmer gliding slowly through the
water that always closes back around him. By now he was almost
brushing against the she-donkey, which, caparisoned with ice, her
stomach and eyes bristling with fine stalactites, her mane and tail
sprinkled with crystals, her eyes the colour of dull silver staring,
moonlike, into the emptiness, seemed to him like a ghost. With
the ends of his fingers he lightly touched the nose of the she-
donkey, then, trembling, he placed both hands on her head, slid
them down her taut neck and, slowly, quite gently, he kissed her.
The ice cracked and melted beneath his palms and imperceptibly
Héloïse's body began to stream with water. The drops slid over her
flanks like a cold silent weeping. And he leant towards her, overwhelmed by boundless emotion. He could no longer control his
hands, they seemed to have become detached from his body, to be
moved by an unfamiliar desire. They delicately fussed around the

œuvrant à la toilette d'un nouveau-né, ou bien d'un mort. Ses doigts effleurèrent les paupières durcies de l'ânesse, et ce fut comme s'il touchait le regard même de la tendresse, de la plus nue des tendresses. Le regard de la douleur, aussi bien, ou celui de la patience. Le regard de l'amour sans écho ni partage, mais demeuré fidèle.

Alors vint à Guillaume la faim des larmes. Son cœur soudain s'affola, ses gestes se firent désordonnés. Il manquait de mains maintenant, il aurait voulu avoir mille mains pour multiplier ses caresses. Il enserra la tête de l'ânesse entre ses paumes et se mit à lécher ses yeux tout piquetés d'infimes fleurs de givre jusqu'à ce qu'elles exsudent un goût de sel. Lui-même pleurait sans s'en rendre compte, et ses larmes coulaient dans les yeux d'Héloïse.

Et il lui vint aussi la faim des mots. Cela se bousculait en lui, éclatait dans tous les coins de son corps en confuse rumeur. Des mots, des noms, lui venaient par essaims. Cela affluait à sa bouche tremblante, s'arrachait par syllabes brumeuses de ses lèvres gercées. Il se mit à dire des choses dérisoires, il appelait l'ânesse «ma belle, mon enfant, mon ange, ma douceur, mon amour, mon Héloïse . . .». Les mots fleurissaient sa gorge de roses de sel et de sang. Il enfouit sa tête contre le cou de l'ânesse.

Héloïse s'effondra d'un coup, la corde et le piquet cassèrent. Elle se renversa d'un bloc sur le flanc avec un bruit sourd de statue descellée de son socle. Ses pattes gelées se tendaient, raides, dans le vide. Alors il comprit, et les larmes et les mots ne suffirent plus à son chagrin, à son amour, à sa folie. Il roula sur le sol, se coucha tout contre l'ânesse et s'enlaça à son cou.

A bout de mots, à bout de larmes et de raison, il se mit à crier. Et c'était un braiment.

Ce fut un cri profond, tout enroué de vent, de terre et de brouillard. Un long cri monocorde, rauque, obstiné. Un cri d'humain et de bête mêlé, mêlé et déchiré.

animal like the hands of a woman washing a new-born baby or even a corpse. His fingers brushed lightly against the hardened eyelids of the she-donkey, and it was as though he were touching the very expression of tenderness, of the most undisguised tendernesses. The expression of grief, as well, or that of patience. The expression of a love that has been neither returned nor shared, but has remained faithful.

Then Guillaume began to crave tears. Suddenly his heart was thrown into turmoil, his movements lost obvious purpose. Now he did not have enough hands, he would have liked to have a thousand hands to multiply his caresses. He clasped the she-donkey's head between his hands and began to lick her eyes, which were dotted all over with minute flowers of frost, until these had a taste of salt. He was crying without realizing it and his tears flowed into Héloïse's eyes.

And he also began to crave words, a craving that went wild within him and that exploded in every part of his body in an inco-herent hubbub. Words, names, came to him in swarms. They flowed to his trembling mouth, were torn in indistinct syllables from his frozen lips. He began to utter laughable phrases, he called the she-donkey 'my beauty, my child, my angel, my sweetness, my love, my Héloïse . . .' The words filled his throat with roses of salt and blood. He buried his head into the neck of the she-donkey.

Héloïse suddenly collapsed, the rope and the stake broke. She fell as one mass on to her side with the muffled sound of a statue pushed off its pedestal. Her frozen legs stuck straight out, stiff, in the emptiness. Then he understood, and the tears and the words were no longer enough to express his grief, his love, his madness. He rolled on the ground, lay right up against the she-donkey and wrapped himself round her neck.

Devoid of words, devoid of tears and of reason, he began to shout. And it was a braying noise.

It was a deep cry, made hoarse by the wind, the earth and the fog. A long, monotonous cry, raucous and relentless. It was a cry that was human and animal combined, combined and torn.

The Character

GLORIA ESCOMEL

Le Personnage

Pierre avait toujours eu peur des atterrissages. Il mâchait rageusement
sa gomme pour se déboucher les oreilles, rangeait machinalement
livres et revues dans sa serviette, mettait ses lunettes de soleil, les
enlevait pour bâiller, essuyer ses yeux, les remettait, se mouchait,
enfouissait son mouchoir au fond de sa poche, le serrait convulsive-
ment . . . Il sentait croître la peur, une peur absurde, irrationnelle; des
mots sourdaient de lui, qu'il marmottait sans leur prêter attention.
«Le temps n'a pas passé pour nos âmes égarées . . . nos âmes égarées . . .
z'âmes z'égarées . . . z'âmes . . . zamezégarées . . .» [1] Il eut un rire
nerveux. Zamezégarées: cela lui rappelait quelque chose, ou quelqu'un.

Qui donc ai-je oublié de prévenir de mon arrivée? se demanda-
t-il soudain, avec angoisse. Pourquoi cette angoisse?

L'avion toucha brutalement le sol, rebondit mollement et le
freinage forcené commença. Pierre, calé dans son fauteuil, poings
crispés, pensa que si l'appareil venait à s'écraser au bout de la
course, l'ami oublié ignorerait sa mort.

La peur, une vieille peur, se liquéfiait dans ses veines, bousculait
son cœur, mouillait ses paumes, s'accrochait aux barbes d'un bon
dieu d'enfance. Mais l'avion finit par s'immobiliser. Pierre oublia sa
panique d'où allait naître une prière grotesque, puisqu'il ne croyait
en aucun dieu. Une dernière fois, il murmura «zamezégarées»
avant de cracher sa gomme dans un cendrier plein de mégots, se
moucha énergiquement, ajusta ses lunettes et se mit à siffloter.

Fafou! C'était elle qu'il avait oublié de prévenir! C'était elle qui
lui avait signalé ce «zamezégarées», cette dissonance dans un
poème, en lui psalmodiant le vers, narquoise. Pierre sentit l'atten-
drissement fondre sur lui ou plutôt, le faire fondre de tendresse
éblouie, tant le sourire narquois de Fafou lui était apparu nette-
ment, comme une photo, ce sourire câlin où l'ironie était coquine

The Character

Pierre had always been afraid of landing. He furiously chewed his gum to unblock his ears, mechanically tidied away books and magazines in his briefcase, put on his sunglasses, took them off again to yawn, to wipe his eyes, put them back on, wiped his nose, stuffed his handkerchief deep into his pocket, convulsively squeezed it . . . He felt his fear increasing, an absurd, irrational fear; words sprang to his mind, which he muttered without paying them any attention. 'Time has not passed for our lost souls . . . our lost souls . . . arlostzoles . . . arlost . . . aaarlostzoles . . .' He laughed nervously. Aaarlostzoles: that reminded him of something, or someone.

'So who have I forgotten to warn about my arrival?' he suddenly wondered, in anguish. Why this anguish?

The aeroplane jarringly touched the ground, bounced gently up and frenziedly began to brake. Pierre, wedged into his seat, fists tightly clenched, thought that if the machine happened to crash at the end of its run, the forgotten friend would be unaware of his death.

Fear, an old fear, turned liquid in his veins, banged against his heart, dampened his palms, clung to the beard of a good childhood god. But the aeroplane eventually came to a halt. Pierre forgot his panic, from which was about to be born a grotesque prayer, for he did not believe in any god. One last time he muttered 'aaarlostzoles' before spitting his gum into an ashtray full of cigarette butts, vigorously wiped his nose, adjusted his glasses and began to whistle.

Fafou! It was her he had forgotten to tell! It was she who had pointed out that 'aaarlostzoles', that dissonance in a poem, while mockingly chanting the line to him. Pierre felt tender emotion melting over him or, rather, making him melt with bedazzled tenderness, so clearly had the mocking smile of Fafou come into his mind, like a photograph, that tender smile in which irony was mischievous

et complice. En ce bref instant, il comprit que c'était elle par-dessus tout qu'il avait désiré revoir, à Paris. Son oubli prit alors une dimension de tragique rétrospectif: s'il était mort au cours de l'atterrissage, elle n'aurait jamais su combien son besoin de la revoir était intense!

Puis un soulagement sans borne d'être encore en vie déferle en lui, avec le plaisir de sentir le souffle de sa respiration devenu profond et régulier, la joie de savoir qu'il est encore plein de désirs, d'envies de rire et d'aimer. Il a laissé le Pierre austère à Montréal, accroché à quelque patère, avec son manteau d'hiver et celui de sa femme triste. Instinctivement, il retrouve la dégaine de l'étudiant, la mèche sur l'œil, le sourire goguenard aux lèvres, qu'il mordille sensuellement. Il pense à Fafou, si délicieusement folle et libre, tragique aussi, sortie d'une ambiance de Carco,[2] d'un poème d'Apollinaire,[3] d'un rêve éclaté de Pierrot.[4]

«Mon Pierrot gourmand», disait-elle, en l'embrassant. Un long désir vibrant monte en lui.

Il prendra la voiture louée, il arrivera à Paris, rêvant de débauches anciennes. Il se souviendra. Ce flot d'images qui ne me quittent plus ne sont en lui que depuis que le prénom de Fafou a été placé entre ses lèvres. C'est pourtant un peu vrai qu'au cours de ce voyage-là je n'avais pas pensé, pour la première fois, à lui écrire pour lui demander si je pourrais la voir. Mais je n'y ai pas davantage pensé à l'atterrissage, pour la bonne raison que cette fois-là j'ai été malade à m'en évanouir, que j'ai repris conscience à côté d'une hôtesse au parfum ambré et que j'étais encore sous le choc du décalage entre ce parfum et le visage rébarbatif de celle qui le portait . . .

Je n'ai pensé à Fafou que plusieurs jours plus tard, en attendant mon neveu devant une agence de voyages, près de Clichy.[5] Et aussitôt je suis entré dans ce café pour téléphoner.

Mais je préfère revenir à Pierre, qui est encore sur la route, plein de joie à l'idée de ces retrouvailles possibles avec Fafou. Il a devant lui une heure ou deux encore, peut-être plus. Il lui faut le temps d'arriver à Paris, de se balader un peu, refaire connaissance, se

and knowing. In that brief moment he realized that it was her above all else that he had wanted to see again in Paris. His oversight then assumed a dimension of retrospective tragedy: if he had died during the landing, she would never have known how intense was his need to see her again!

Then an infinite relief at still being alive unfolded within him, with the pleasure of feeling his breathing, which had become deep and regular, the joy of knowing that he was still full of desires, longings to laugh and love. He had left the austere Pierre in Montreal, hanging on some coat-peg, with his winter coat and that of his sad wife. Instinctively, he thought of his gawkiness as a student, the fringe over his eyes, the mocking smile on his lips, at which he sensuously chewed. He thought about Fafou, so exquisitely mad and free, though tragic at the same time, having sprung from an atmosphere created by Carco, from a poem by Apollinaire, a shattered dream by Pierrot.

'My greedy Pierrot,' she said, as she kissed him. A long, trembling desire rose within him.

He will take the hire car, he will get to Paris, dreaming of former debauchery. He will remember. That flood of images which I cannot get out of my mind has only been with him since Fafou's name was placed on his lips. Yet it is not entirely true that during this voyage I had not thought, for the first time, to write to her to ask if I could see her. But I did not think more about it when I landed, for the simple reason that I was so ill that I fainted, that I regained consciousness next to an air hostess wearing ambergris perfume, and that I could not get over the shock of the discrepancy between that perfume and the ugly face of the woman wearing it . . .

I did not think about Fafou until several days later, whilst waiting for my nephew outside a travel agency, near Clichy. And I immediately went into a café to make a telephone call.

But I prefer to come back to Pierre, who is still on the road, joyful at the thought of this possible reunion with Fafou. He still has an hour or two ahead of him, perhaps longer. He needs the time to get to Paris, to wander about a bit, to refamiliarize himself, to find a

trouver un petit hôtel bon marché, s'installer . . . Il n'a pas, lui, de famille qui l'attend à Paris.

Lui, l'amertume l'a quitté depuis longtemps. Celle-ci, du moins. Il est trop habitué à l'autre, celle qui ternit sa vie quotidienne, la mienne, que j'étais venu oublier à Paris.

Oui, Fafou l'avait aussi fait souffrir monstrueusement. Même lorsqu'elle lui disait: «Et tu crois que c'est Frantz qui a le meilleur rôle? Tu ne me vois tout de même pas, mon amour, t'appeler papa? Laisse les grands jouer à la famille: tu restes mon grand fou, mon amour, mon Pierrot gourmand . . .»

«Je te donnerai des rendez-vous au coin des rues perdues, disait-elle, nous irons nous aimer dans des mansardes . . .»

Pierre avait vingt ans. Non: vingt et un. Il avait joué et perdu. Mais il y a quinze ans de cela. C'était sa première maîtresse . . . Avec quelques années de plus, il l'aurait peut-être emporté sur l'autre, père légitime ou pas. Maintenant, le voilà enchaîné à sa femme, à la tristesse morne de la vie besogneuse. Mais il n'a pas oublié Fafou, sa fantaisie, son pathétique appétit de vivre, sa sensualité débordante, exigeante, à la base de tout le drame.

Fafou. Voilà que j'étais prêt à oublier ce drame, à la réduire à cette seule fantaisie un peu superficielle, celle dont j'avais le plus besoin, et comme toutes les autres fois, voilà que je replonge en une tristesse stupéfiée.

«Ne me quitte pas!» avais-je supplié, sans aucun orgueil. Déjà.

Chasser cette image, en rechercher d'autres qui se mêlent en ma mémoire à la saveur de son rouge à lèvres. «Et nos baisers mordus-sanglants[6] faisaient pleurer nos fées marraines . . .» Apollinaire, sa passion. Prévert,[7] Carco, ses engouements, toute cette ambiance.

Sa voix contre ma bouche noyait mes paroles sous les baisers, les morsures: «Mais je ne te quitte pas, j'épouse Frantz, à cause du bébé, c'est tout . . .»

Mes larmes donnaient à nos baisers un goût de sel, de profonde débâcle. Quel âge aura l'enfant, cet enfant, qui me l'a volé? Quinze ans . . . Déjà? Le temps n'a peut-être pas passé pour Pierre, ni pour moi. Mais je peux le mesurer à l'âge de cet enfant. Fafou disait

cheap little hotel, to settle in . . . He does not have any relations waiting for him in Paris.

As for him, bitterness left him long ago. In this matter at least. He is too accustomed to the other bitterness, the one that tarnishes his daily life, mine, that I had come to Paris to forget.

Yes, Fafou had also made him suffer terribly. Even when she said to him: 'And so you think that it is Frantz who has the better role? Come on, darling, you cannot see me calling you 'Daddy'? Let the grown-ups play at families: you are still my mad passion, darling, my greedy Pierrot . . .'

'I'll meet you at the corner of the out-of-the-way streets,' she said. 'We'll go and make love in garrets . . .'

Pierre was twenty. No: twenty-one. He had played and lost. But that was fifteen years ago. She was his first mistress . . . If he had been a few years older, he would perhaps have got the better of the other man, whether he was the legitimate father or not. Now, here he is, chained to his wife, to the depressing sadness of a life of drudgery. But he has not forgotten Fafou, her fantasy, her moving appetite for life, her excessive, demanding sensuality, which is at the heart of the entire drama.

Fafou. And there I was, ready to forget that drama, to reduce her to the level of a mere, somewhat superficial, fantasy, which I most needed, and as on every other occasion, here I am plunging back into stupefied sadness.

'Do not leave me!' I had begged, without any pride. Already.

Chase away that image, seek others which are confused in my memory with the taste of her lipstick. 'And our passionate, blood-red kisses made our fairy godmothers cry . . .' Apollinaire, her passion. Prévert, Carco, her infatuations, all that atmosphere.

Her voice against my mouth drowned my words beneath the kisses, the bites: 'But I am not leaving you, I am marrying Frantz, because of the baby, that's all . . .'

My tears gave our kisses the taste of salt, of utter defeat. How old will the child be, that child, who stole him from me? Fifteen . . . Already? Time has perhaps not passed for Pierre, nor for me. But I can gauge it by the age of that child. Fafou

toujours «d'enfant». Jamais «mon» enfant, ni le nôtre. Encore moins «le tien».

Un mot de trop. Juste un mot de trop pour que se creuse la distance, irrémédiable. Non, cet enfant ne pouvait être le mien. Mais il aurait pu être celui de Pierre, ou de cet autre, là, qui feint de parler pour lui.

Pierre accélère, fonce vers Paris, heureux de la vitesse qui fait défiler le paysage au rythme de ses envies, du vent qui s'engouffre par les fenêtres ouvertes, le décoiffe, rafraîchit son torse humide, heureux surtout d'être seul dans la voiture, de s'imaginer Fafou à ses côtés, bientôt, bientôt, le temps d'arriver, de l'appeler . . .

Le fils de Frantz a donc quinze ans, pense-t-il, quel âge aurait eu l'autre bébé, celui qui n'était pas né, l'enfant condensé en quelques semaines d'espoir, dont elle ne pouvait parler sans larmes? «Il aurait été si mignon, murmurait-elle, il aurait eu les yeux verts . . .» Pierre peut aujourd'hui se défendre de l'émotion d'hier, en se disant: «Non, mais quel mélo!»[8] cette phrase est inscrite en sa mémoire avec l'exacte intonation de la voix de Fafou, un peu rauque, un peu nasale, à travers les larmes et chaque fois qu'il l'entend, il en a la chair de poule, bien qu'à chaque fois, pour s'en défendre, il répète: «Non, mais quel mélo!»

Comme Pierre, j'ai beau hausser les épaules, me passer la main sur le bras, je n'ai pu oublier cette phrase anodine et fleur bleue, si sobre pourtant, par rapport à sa souffrance. Pendant combien de nuits et de jours de regrets cette phrase n'est-elle pas venue résonner en moi? Cet enfant-là, d'avant Frantz, cet enfant-là aurait pu nous réunir au lieu de nous séparer. Je voudrais pouvoir retrouver ma ferveur de l'époque, nos projets insensés, ce romantisme exacerbé, jusqu'à mon manque de réalisme qui me faisait entrevoir toutes choses aussi simplement: j'adoptais l'enfant, j'épousais la mère, mes parents ne pouvaient s'opposer à ce mariage, malgré mes vingt ans, puisque j'allais prétendre que l'enfant était le mien . . .

Me raccrocher à Pierre qui roule à tombeau ouvert sur un

always said 'the child'. Never 'my' child, nor ours. Even less 'yours'.

One word too many. Just one word too many for distance to grow wider, irremediably so. No, that child could not be mine. But it could have been Pierre's, or that other man's, the one who pretends to speak for him.

Pierre accelerated, belted towards Paris, happy with the speed which made the countryside unravel at the rhythm of his desires, with the wind which swept in through the open windows, blowing his hair, cooling his damp body, above all happy to be alone in the car, to imagine Fafou by his side, soon, soon, the time that it would take to get there, to call her . . .

So, Frantz's son is fifteen, he thought, how old would the other baby have been, the one who had not been born, the child condensed into a few weeks of hope, about whom she could not talk without crying? 'He would have been so cute,' she murmured, 'he would have had green eyes . . .' Today Pierre can protect himself against emotions from the past by saying to himself: 'No, how melodramatic!', this phrase is etched in his memory with precisely the intonation of Fafou's voice, slightly hoarse, slightly nasal, through the tears, and every time he hears it, he gets goose pimples, even though each time, to protect himself, he repeats: 'No, how melodramatic!'

As with Pierre, it is pointless me shrugging my shoulders, running my hand over my arm, I have not been able to forget that innocuous and naïvely sentimental phrase, which is yet so sober, in relation to her suffering. For how many nights and days of regret has this phrase not come and echoed in my head? That child, the one before Frantz came along, could have brought us together instead of separating us. How I wish I could rediscover my ardour of those days, our wild plans, that exaggerated romanticism, even my failure to be realistic, which made me see everything in such simple terms: I would adopt the child, I would marry the mother, my parents could not oppose the marriage, in spite of my being only twenty, since I would claim that the child was mine . . .

Cling to Pierre, who is driving at breakneck speed towards a

Paris de légende où gît sa jeunesse et l'oubli qu'il cherche, me dire qu'il est plus léger que moi, qu'il a été capable de surmonter la grisaille, capable de croire encore au bonheur, me dire que c'est lui qui pense à sa femme triste, se reprochant de n'avoir su la rendre heureuse, malgré toute sa bonne volonté, son amour des premières années, sa gaieté d'alors, son enthousiasme à vouloir s'occuper de son fils, ce voyou dont il craint aujourd'hui les mauvais coups, gâté par sa mère au point de l'obliger, lui, Pierre, à endosser le mauvais rôle, père fouettard, parâtre austère à trente-cinq ans, lui qui voulait demeurer l'éternel gamin enjoué de son adolescence, qui doit maintenant chasser son insouciance et sa fantaisie pour se raidir face à l'autre, de vingt ans son cadet, dont les fantaisies s'égarent en drogues de moins en moins innocentes, trafics douteux, insolences cruelles qui ont fini par gâcher sa vie et celle d'Adrienne en si peu d'années de mariage . . .

J'avais tout investi en elle, mon espoir et ma joie, mon amour aussi. Mais les quêtes sont finies. Mon devoir est auprès de cette femme amorphe, mais au milieu de cette mort lente, mes vacances étaient comme une bouffée d'air frais, comme pour Pierre, une indispensable bouffée de jeunesse qu'il vient chercher sur les lieux de son passé, de son premier amour. Fafou, Fafou et les autres, amis, anciennes maîtresses avec lesquelles il a gardé de bons rapports et qu'il compte revoir, se pardonnant d'avance ses premières infidélités à Adrienne.

Il arrivera bientôt à Paris, la circulation ralentit, il doit emprunter des autoroutes nouvelles, qu'il connaît mal, il ne sait pas très bien comment se rendre au quartier des Invalides,[9] ne s'est pas décidé entre les Invalides et Montparnasse,[10] d'ailleurs, tout ce qu'il sait s'estompe légèrement, même l'indicatif téléphonique de Fafou: Suffren ou Ségur, se demande-t-il, anxieux soudain, comme s'il ne savait pas que son nom figure encore au Bottin,[11] qu'il y a plus de vingt-cinq ans que ses parents habitent le même appartement, ont le même numéro de téléphone . . .

Mais je veux qu'il roule encore et se perde à travers les rues de ces quartiers où nous avons tant erré, certains soirs, que je suis revenu

legendary Paris where lies his youth and the oblivion that he is seeking, tell myself that he is more superficial than me, that he was capable of overcoming the dullness, capable of still believing in happiness, tell myself that it is he who thinks of his sad wife, reproaching himself for never having been able to make her happy, in spite of all his good will, his love in the early years, his happiness in those days, his eagerness to want to take care of her son, that thug whose dirty tricks he fears nowadays, spoilt by his mother to the point of forcing him, Pierre, to assume the nasty role, that of Mr Bogeyman, the austere stepfather at the age of thirty-five, he who wanted to remain the eternal, cheerful youth of his teenage years, who must now chase away his happy-go-lucky attitude and his fantasy in order to be firm with that other, twenty years his junior, whose fantasies drift off into drugs that are increasingly less innocent, shady deals, acts of cruel arrogance that have eventually ruined his life and that of Adrienne in so few years of marriage . . .

I had invested everything in her, my hope and my joy, my love also. But the quest is over. My duty lies with that amorphous woman, but in the midst of this slow death, my holidays were like a breath of fresh air, as with Pierre, a vital breath of youth that he has come to seek in the places of his past, of his first love. Fafou, Fafou and the others, friends, former mistresses with whom he has maintained good relations and whom he intends to see again, forgiving himself in advance for his first infidelities to Adrienne.

He will soon reach Paris, the traffic slows down, he must take new motorways, which he does not know well, he does not know exactly how to get to the district of the Invalides, has not yet decided between the Invalides and Montparnasse, besides, everything that he knows is becoming slightly hazy, even the dialling code for Fafou: 'Suffren or Ségur,' he wonders, suddenly anxious, as if he did not know that her name is still in the directory, that her parents have lived in the same flat for more than twenty-five years, have the same telephone number . . .

But I want him to still be driving and to get lost in the streets of those districts where we wandered so often, some evenings, and that

parcourir, ces dernières nuits, et où, probablement, il ira se promener, lui aussi, quelques pages plus tard.

Pierre, faux masque. Je me relis, et ce récit sonne faux, avec son style facile, truffé de clichés, mais comme cela banalise et apaise, ramène à la norme, et comme ce simple subterfuge me calme, de savoir qu'à travers Pierre, je vais retrouver Fafou, entendre sa voix au téléphone, me promener dans ces rues, comme il y a quinze ou seize ans, l'embrasser, respirer ce parfum musqué dont le nom m'échappe. A travers lui je pourrai me permettre d'affronter ces lambeaux du passé, les reconstituer, tenir à distance l'indicible douleur. Il est trop tôt sans doute pour sublimer autrement, pour faire du style . . . trop tôt . . . ou trop tard.

Et plonger dans ce passé sous le nom de Pierre ou le mien, quelle importance, au fond. C'est Fafou que je cherche, c'est là ma quête, ma reconquête devant laquelle je peux bien, pour une fois, m'effacer.

Pierre, donc, au volant de sa voiture, arrive, fou de joie à l'idée de te retrouver. Moi, j'arrivais terne et sans joie, voulant puiser auprès des témoins de ma jeunesse un peu de ce que j'avais été, pour me prouver que le temps n'avait pas passé, que rien encore n'était irrémédiable.

Te souviens-tu? Peux-tu te souvenir de tout ce qui nous unissait? Où donc est ta mémoire, mon oiseau fou libéré de sa cage, où? La cage et l'oiseau avaient-ils même souffle? Si dense est le silence de cette nuit où je viens de créer Pierre, ma première imposture, que je me demande si ce faux respect ne te trahit pas davantage que tout le reste.

Mais voilà que par le truchement de ces quelques pages manuscrites, ce Pierre-là qui m'aide tant s'est mis à vivre dans mon esprit, à s'imposer entre moi et moi, toi et moi, imperceptiblement encore.

Il a mon visage, sans doute, celui que j'entrevois dans des miroirs ou des vitres qui me renvoient mon reflet, celui, peut-être, que tu regardais entre deux baisers, quoique je ne sache pas très bien à quoi ressemblait mon visage lorsqu'il était penché vers toi . . . Je ne revois que le tien, dont l'expression me troublait tellement en ces instants où la tendresse virait au désir, comme le rose au pourpre et que je

I have come back to wander, these last few nights, and where he will probably go for a stroll, he too, in a few pages' time.

Pierre, false mask. I reread what I have written, and this tale does not ring true, with its simple style, stuffed with clichés, but how it trivializes and appeases, brings one back to normality, and how this simple subterfuge calms me, knowing that through Pierre I am going to find Fafou, hear her voice on the telephone, stroll in those streets, as I did fifteen or sixteen years ago, kiss her, breathe that musky perfume whose name escapes me. Through him I will be able to allow myself to confront those fragments of the past, rebuild them, keep the indescribable grief at bay. It is probably too soon to refine my thoughts in any other way, to write in a better style . . . too soon . . . or too late.

And to plunge into that past under the name of Pierre or my own, what does it matter in the end. It is Fafou that I am seeking, she is my quest, my reconquest in the presence of whom I can, for once, become invisible.

So Pierre arrives, at the wheel of his car, wild with joy at the thought of seeing you again. I arrived gloomy and joyless, wanting to draw from those who had witnessed my youth a little of what I had been, to prove to myself that time had not passed, nothing was yet beyond repair.

Do you remember? Can you remember everything which brought us together? So where is your memory, my mad bird freed from its cage, where? Were the cage and the bird ever real? So deep is the silence of this night in which I have just created Pierre, my first deception, that I wonder if this fake respect does not betray you more than all the rest.

But with the aid of these few handwritten pages, that Pierre, who is such a help to me, has begun to grow in my mind, to stand between me and me, you and me, though still barely visible.

His face is probably like mine, the one that I glimpse reflected in mirrors or windows, the one you perhaps looked at between two kisses, although I do not really know what my face resembled when it was leant towards you . . . I can only see yours, whose expression disturbed me so much at those moments when tenderness turned to desire, as pink turns to crimson, and which I would like to be able

voudrais pouvoir décrire, pour mieux m'en souvenir. Mais toi, quel visage contemplais-tu en ces minutes, pour me traiter d'ange pervers, d'enfant sauvage, de Pierrot gourmand? Ta mémoire, Fafou, quelles images a-t-elle conservées de moi, à quels signes me reconnaîtras-tu, si par hasard, dans la rue, tu me retrouvais vieilli, dans quelques années?

Pierre a fini par arriver dans ton quartier, le voilà qui cherche un hôtel et que j'hésite à lui en donner un, moi qui ne me souviens que d'un seul, un peu plus loin, sur la rue de Vaugirard, que je ne veux pas relier à toi . . .

Irrésistiblement, je sens qu'il cherche une cabine téléphonique alors que ce n'est pas de ce quartier-ci que j'ai voulu t'appeler, alors que j'aurais voulu qu'avant de t'appeler il ait le temps de vagabonder dans les rues, à la recherche de nos souvenirs . . . Irrésistiblement, il ira sans doute s'enfermer dans une cabine étroite qui sent le mégot, l'écouteur à la main, il entendra cette sonnerie grelottante qui éveillera tant de souvenirs heureux et malheureux . . . Mais c'étaient mes souvenirs ! Les miens, pas ceux de Pierre! Et j'hésite à donner à ce zombi ces émotions trop intimes, ces sensations qui furent miennes, cette vie qui m'appartient encore, à moi et non à cet usurpateur qui endosse si facilement en quelques heures de rêverie quelques défroques de mon passé, ce passé où, pourtant, je ne voulais retrouver que nous deux. Et voilà que par sa faute, le fil ténu de mes sensations se brise et que je me perds dans les méandres de ce fleuve de mémoire où j'ai voulu m'aventurer à ta recherche, trop lâche pour partir seul.

C'est si loin, déjà, le domaine où je dois te retrouver et il y a si longtemps de cela!

J'aurais voulu évoquer le jour de notre rencontre, recommencer par le commencement, fixer les instantanés de notre amour, nous revoir comme à travers un film dont je serais à la fois le cameraman et la caméra vibrante, l'œil et l'acteur qui te tiendrait dans ses bras, décrire les expressions, exhumer tes paroles, faire revivre ces quelques mois, ces quelques années qui t'ont contenue dans ma vie, mais les mots glissent comme des pieuvres, étouffent ce qu'ils saisissent. Certaines scènes se superposent, dérivent, algues lentes dans les eaux de ma mémoire. Et cela m'est aussi insupportable que ma vanité à

to describe, better to remember. But you, what face did you gaze upon in those minutes, to call me a depraved angel, a wild child, a greedy Pierrot? What images has your memory retained of me, Fafou, by what signs would you recognize me if, by chance, in the street, you met me, grown old, in a few years' time?

Pierre eventually got to your district, here he is looking for a hotel and I am hesitating to give him one, I who remember only one, a little further on, in the rue Vaugirard, that I do not want to link with you . . .

I cannot help feeling that he is looking for a telephone booth although it was not from this district that I wanted to call you, although, before he called you, I would have liked him to have the time to wander about the streets, looking for our memories . . . He will probably not be able to help shutting himself into a narrow booth that reeks of cigarettes and, the receiver in his hand, he will hear that quivering ring which will evoke so many happy and unhappy memories . . . But they were my memories! Mine, not Pierre's! And I hesitate to give to this zombie these emotions that are so intimate, these feelings that were mine, this life which still belongs to me, to me and not to that usurper who so easily, and in a few hours of daydreaming, takes for his own a few cast-offs of my past, that past in which, however, I only wanted to find the two of us. And through his fault, the slender thread of my feelings breaks and I become lost in the meanderings of that river of memory in which I wanted to venture in search of you, too cowardly to set off alone.

The place where I must find you is already so far away, and so long ago at that!

I would have liked to evoke the day we met, to begin again at the beginning, to fix the snapshots of our love, to see ourselves as though in a film of which I would be both cameraman and the trembling camera, the eye and the actor who held you in his arms, to describe the expressions, to dig up your words, to bring back to life those few months, those few years that held you in my life, but the words slide away like octopuses, stifle what they seize. Certain scenes become superimposed, drift away, slowly like seaweed in the waters of my memory. And that is as unbearable to me as my

vouloir ressusciter par des mots le temps qui s'engouffre dans les charniers du vécu.

Mais à trop différer, les images s'enfuient. Quels que soient les mots, les laisser couler, me ramener vers ce grand amphi où nous nous sommes connus.

J'étais assis au centre et, à mes côtés, il y avait cette place vide où tu viendrais t'asseoir. Je t'ai vue venir par l'allée de droite, de ta démarche nonchalante, balancée. Ce sont là des clichés, je sais, mais est-ce ma faute s'il n'y a pas d'autres mots qui conviennent mieux à ta démarche, parce que dès le début j'ai associé des clichés à ce pas qui était le tien et qu'à présent ces mots-là collent comme glu au film de mes souvenirs, au point qu'ils en déclenchent les images pour moi seul dès que je les prononce, comme on prononcerait des mots de passe? Tu me regardais, alors que je croyais tes yeux posés sur le fauteuil libre; tu avais l'art de fixer ce qui semblait te distraire. «Tu permets?», m'as-tu dit en prenant place. La gorge nouée par un désir brutal né de ton parfum, je n'avais pas répondu et tu t'étais assise avec un sourire amusé.

Pourquoi le nom de ce parfum m'échappe-t-il encore, alors que ma mémoire est envahie par lui et qu'en cet instant mes narines le hument encore, par-delà l'odeur de ma cigarette, si distinctement, à travers tant d'années?

Je n'ose relire ces quelques lignes qu'il m'a fallu si longtemps pour écrire afin de pouvoir de nouveau être envahi tout entier par ce parfum: la scène de notre rencontre que je croyais avoir oubliée m'est revenue si totalement, elle aussi! Je sais, oui, je sais que pour un tiers ces quelques mots ne pourront pas tout dire: maigre conquête des mots, qui comble une absence et ressuscite le temps.

Me voici de nouveau démuni, épuisé, vidé: que peut ce pauvre souvenir contre le Temps? Que peut ma joie puérile, quand je retrouve le mot juste pour te décrire, que peut ma joie contre le Temps? Tu avais l'air canaille, Fafou, canaille, oui, mais je sais que ce mot n'a de sens que pour moi, pour l'image de toi qu'il évoque en moi, ce sourcil levé, cet œil brun pervers mais enfantin et joueur, et je n'ose imaginer à quelles images un autre

vanity in wanting to use my words to bring back that time in my life which is sinking into the mass graves of the past.

But in delaying for too long, the images are fleeing. Whatever the words, let them flow and lead me towards that great amphitheatre where we got to know each other.

I was sitting in the middle and, at my side, there was this empty seat where you would come and sit down. I saw you approaching along the right-hand aisle, with your nonchalant, swaying walk. These are clichés, I know, but is it my fault if there are not any other words that better describe your walk, because I immediately associated clichés with that tread of yours, and for the moment those words stick like glue to the film that is my memories, to the extent that they trigger off images for me alone as soon as I pronounce them, as one would pronounce passwords? You were looking at me, although I thought your eyes were fixed on the empty seat; you had a knack of staring at what seemed to amuse you. 'May I?' you said to me as you took your seat. With a lump in my throat brought on by a wild desire sparked off by your perfume, I had not replied and you had sat down with an amused smile on your face.

Why does the name of that perfume still escape me, when my memory is overcome by it and when at this very moment I can still smell it, over the smell of my cigarette, so distinctly, across so many years?

I dare not reread these few lines that it has taken me so long to write in order that I might once again be totally overcome by that perfume: the scene of our meeting, which I thought I had forgotten, has come back to me in such completeness, it too! Yes, I know that these few words will not express everything to a third party: a meagre victory of words, which fills an absence and brings time back to life.

Here I am again, destitute, worn out, emptied: what can this pathetic memory do against Time? What can my childish joy do, when I find precisely the right word to describe you, what can my joy do against Time? You looked like a rogue, Fafou, yes like a rogue, but I know that this word only means something to me, because of the image of you that it evokes in me, that raised eyebrow, that brown eye, perverse but child-like and playful, and I dare not imagine

pourrait penser en lisant ce simple mot par lequel tu aimais bien que
je te nomme: «canaille». J'ai trop peur que cet autre manque de
nuances, ne sache pas avec quelle tendresse je te nommais ainsi,
qu'il ajoute à ton portrait déjà si incomplet les traits d'une autre
femme, les préjugés qui peuvent naître de cet adjectif-cliché. Le
moindre mot me fait trébucher, le moindre adjectif me fait peur,
tandis qu'alors, dans notre innocence romanesque nous nous
soûlions de ces clichés, nous rencontrions à travers eux, t'en
souviens-tu, nous en amusions comme des enfants qui jouent avec
des couleurs et des images toutes préparées d'avance, qu'il s'agissait
de combiner seulement de manière insolite pour que nous les trou-
vions beaux: vers de quatre sous,[12] paroles de chansons, midinettes
fleur bleue panache et bohème folklorique, mais fous rires d'esprits
cultivés, distance légère que les bienséances intellectuelles nous
faisaient prendre aussi, le moment de fièvre tombée . . . Depuis trop
longtemps, Fafou, canaille, oiseau fou, gitane, la fièvre est tombée
qui ne me permet plus d'écrire aussi librement qu'alors; les mots
aujourd'hui me font peur, et pas seulement parce que je redoute un
lecteur sévère, non, pas seulement pour cela . . . Et je voudrais hurler
ma peur, ma peine, ton absence que les mots ne comblent pas, que
rien ne peut plus effacer, sinon les mots pourraient te faire revivre
aux yeux d'un tiers, telle que tu étais, exactement telle que tu étais et
non pas telle qu'il pourrait t'imaginer si jamais les adjectifs que
j'emploie n'ont pas pour lui la même saveur, la même musique . . .

Je dois même me méfier de moi, ne pas laisser des mots posté-
rieurs s'adresser à toi. Tout à l'heure j'écrivais: oiseau fou, gitane et
j'ai pensé «mon amour», failli l'écrire, raturé immédiatement les
quelques lettres qui couraient à l'imposture. Jamais je ne t'ai appelée
mon amour, et il aurait suffi que je pense à toi en ces termes pour
que d'autres visages de femmes viennent insidieusement se super-
poser au tien comme des reflets . . .

Et je reviens à ce parfum ambré, à mon besoin de le décrire, alors
qu'il me suffit de l'évoquer pour qu'il m'envahisse, me plonge en
cette transe légère du désir . . . Esclave de l'écriture, qui ne peut
recréer qu'en prenant des distances, pourquoi me force-t-il ce soir à
circonscrire les émotions, les sensations, les événements, au lieu de

what images someone else would think of, reading that single word by which you loved me to call you: 'rogue'. I am too afraid that the other man lacks subtleties, that he does not know how affectionately I called you this, that he adds to your portrait, which is already so incomplete, the features of another woman, the prejudices that can arise from this clichéd adjective. The slightest word makes me stumble, the slightest adjective makes me afraid, whereas then, in our romantic innocence we got drunk on those clichés, met through them, do you remember, we had fun like children who play with colours and pictures prepared in advance, it was just a matter of combining them in an unusual way for us to find them beautiful: worthless lines of verse, words from songs, the panache of hopelessly romantic shop-girls and bohemian folklore, but giggles from cultured minds, a tiny distance that we were obliged to keep by the intellectual rules of good taste, the moment when our fever abated . . . It is too long, Fafou, rogue, mad bird, gypsy-girl, since the fever abated, which no longer allows me to write as freely as before; nowadays words frighten me, and not just because I dread a critical reader, no, not just for that reason . . . And I would like to scream my fear, my grief, your absence that words do not fill, that nothing can wipe away any more, otherwise words would be able to make you live again in the eyes of a third party, just as you were, exactly as you were and not as he might imagine you if ever the adjectives that I am using do not have for him the same flavour, the same music . . .

I must even mistrust myself, not allow subsequent words to be directed to you. Just now I was writing: mad bird, gypsy-girl and I thought 'my darling', I almost wrote it but I immediately crossed out the few letters that were bordering on deception. I have never called you 'my darling', and I would only have had to think of you in those terms for the faces of other women to come and insidiously superimpose themselves on yours like reflections . . .

And I return to that musky perfume, to my need to describe it, when I only need to evoke it for it to overcome me, to plunge me into that light trance of desire . . . A slave to writing, who can only recreate by assuming a distance, why does it force me this evening to circumscribe emotions, feelings, events, instead of allowing me to

me laisser emporter par cette marée mélancolique, où des souvenirs, parfois, émergent, vivaces comme le présent dont ils ont la limpidité, la nitescence? Sans doute parce que revivre ne me suffit plus, qu'il faut aussi que tu revives avec moi.

Ces pages, pistes de décollage ou de décodage, ne suffisent pas: les signes me manquent. Il me semble aborder un langage inconnu. J'examine chaque mot qui te désigne, je le soupèse, le goûte, le respire, le prononce, le répète et l'écoute, le palpe, le hume et le rejette finalement, découragé. Ses vibrations ne te conviennent pas, ne semblent pas propices. Et pourtant, il ne me reste que les mots pour t'atteindre à nouveau, te ramener à moi d'aussi loin que tu sois, difficile reconquête. Pourrais-je rejeter les mots, comme Orphée[13] sa lyre pour mieux courir vers Eurydice, était-ce là son erreur?

Comment te ramener à moi, sinon en éveillant dans ta mémoire tous les souvenirs qui te liaient à moi, que j'ai laissé s'atténuer, en ressuscitant l'émotion et non plus en l'évoquant pour moi seul?

Te souviens-tu? Dans ce grand amphithéâtre, lorsque je t'ai vue venir vers moi, j'aurais voulu être invisible pour mieux te regarder réagir naturellement. Mais j'étais plongé en moi-même te contemplant. Ce n'est donc pas de cela que tu peux te souvenir, mais de moi, lorsque tu m'as vu. Tu m'avais dit: «Je n'ai vu que tes yeux, au centre de l'amphi, les seuls vivants, les seuls qui me voyaient exister. C'était comme s'ils m'appelaient.»

J'ai besoin de te croire, aujourd'hui. A l'époque, cela me semblait trop beau pour être vrai. J'essaye de me mettre à ta place lorsque tu étais entrée par la porte de droite, je me souviens parfaitement de la vue d'ensemble que tu as pu avoir – tant de fois la perspective de cette centaine de têtes émergeant des dossiers en rangées uniformes m'a donné le vertige! – il ne m'est pas difficile, non, de laisser cette image remonter en moi, pas plus que de focaliser le centre et de m'y voir, me retournant par hasard en cet instant précis, mais la vision s'estompe dès que j'aperçois mon propre visage: tout se brouille alors, se ternit, tes traits remplacent les miens, je ne me souviens plus que de moi te regardant me regarder de cet œil noir, canaille sous la longue mèche qui traçait sur

be carried away on this tide of melancholy from which memories occasionally emerge, as undying as the present whose clearness and glow they have? Probably because living again is no longer enough for me, because you must also live again with me.

These pages, runways or decodings, are not enough: I lack the signs. I feel as though I am tackling an unfamiliar language. I examine each word which refers to you, I weigh it up, I taste it, I breathe it, I pronounce it, I repeat it and listen to it, I feel it, I smell it and finally I reject it, disheartened. Its resonance does not suit you, does not seem fitting. And yet, I only have words left to reach you again, to bring you to me from as far away as you are, a difficult reconquest. Could I throw words away as Orpheus threw away his lyre in order to be able to run more easily to Eurydice, was that his mistake?

How can I bring you to me, other than by waking in your mind all the memories that linked you to me, which I have allowed to grow fainter, by breathing new life into the emotion and by ceasing to evoke it for me alone?

Do you remember? In that great amphitheatre, when I saw you coming towards me, I would have liked to be invisible in order more easily to watch you reacting naturally. But I was immersed in myself as I watched you. So it is not that which you can remember, but me, when you saw me. You had said to me: 'I only saw your eyes, in the middle of the amphitheatre, the only ones that were alive, the only ones which saw that I existed. It was as though they were calling to me.'

I need to believe you, today. At the time, it all seemed too beautiful to be true. I try to put myself in your place when you came in through the door on the right, I remember perfectly the general view that you might have had – how often has the vision of those hundred or so heads sticking out of chair-backs in identical rows made my head spin! – no, it is not difficult for me to allow that image to rise up in me, and no more difficult than to focus on the centre and to see myself there, by chance turning round at that precise moment, but the vision becomes blurred as soon as I spot my own face: everything becomes confused, becomes dull, your features replace mine, I no longer remember anything other than me looking at you looking at me with that dark eye, roguish beneath the long

ta tempe et ta joue une courbe molle et caressante. Mais toi, toi, que voyais-tu en moi qui ait pu t'émouvoir? Je me regarde en cet instant où tu ne peux plus me voir, sachant que ce n'est plus tout à fait le même visage d'il y a quinze ans, mais que tu le reconnaîtrais sans doute . . .

Pourrait-elle vraiment le reconnaître?

La croisée entrouverte sur la nuit me renvoie un reflet suffisamment imprécis pour estomper les quelques rides naissantes, ces lignes amères qui partent du nez, ces pattes d'oie enjouées cicatrices du sourire, et je m'étonne comme d'habitude face à ce visage que je dois identifier mien. Mais il m'est plus précieux cette nuit: c'est par ce visage que tu te souviens de moi, par lui, que tu avais aimé . . .

Alors pourquoi le grimer, me cacher derrière ce masque? Fafou, c'est moi qui parle à travers cet homme, c'est de moi, non de lui que tu dois te souvenir! Homme-plume, il ne sert qu'à te lancer dans un livre-bouteille à la mer, son visage n'est pas le mien, mais je suis là, me reconnais-tu?

Je sais que les visages ne sont qu'écorces, mais ce sont les formes que nous avons aimées. Quel visage aurait-il, cet homme qui s'attarde à rêver sa première maîtresse en ce jeu narcissique où le reflet conduit à la mort? Je le situe ici, pourtant, dans cet appartement où nous nous sommes aimées. Ici? Non, plus bas, dans la cave, t'en souviens-tu? Lorsque nous étions arrivées, ma sœur était avec des amis, et j'avais prétexté vouloir te montrer de vieux daguerréotypes[14]. . . . Dans la cave, oui. Et maintenant, cet autre-là, qui aurait pu t'aimer au grand jour, parle de son visage, alors que c'est le mien que tu aimais, quelle que soit la ressemblance qu'il puisse y avoir entre nous deux! Pierre le gênait – moi aussi – mais c'est lui qui s'en est débarrassé d'un coup de plume.

Pierre, que nous avons abandonné sur la route, a déjà eu le temps d'arriver à Paris, d'entrer dans ce bistro, de demander un jeton à la caisse, Canadien s'émouvant de ces archaïsmes parisiens. L'écouteur à la main, il vient d'entendre les sonneries qu'il reconnaît bien . . . Et la voix de ta mère . . . Non.

Je reviens à toi, Fafou, le visage lavé, comme au premier jour. Je ne me cacherai plus. Je ne suis ni Pierre, ni cet autre, là, qui a feint d'être Pierre ou moimême. Et pourtant, l'image est lancée, Pierre a reconnu la voix de ta mère. Il répète la scène que j'ai jouée avant lui: il se nomme, s'explique, demande de tes nouvelles . . . Sonde le malaise, à l'autre bout de la ligne,

strand of hair that curled softly and caressingly over your temple and your cheek. But you, what did you see in me that might have moved you? I am looking at myself at this moment in a place where you can no longer see me, knowing that it is no longer quite the same face as the one of fifteen years ago, but you would probably recognize it . . .

Could she really recognize him?

The window that is half-open on to the night sends me back a reflection that is sufficiently lacking in detail to soften the few nascent wrinkles, those bitter lines that start at the nose, those cheery crow's-feet scars of one's smile and, as usual when looking at this face, I am amazed that I must identify it as my own. But it is more precious to me tonight: it is with this face that you remember me, this is the face that you had loved . . .

So why put on make-up, hide myself behind this mask? Fafou, it is I who speak through this man, it is I, not him, that you must remember! A scribe, his only use is to throw you like a message in a bottle into the sea, his face is not mine, but I am here, do you recognize me?

I know that faces are merely like peel, but they are the shapes that we have loved. What face would this man have, the one who is slow to dream of his first mistress in this narcissistic game in which reflection leads to death? I place him here, however, in this flat where we loved each other. Here? No, lower, in the cellar, do you remember it? When we had arrived, my sister was with friends, and I had pretended to want to show you some old daguerreotypes . . . yes, in the cellar. And now, that other man, who could have loved you in broad daylight, talks about his face, whereas it was mine that you loved, whatever the resemblance that there might be between us both! Pierre embarrassed him – me too – but it was he who got rid of him with a stroke of the pen.

Pierre, whom we left on the road, has already had the time to get to Paris, to go into that bistro, to ask for a telephone token at the bar, a Canadian moved by these Parisian archaisms. With the receiver in his hand, he has just heard the ringing that he easily recognizes . . . And your mother's voice . . . No.

I am coming back to you, Fafou, with my face washed, as on the first day. I shall not hide myself any more. I am neither Pierre, nor that other man, who pretended to be Pierre or myself. And yet, the image has been launched, Pierre has recognized your mother's voice. He goes through the scene that I played before him: he gives his name, explains who he is, asks about you . . . Probes the uneasiness, at

entend même ta mère demander à Cyril: «Va jouer dans l'autre pièce, veux-tu mon chéri?», pense que ce n'est pas ainsi que l'on s'adresse à un garçon de quinze ans, redoute déjà les propos moralisateurs que ta mère pourrait lui tenir, maintenant qu'elle est seule avec lui, elle qui avait tout appris de votre liaison . . .

Mais c'est moi, moi seule qui peux entendre ces mots qui me glacent, ridicules dans leur formule désuète, impitoyables.

J'ai eu besoin de lui, pourtant, pour revivre cette scène, mais il peut me quitter maintenant. Je suis seule à présent, pour recevoir les paroles de cette femme vieillie, qui me glacent et m'exaucent, au-delà des années: «Elle vous a tellement aimée, si vous saviez!» Sait-elle de quel amour ou l'a-t-elle oublié, elle qui maintenant, après m'avoir chassée de chez vous comme un démon, me demande aujourd'hui de retourner la voir?

J'irai. Dans quelques jours, lorsque je serai capable d'affronter la rue, les marches, l'appartement que tu n'habites plus, j'irai; mais auparavant, il faudra que je cherche de quel masque je dois me revêtir pour l'affronter. Ici, j'ai d'abord emprunté celui de Pierre et j'ai eu besoin d'une autre voix pour le démasquer, voix que j'ai cru être la mienne, jusqu'au premier accord masculin qui m'a échappé, contre lequel je n'ai pas résisté, par respect pour ta mémoire auprès de ta famille et de tous ceux qui ne pouvaient être au courant de notre amour. Faux respect qui me chasse de ta vie, m'estompe, comme un reflet délavé par les années; après tout, ne sommes-nous pas un peu oubliées, toi dans ton mariage, moi dans le mien, à peine transposé ici?

Ironiquement, c'est à ta mère que je dois de savoir que tu ne m'as jamais oubliée: «Elle nous a si souvent parlé de vous, comment pourrais-je ne pas me souvenir?» Vous auriez pu, Madame, ne retenir de moi que l'épisode de cette lettre qui nous avait découvertes et soulevé votre colère. Mais non: depuis, votre indiscrétion – que je bénis aujourd'hui – vous a poussé à lire le journal de Fafou, mes lettres qu'elle avait conservées, à comprendre que notre amour n'était pas damné comme des poèmes vous l'ont fait croire, les fleurs du mâle[15] n'ayant pas donné le bonheur à Fafou comme vous l'aviez innocemment cru, malgré l'enfant au nom de qui tout fut brisé, ravagé . . . «Peut-être, disiez-vous encore, l'auriez-vous rendue plus heureuse, qui sait?» Qui sait? Mots chuchotés, qui me reviennent par bribes, auxquels, sur le moment, je ne pouvais prêter attention . . .

Oui, j'ai besoin d'affronter tous mes masques avant d'aller la rencontrer. De tous mes masques, recomposer le mien d'alors, il y a quinze ans, pour pouvoir m'emparer de ce que nulle autre que moi doit entendre.

the other end of the line, he can even hear your mother asking Cyril: 'Go and play in the other room, will you, darling?', he thinks that this is not how one talks to a fifteen-year-old boy, already dreads the moralizing comments that your mother might make to him, now that she is alone with him, she who had learnt everything about your affair . . .

But it is I, I alone, who can hear those words which chill me, ridiculous because of their old-fashioned expression, pitiless.

I needed him, however, to relive this scene, but he can leave me now. For the moment I am alone, in order to hear this old woman's words, which chill me and yet answer my prayers, across the years: 'She was so in love with you, if you only knew!' Does she know with what love or has she forgotten, she who now, after chasing me away from your house as though I were a demon, today asks me to go back and see her?

I shall go. In a few days, when I am able to confront the street, the steps, the flat that you no longer live in, I shall go; but before then I shall have to think what mask I must wear in order to confront it. In this account, I initially borrowed Pierre's and I needed another voice to take it off, a voice that I thought was mine, until the first masculine agreement that I missed, against which I did not put up any resistance, out of respect for your memory amongst your family and all those who could not have been aware of our love. A misguided respect that chases me from your life, blurs my image, like a reflection faded by the waters of time; after all, haven't we forgotten each other just a little, you in your marriage, me in mine, hardly mentioned in these pages?

Ironically, I am in debt to your mother for knowing that you have never forgotten me: 'She has talked to us about you so often, how could I not remember?' Madame, you might have remembered about me only the episode of that letter which gave us away and which made you so angry. But no: since then, your indiscretion – for which I thank God today – made you read Fafou's diary, my letters, which she had kept, and realize that our love was not damned as some poems led you to believe, the flowers of the male not having given happiness to Fafou as you had naively believed, in spite of the child, in whose name everything was shattered, torn apart . . . 'Perhaps,' you also used to say, 'you would have made her happier, who knows?' Who knows? Words spoken softly, which come back to me in snatches, which, at the time, I could not pay any attention to . . .

Yes, I need to face up to all my masks before going to meet her. From all my masks, I must reconstruct mine from that time, fifteen years ago, so I can seize that which no woman but me must hear.

Flottent en moi, incohérentes, des images comme des feuilles mortes sur un lac. Et je suis tour à tour l'eau stagnante qui les porte, et les feuilles, toutes deux prisonnières des rives, figées pour l'éternité.

Pierre n'arrivera pas au but: c'est inutile. Et celui qui se contemple encore sur les vitres d'une fenêtre entrouverte sur la nuit restera là, à s'interroger sur son visage que tu n'as pas connu. Aucun des deux ne parviendra au but. Et moi, je sais aussi que j'ai failli au mien. Entre ces pages, non écrites, des évocations de toi, images limpides, flottent comme les feuilles sur un lac, mais aucun mot n'a su les ressusciter.

Mes subterfuges ne t'ont pas tirée de l'ombre où tu te terres, ne t'ont pas alertée, là où tu t'es cachée, ils n'ont fait que raviver ma propre angoisse. Ton image lumineuse, ton parfum, ta peau, la brillance de tes yeux noirs, tes lèvres, tout s'enlise en un fatras de poussière. Se peut-il que la mort soit cette conscience marécageuse, uniquement capable de contempler le passé qui se désagrège dans le néant du temps?

Ce récit, entrepris dans le seul but de te faire revivre — mais est-ce revivre que de se voir condamnée à refaire des gestes anciens, comme une marionnette entre les mains d'une autre — ce récit ne peut aboutir qu'à la désespérante mais humble acceptation de ces mots de ta mère, au téléphone, que moi seule pouvais entendre:

«Fafou n'est plus de ce monde.»

Like dead leaves on a lake, incoherent images float through my mind. First I am the stagnant water that carries them, then the leaves, both prisoners between the riverbanks, fixed for all eternity.

Pierre will not reach his goal: there is no point. And he who still looks at himself on the panes of a window half-opened on to the night will stay there, wondering about his face that you did not know. Neither of them will reach their goal. And I too know that I have failed to reach mine. In these pages, not yet written, are evocations of you, clear images, which float like the leaves on a lake, but no word could bring them to life.

My subterfuges have not pulled you out of the shadow in which you are hiding, have not warned you, there where you have hidden, they have merely rekindled my own anguish. Your shining image, your scent, your skin, the brilliance of your dark eyes, your lips, everything sinks into a mishmash of dust. Is it possible that death is that swampy conscience, uniquely capable of contemplating the past which disperses into the emptiness of time?

This account, undertaken with the sole intention of bringing you back to life – but can it be termed bringing back to life if one merely sees oneself condemned to recreating old gestures, like a puppet in someone else's hands – this account can only lead to the hopeless but humble acceptance of your mother's words, spoken on the telephone, that only I could hear:

'Fafou is no longer of this world.'

Self-destruction

RENÉ BELLETTO

Autodestruction

Je fais un long voyage entre deux capitales.

Une amie, qui connaît mon dégoût des hôtels, plus invincible encore que ma crainte de la solitude, m'a remis avant mon départ les clés d'une maison qu'elle possède et située, loin des villes et des routes, à mi-chemin entre mon point de départ et mon point d'arrivée. Je pourrai ainsi dormir autant qu'il me plaira – couper le voyage – et laisser reposer ma voiture – vieille, délavée, coussins nauséabonds, moteur qui tape, radiateur fuyant, les portières s'ouvrent seules et le bouton de la radio, actionné, émet mystérieusement des jets puissants d'huile noire.

– et quand j'arrive en vue de la maison, par une nuit d'orage, il est temps, car le moteur, noyé, s'éteint dans les hoquets, et le véhicule se blottit contre une haie de houx comme une chienne malade.

Je m'en inquiéterai demain.

Chargé de bagages la pluie me bat sur l'étroit chemin ruisselant où je me courbe talonné par la peur du refroidissement dans un lit inconnu fiévreux (le robinetier qui employait mon père lui ayant demandé s'il pleuvait dehors un jour que mon père, le cheveu dégouttant de brillantine, mon père lui répondit), vite, vite, du feu, un bain fumant, des serviettes bien râpeuses, le manger et le dormir!

C'est une maison d'un étage.[1]

Je ferai à mon amie un présent[2] de prix – une sculpture, un violon, douze livres – oui, douze beaux volumes –, et nous resterons silencieux de longues heures comme par le passé – sa maison est un petit paradis. Paradis.

*

Self-destruction

I am on a long journey between two capital cities.

Before I set off, a female friend, who knows my intense dislike of hotels, which is even more insuperable than my fear of being alone, handed me the keys to a house she owns, which is situated, a long way from any town or road, halfway between my point of departure and my destination. I will therefore be able to sleep as much as I like – to break the journey – and to give a rest to my car, which is old, faded in colour, with disgusting seat cushions, an engine that thumps, a radiator that leaks, doors that open by themselves and a radio button that, when turned on, mysteriously squirts out powerful gushes of black oil.

– and when the house comes into sight, one stormy night, it is time, for the engine, which is flooded, splutters to a halt, and the car huddles against a hedge of holly like a sick dog.

I'll worry about it tomorrow.

I am laden with luggage, and the rain is beating down on me on the narrow path, streaming with water, along which I am bent, driven by the fear of catching a feverish chill in a strange bed (the tap-maker who used to employ my father having asked him one day if it was raining outside when my father, his hair dripping with brilliantine, my father replied to him), quickly, quickly, a fire, a steaming hot bath, really rough towels, eat and sleep!

It is a house with a ground and first floor.

I will give my friend an expensive gift – a sculpture, a violin, twelve books – yes, twelve fine volumes – and we will remain silent for hours on end, as we did in the past – her house is a minor paradise. A paradise.

*

Lavé d'abondance, peigné fin, rasé jusqu'au muscle, rassasié sans
vergogne, j'attends que le feu s'apaise dans la grande cheminée
rose et je monte à l'étage où je trouve plus douillette encore la
chambre où je vais dormir d'un trait. Un refroidissement! Ha, ha!
Foin des idées noires! Déshabillé, je me glisse dans le lit comme pour
ne pas le défaire.

Or un malin sommeil se plaît à m'échapper.

Je pense dans la nuit.

Le silence a chassé la pluie. Seules des gouttes obstinées . . .

Et malgré le confort qui me ceint de toutes parts, et bien, aussi, que
j'aie quelque réticence à admettre une quelconque ressemblance entre
moi-même et quiconque, néanmoins, si quelqu'un me poussait dans
mes tout derniers retranchements, je finirais par admettre qu'entre
Robinson Crusoë[3] – *Robinessonne Krouzô*, prononcé à l'anglaise par un
maître un jour gris de lycée, interminable hilarité – et moi . . . Mais si
peu à la réflexion. Il est seul dans une île. Je me souviens qu'en dépit
de la chaleur accablante, il dissimule ses parties honteuses derrière une
peau de bête, prétextant que les mouvements de cette espèce de jupe
produisent de petits courants d'air qui le rafraîchissent. *Robinessonne.*

J'avais cru mon sommeil impérieux et je n'ai pas – indifférence
peu concevable, mais passons – examiné avant d'éteindre les nom-
breux livres qui bombent une bibliothèque en acajou massif. La
certitude que je ne dormirai pas de sitôt, l'excitation provoquée
en moi par le calme absolu qui m'entoure, un bien-être eupho-
rique aussi, né d'une fatigue toujours présente mais dissoute, font
que j'allume et me relève en souplesse et bondis de-ci de-là dans
la pièce, béat, jusqu'à la bibliothèque d'acajou sombre et
finement poussiéreux dont la clé tourne pour ainsi dire seule:
que de livres!

Sur plusieurs rangées, aussi profond que mon bras puisse
atteindre et encore au-delà (le meuble trompe, on l'eût dit moins
épais), une infinité de livres s'offrent à moi. A cette vue, à ce
toucher, à ce sentir de cuir lisse et de papier ranci, je perds tout sens
commun et j'applaudis en sautant sur place avec de petits cris et

Washed thoroughly clean, hair neatly combed, shaved as close as can be, hunger shamelessly satisfied, I wait for the fire to die down in the large pink fireplace and then go upstairs where I find the even cosier bedroom in which I am going to sleep without waking. A chill! No way! A plague on such foolish notions! Undressed, I slide into the bed as though not to disturb the sheets.

Then crafty sleep delights in eluding me.

I spend the night in thought.

Silence has chased away the rain. Just persistent drips . . .

And despite the all-embracing feeling of comfort and although I am also slightly reluctant to admit to some resemblance or other between myself and anyone else, nevertheless if driven into a corner I would eventually admit that between Robinson Crusoe – pronounced *Robinessonne Krouzô* in the English way by a teacher one grey day at the lycée, the source of interminable mirth – and me . . . But on reflection so little. He is alone on an island. I remember that in spite of the oppressive heat, he conceals the shameful parts of his body beneath an animal skin, claiming that the movement of this sort of skirt makes draughts to keep him cool. *Robinessonne.*

I had thought that sleep would come immediately and before putting the light out I have not – with scarcely conceivable indifference, but let's not tarry over it – examined the many books that are bulging out of the solid mahogany bookcase. The certainty that I will not fall asleep immediately, the excitement stirred in me by the total calm that surrounds me, a feeling of well-being that is also one of euphoria, born from an ever-present though indefinable tiredness, combine to make me turn on the light and slide smoothly out of bed, and I leap hither and thither in the room, blissfully happy, until I reach the dark mahogany bookcase, covered in a fine dust, whose key turns almost by itself: so many books!

In several rows, as deep as my arm can reach and even further (the bookcase is deceptive, one would have said that it was not so deep), an infinite number of books offer themselves to me. Seeing, touching, smelling this smooth leather and musty paper, I lose all my common sense and I clap my hands, as I jump on the spot,

seule la crainte (mes essors élastiques m'arrachant toujours plus loin du sol) de défoncer le plafond dans une explosion de plâtre et une chute de petits moellons (mes yeux hagards dans le noir du grenier, les souris accourant pour me ronger la tête) m'immobilise à la raison.

Gravement, je feuillette des milliers de volumes sans m'attacher à aucun, sauf à une plaquette pourtant, tard dans la nuit, dernière saisie, un ravissant petit format sans nom d'auteur, quelques pages à peine de beaux caractères nets que je vais pouvoir aisément déchiffrer du premier au dernier.

Ma lecture commence.

Autodestruction

Je fais un long voyage entre deux capitales.

Une amie, qui connaît mon dégoût des hôtels, plus invincible encore que ma crainte de la solitude, m'a remis avant mon départ les clés d'une maison qu'elle possède et située, loin des villes et des routes, à mi-chemin entre mon point de départ et mon point d'arrivée. Je pourrai ainsi . . .

Fort drôle! Voilà mon histoire narrée par le menu détail! Je m'arrache non sans peine à la phrase: cette rupture, cette suspension, ce simple effort de réflexion m'empêchent, je le sais, de sombrer dans le vertige d'un éternel recommencement et me permettent de

uttering brief cries (my springy leaps lift me ever further off the
ground) and it is only the fear of going through the ceiling in an
explosion of plaster and a clatter of small stones (wild-eyed in the
attic as the mice run up to gnaw at my head) that keeps me within
the bounds of reason.

Solemnly, I leaf through thousands of volumes without seizing on
a single one, that is with the exception of a slender volume, late into
the night, the last that I grasp, a delightful, small tome which does
not bear the name of its author, barely more than a few pages,
beautifully and clearly printed, that I am easily going to be able to
read from the first letter to the last.

I begin to read.

Self-destruction

I am on a long journey between two capital cities.

Before I set off, a female friend, who knows my intense dislike of
hotels, which is even more insuperable than my fear of being alone,
handed me the keys to a house she owns, which is situated, a long
way from any town or road, halfway between my point of departure
and my destination. I will therefore be able to . . .

How strange! Here is my story told down to the smallest detail. With
great difficulty I tear myself away from the sentence: this break, this
pause, this mere effort to think prevents me, I know, from sinking
into the dizziness of perpetually restarting and allows me to continue

continuer sans qu'aucune inquiétude encore ne se mêle à mon amusement hautain: cette coïncidence, ce jeu: fort drôles.

. . . dormir autant qu'il me plaira – couper le voyage – et laisser reposer ma voiture . . .

L'impotence de mon véhicule, la pluie brutale, ma vie dans la maison, mes souvenirs, la fuite du sommeil, mon désir de lecture: quelle exactitude, dieu du ciel! Comment ce prodige est-il possible? Cette première question ouvre une faille par où s'insinue mon trouble rôdeur et vigilant. Tout est dit, et quand je suis au passage suivant:

. . . je feuillette des milliers de volumes sans m'attacher à aucun, sauf à une plaquette pourtant, . . .

l'illusion d'échapper à l'infini des mots ne pèse rien en regard du piège éternel qu'ils me tendent, me dis-je, et mon malaise épars se ramasse et durcit et devient PEUR, et je lève les yeux, car ce que je lis rapporte un passé de plus en plus proche, rapportera bientôt mon geste, ma réflexion, mon activité du moment – comme un regard jeté-repris aussitôt m'en **assure** –, d'où je conclus que mon avenir gît dans les pages, ma vie, et tout entière absente en un seul point du temps?

Texte maudit, je vais te piétiner, te jeter du haut d'une tour, te souiller au-delà de toute expression, arracher tes pages une à une et les piler dans un mortier de goudron ardent, malmener chacun de tes caractères (j'y reviendrai) et leur donner forme inhumaine d'indécryptables hiéroglyphes!

Ou plutôt devrais-je te lire calmement, mot à mot, et par là te rendre inoffensif, selon une démarche de l'esprit que je ne parviens toujours pas à élucider?

Hélas, la terreur me dicte son incompréhensible loi: je veux savoir, un peu, pas trop, non je ne me précipiterai pas sur la dernière page, le dernier mot, mais je regarderai par éclairs, brèves explorations, foudroyants sondages qui disloqueront mon corps, mes

without any worry interfering with my lofty pleasure: this coincidence, this game: how strange.

. . . sleep as much as I like – to break the journey – and to give my car a rest . . .

The uselessness of my car, the harsh rain, my life in the house, my memories, the flight of sleep, my desire to read: how precise, heavens above! What has made this coincidence possible? This initial question creates an opening through which creeps my wandering, watchful distress. Everything is there, and when I come to the following extract:

. . . I leaf through thousands of volumes without seizing on a single one, that is with the exception of a slender volume . . .

the illusion of escaping from the infinity created by the words counts for nothing, I tell myself, compared with the eternal trap that they are setting for me, and my ill-defined discomfort takes form and hardens and becomes FEAR, and I look up, for what I am reading recalls a past that is getting ever closer, that will soon recall my movement, my thoughts, what I am doing now – as a glance cast and immediately returned **assures** me – from which I conclude that my future lies in these pages, my life, and will it be completely over at a single moment in time?

Wretched text, I am going to trample on you, throw you from the top of a tower, sully you more than I can adequately express, tear out your pages one by one and pile them up in a mortar of burning tar, maltreat each of your characters (I'll come back to this) and give them the inhuman form of undecipherable hieroglyphics!

Or rather, should I read you calmly, word by word, and thus render you harmless, by a mental process that I cannot yet manage to convey adequately?

Alas, terror imposes on me its incomprehensible law: I want to know, a little, not too much, no I will not rush to the last page, the last word, but I will take darting glances, make brief explorations, lightning soundings that will dislocate my body, my limbs and my

membres et mon visage de curiosité fébrile et désordonnée avant que je me raidisse avec nerf, comme ces personnages au squelette de ficelle qu'on manœuvre du pouce – paralysé par ce que j'aurai vu.

Une phrase me sollicite d'abord, peut-être à cause des guillemets qui la détachent: «C'est alors que j'entends des pas dans l'escalier.» Damnation! J'entends des pas dans l'escalier! Quoi d'autre pouvait autant m'effrayer? J'écoute et je perçois distinctement des chocs mous, lourds, espacés! Et qui ne sont pas d'une démarche humaine! Je tourne une page du petit livre sur lequel se crispent et blêmissent les doigts de ma main gauche et ces autres mots m'éblouissent, isolés par deux bandes blanches:

Non, ce n'est pas un homme qui se meut sans grâce dans l'escalier, mais c'est un monstre abject et lent. Le voici maintenant devant la porte de ma chambre. Il va entrer. Sauter par la fenêtre est mon seul espoir de fuite périlleuse, puis, ne pas courir à la route dans la campagne nue, mais contourner la maison, et me perdre dans la forêt.

Silence.

Jamais silence ne fut moins supportable. Rien ne pouvait m'effrayer comme un monstre.

Je me précipite vers la porte (et la main de la folie se referme avec un crissement d'ongles durs à l'endroit précis de l'espace que ma tête occupait un instant auparavant), et j'ouvre.[4]

J'ouvre. Ah! l'horrible chose!

Le monstre se tient là, devant moi, immense et tremblotant, boursouflé d'abcès visqueux d'où s'écoule – et glisse au sol, et ruisselle à mes pieds! – un liquide fétide et fumant, et ses yeux! ses yeux, si l'on peut désigner du nom d'yeux ces vastes cavités asymétriques comme emplies d'une purée grasse à la surface de laquelle viennent crever de petites bulles verdâtres! Ah! le beau monstre!

Je recule vers la fenêtre, il s'avance vers moi en émettant un long rire sans joie!

Mes habits sont posés sur une chaise, pliés avec soin dans l'ordre où je les ai ôtés. J'aurais presque le temps de les passer avant la chute (le froid, la fièvre, la chambre moite – souvenirs de maux et

face with feverish, wild curiosity before I stiffen my resolve like those characters with string skeletons that one works with one's thumb – paralysed by what I will have seen.

A sentence immediately catches my eye, perhaps because of the speech marks, which make it stand out: 'It was then that I heard footsteps on the staircase.' Damnation! I can hear footsteps on the staircase! What else could make me so afraid? I listen and I can clearly make out muffled, heavy, regular steps! And these are not sounds made by a human tread! I turn a page of the tiny book on which the fingers of my left hand are tense and pale, and these other words dazzle me, separated by two blank lines:

No, it is not a man who is moving gracelessly on the staircase: it is a despicable, slow monster. There it is now, outside my bedroom door. It is about to come in. My only hope of a perilous escape is to jump through the window, then not to run to the road in the open countryside but to go round the house and get lost in the forest.

Silence.

Never was a silence more unbearable. Nothing could terrify me as much as a monster.

I rushed towards the door (and the hand of madness closed with the screech of hard fingernails at the precise point in space occupied by my head a moment before) and I opened the door.

I opened the door. Oh, what a dreadful sight!

The monster was standing there, before me, huge and quivering, swollen with slimy abscesses from which oozed – and slid to the ground, and flowed at my feet! – a fetid, fuming liquid, and its eyes! its eyes! if it is possible to call eyes those vast asymmetric cavities, which looked filled with a fatty purée on the surface of which had just burst small, greenish bubbles! Ah! a monster indeed.

I stepped back towards the window and it came towards me, letting out a long, joyless laugh.

My clothes were on a chair, carefully folded in the order in which I had taken them off. I would nearly have time to slip them on before I fell (cold, fever, the damp room – memories of evil and a

d'âme rendue, hors de mon esprit!), tellement sa progression est timide – implacable néanmoins –, mais la peur m'en empêche. Je me contente d'enfiler sans me baisser ces chaussures, là, qui m'évoquent le temps heureux où je les achetai en solde dans les rues animées de la vieille ville.

Le monstre s'approche et étend dans ma direction une main, si l'on peut désigner du nom de main . . .

J'ouvre la fenêtre, et je saute, le livre serré contre ma poitrine, un doigt glissé à l'intérieur en guise de signet.

Je cours sous la lune dans la forêt frileuse, gémissant de la chute et soupirant après une bonne pèlerine, comme jadis dans une région de montagne, je m'en souviens comme si c'était hier, et encore aujourd'hui je me demande si ce n'était pas en effet hier, vacances glorieuses – enfants de mon âge, murmures à l'oreille, longs jours, brèves nuits, confiture léchée et pain jeté, monde immobile – vacances éternelles où j'allais, vêtu d'une pèlerine qui balayait les graviers de la route, marchant derrière le troupeau de moutons, marchant jusqu'à la pâture, septembre était venu, et rêvant déjà de la brûlante époque des foins, juché sur la charrette où j'ordonnais l'herbe et la piétinais, plein de l'orgueil des fourches évitées, retours impériaux à la ferme, monde immobile et soumis, paroles tues – aveugle, insensible, je cours dans la forêt jusqu'à bout de souffle.

Je dois m'arrêter. Devant moi, une rivière profonde.

Halètements.

J'ai oublié le monstre, mais la peur ne m'a pas quitté.

Bruits dans mon dos: frissons des hautes fougères, trépignements d'écureuils, tourbillons d'aiguilles de pin?

Je me retourne et je vois.

Les arbres enflent à leur base comme s'ils se dédoublaient. Malédiction! Chacun dissimulait un monstre, les ignobles créatures sont légion! Une infinité de monstres me coupent toute issue!

Le temps est venu d'oser.

J'ouvre la plaquette à la dernière page. Mes yeux saillent à

soul delivered, out of my mind!) so slowly did it move – no less
unrelenting for all that – but fear prevented me. Without bending
down, I merely slipped on those shoes, which brought back that
happy time when I bought them in a sale in the busy streets of the
old town.

The monster moved forward and stretched out a hand towards
me, if it is possible to call a hand . . .

I opened the window and I jumped, the book held tight against
my chest, a finger slipped inside like a bookmark.

I ran in the moonlight through the cold forest, groaning from my
fall and yearning for a warm cape, such as I had worn long ago in a
mountainous area, I remembered it as if it were yesterday, and even
today I wonder if it was not indeed yesterday, those glorious holidays – children of my own age, whisperings, long days, short nights,
jam licked and bread thrown away, an unchanging world – ever-
lasting holidays when I went about, dressed in a cape which swept
the gravel on the road, walking behind the flock of sheep, walking to
the grazing grounds, September had come, and already dreaming of
the baking hot hay-making season, perched on the cart in which I
arranged the hay and trampled it, full of pride at all the forks I had
avoided, imperial return journeys to the farm, an unchanging and
submissive world, where words remained unspoken – blind, numb, I
ran through the forest until I was out of breath.

I had to stop. Before me lay a deep river.

Panting.

I had forgotten the monster but I had not lost my fear.

Noises at my back: shivers in the tall ferns, squirrels stamping, whirls
of pine needles.

I turned and I saw.

The trees were swelling at their bases, as if they were unfolding.
Curses! Each one hiding a monster, there were hundreds of the vile
creatures! An infinite number of monsters were cutting off all chance
of escape!

The time had come to be daring.

I opened the small tome at the last page. My eyes were bulging as I

la lecture de la dernière phrase, embellie de guillemets narquois.

Hurlant de rage, pestant contre ce dénouement cruel et sans surprise, mais inévitable, je me précipite vers la rivière où je jette le livre que l'eau avale, et les derniers mots lus continuent de s'inscrire douloureusement dans la matière cérébrale où ils se figent et durcissent: «A la mort indicible qu'ils me réservent, je préfère l'eau noire de la rivière!»

read the last sentence, made more appealing by its sardonic speech marks.

Yelling with anger, cursing this cruel, unsurprising but inevitable ending, I rushed towards the river, threw in the book, which the water swallowed, and the last words continued to inscribe themselves painfully into my brain, where they set and grew hard: 'I preferred the black water of the river to the unspeakable death they reserved for me!'

You Never Die

ALAIN GERBER

On ne meurt jamais

Laurentides[1] (Québec), octobre 1953

J'avais prévenu l'institutrice. Elle n'a pas fait de difficultés: nous sommes amies d'enfance, Marie-Jeanne et moi.

J'ai essayé de lire un peu, mais je n'avais guère la tête à ça. Pour me calmer, je n'ai rien trouvé de mieux que de tourner en rond, ne lâchant le réveil des yeux que pour consulter la pendule. Dans la cuisine, un linge de toile écrue protégeait la jatte où la pâte était en train de reposer.

J'ai quitté si tôt la maison qu'au magasin, j'étais à peu près la seule cliente. Mon sac de guimauves sous le bras, j'ai flâné entre les rayons, détaillant les étiquettes de produits que je n'avais nulle intention d'acheter. Pour finir, j'ai failli oublier mon paquet à la caisse.

La petite mère m'attendait sur le perron de l'école, les pieds joints dans une flaque de soleil qui commençait à roussir.

L'air était imprégné d'une senteur d'écorce. Il y avait aussi des fragrances de feu, de sciure, de toile humide et de labours. Puis un vague fumet de bêtes sauvages, que j'imaginais sans doute.

Tout le long du chemin, j'avais exposé mon coude à la portière afin de sentir sur moi cette chaleur capiteuse et fragile des automnes. Au seuil de la saison indienne, la forêt se préparait à une éblouissante agonie – la forêt de chez nous, pleine de secrets modestes.

On s'est souri, avec Céline. Moi tout émue, tâchant que ça ne paraisse pas trop. Elle presque grave, à sa façon d'enfant. On a ramené l'auto. Elle a soulevé un coin du linge. Elle était ravie; elle a battu des mains. On a mangé une ou deux guimauves avant de prendre nos vestes et de boucler la maison.

On a marché sur le chemin de terre, jusqu'au ponton, près des

You Never Die

Laurentides (Quebec), October 1953

I had warned the primary-school teacher. She did not raise any objections: Marie-Jeanne and I have been friends since childhood.

I tried to read a little, but my mind could hardly focus. I could not find anything better to calm myself down than to walk around, only taking my eyes off the alarm to consult the clock. In the kitchen, an unbleached linen cloth was covering the bowl in which the dough was resting.

I left the house so early that I was just about the only customer in the shop. With my bag of marshmallows under my arm, I strolled up and down the aisles, examining the labels on produce that I had no intention of buying. In the end I nearly left my packet behind at the check-out.

The little mother was waiting for me on the stone staircase to the school, her feet touching in a pool of sunlight that was beginning to glow red.

A smell of bark filled the air. There were also wafts of fire, saw-dust, damp cloth and ploughing. Then a vague aroma of wild animals, which I probably imagined.

Throughout the journey I had had my elbow out of the window in order to feel on me the heady, fragile warmth of autumn. On the threshold of the Indian summer, the forest was getting ready for its dazzling death throe – the forest near where we live, full of modest secrets.

Céline and I smiled at each other. I was quite moved, though I tried not to show it too much. She was almost serious, in her childish way. We took the car back. She raised a corner of the cloth. She was delighted; she clapped her hands. We ate one or two marshmallows before taking our jackets and locking the house.

We walked down the earth path, as far as the landing-stage, near

bouleaux dont la ramure, tôt le matin, étincelle dans la lumière rosée, comme un précieux métal.

Sous notre nez, toute une famille de corneilles s'est arrachée d'un buisson dans un bruit de papier qu'on froisse. On a eu un petit sursaut. Riant de notre frayeur, on leur a fait des signes une fois qu'elles étaient en l'air. Céline est restée un moment la nuque à la renverse, baignant son visage dans le ciel, les paupières closes. Ses lèvres formaient des mots que je n'entendais pas.

Depuis le jour de ma naissance, la vieille barque de mon père porte mon nom. Il se devine encore bien que les lettres, au fil du temps, aient pris la teinte de la cendre. J'ai installé Céline à l'arrière, sur une couverture pliée. J'ai boutonné sa veste. J'ai enfilé la mienne. Sur l'eau, il fait toujours un peu frais, et puis le soir n'allait plus tarder à venir.

Dans ces instants-là, parler n'est pas nécessaire. Le dos au lac, je me suis mise à ramer. Une grosse truite mouchetée a glissé tout contre notre bord, entre deux eaux.

On n'oublie pas. On n'oublie rien. Peser sur les poignées, enfoncer les pelles, aller sur les pistes de jadis, garder ses mots pour soi, reconnaître les arbres et les oiseaux: en toutes ces matières, Papa était un merveilleux professeur.

«Laure, disait-il pourtant, tu n'as pas besoin d'apprendre ces choses. Elles sont en toi. Il faut seulement que tu les retrouves.» Et aussi: «Regarde le monde: il est à toi.» Pour me taquiner, enfin, il ajoutait souvent: «Le monde a le goût des jolies filles. Regarde-le comme un amoureux.»

Nous voici au milieu de l'eau, au centre de notre infini à nous. Rien qu'un instant, je lâche les avirons.

«Écoute!»

Des oiseaux s'interpellent. Ils chantent autour du silence, mais sans le troubler. Leur musique lui servirait plutôt de faire-valoir.

«Laisse traîner ta main dans l'eau. Hein donc, que c'est bon froid?» Combien de fois ai-je entendu cette phrase? Maintenant, il m'appartient de la prononcer. Un jour, ma Céline, tu diras ces mots à quelqu'un. Mot pour mot les mêmes, de façon que ce monde n'ait jamais l'idée de finir. Jamais de la vie.

the silver birches whose foliage, in the early morning, twinkles with the light from the dew, like a precious metal.

Before our eyes, a whole family of crows burst out of a bush with a noise like the rustling of paper. It startled us a little. Laughing at our fright, we gestured to them as soon as they were in flight. Céline stood for a moment, head bent backwards, bathing her face in the open sky, her eyelids closed. Her lips formed words that I could not hear.

Since the day I was born, my father's old boat has borne my name. You can still make it out, though the letters have become the colour of ash as the years have gone by. I settled Céline down at the stern, on a folded blanket. I buttoned up her jacket. I slipped mine on. It is always a little cool on the water and at that time evening would not be long in coming.

You do not need to speak at times like these. With my back to the lake, I began to row. Close up, a fat speckled trout slipped past, in the shallows.

You do not forget. You do not forget anything. Pushing down on the handles, burying the blades, going down the paths of old, keeping your words to yourself, recognizing the trees and the birds: father was a marvellous teacher in all these subjects.

'Laure,' he used to say, however, 'you don't need to learn these things. They are in you. You only have to find them.' And also: 'Look at the world: it belongs to you.' Indeed, to tease me, he often added: 'The world has a taste for pretty girls. Look at it as you would a lover.'

There we were in the middle of the water, in the centre of our own infinity. Just for a moment, I let go of the oars.

'Listen!'

Birds were calling to each other. They sang around the silence, without disturbing it. Their music would act more as a foil.

'Let your hand trail in the water. It's cold, isn't it?' How many times have I heard that sentence? Now it is my turn to enunciate it. One day, dear Céline, you will say these words to someone. Word for word, the same words, in order that this world never gets the idea of ending. Never, no never.

Chaque jour, chaque minute est une saison. Unique et vieille comme le monde. Il y a, il y aura des millions d'automnes rien que pour nous. Les feuilles reviennent sur les arbres, on revient sur la terre, éternellement.

Regarde, ma fille. Regardons-nous. «Ce qu'on ne dit pas, ce sont les plus beaux mots, ma Laure. On n'a pas besoin de les apprendre; on n'est même pas capable de les oublier. On est capable d'être là. Comme ça d'être bien. La raison? Oh! la raison, on s'en fiche.»

Là-bas sur l'autre rive, un pêcheur s'est installé. Costumé en pêcheur. Immobile comme un pêcheur. Chaque chose est à sa place.

Regarde bien tout, tout doucement. Moi je te regarderai – tu n'en sauras même rien. Le reflet d'argent, paisible au milieu des érables, c'est le clocher de notre église. Le vois-tu?

Maintenant la Laure ne bouge plus. Tout s'est arrêté. Quelque chose d'invisible et de lent descend du haut des arbres et se laisse glisser au fond de notre lac. Alors les oiseaux se taisent. C'est l'heure où les échos de la vie se baignent avant d'aller dormir. Le paysage retient son souffle. Le miroitement de l'eau s'est figé, les ronds à la surface, la glissure des nuages, les nuances des couleurs, les ombres, le pourtour de chaque chose . . . Le monde est une belle image dans un livre: on est dessus.

Bientôt, tu entendras comme un soupir. L'image sera brouillée. Les arbres se balanceront, une fine brise ridera le miroir du lac, depuis cette pointe jusqu'à cette autre, et l'on repartira. En tirant un peu plus sur les rames, cette fois, tandis qu'entre les troncs, dans le plus creux du monde, s'avancera la noirceur encore timide, dissimulée dans une espèce de poussière assoupie, suspendue au-dessus du rivage comme une haleine de miel.

Nous rentrons, ma Laure. Ma Céline, on s'en revient. Encore une fois on a tout vu. Tout reste à voir. On reviendra. Jamais la nuit ne tombe pour de bon. Un jour, toujours, l'hiver s'en va, la neige s'envole, les voisins donnent une fête, on s'endort au matin.

Le pêcheur a rassemblé ses affaires. Il accroche son pliant à son bras et se met en route. On dirait qu'il va du même côté que nous.

Each day, each minute, is a season. As unique and as old as the world. There are, there will be, millions of autumns, just for us. The leaves return to the trees, we come back to the earth, eternally.

Look, darling daughter. Let's look at each other. 'What we don't say are often the most beautiful words, darling Laure. We don't need to learn them; we cannot even forget them. We can be here. Feeling good, like this. The reason? Oh, the reason, who cares!'

On the other bank, over there, a fisherman has settled down. Dressed like a fisherman. Motionless like a fisherman. Everything is in its place.

Look carefully at everything, quietly. I shall look at you, you will not even know anything about it. The silver reflection, peaceful in the midst of the maple trees, is the tower of our church. Can you see it?

Laure is no longer moving now. Everything has come to a halt. Something invisible and slow is coming down from the tops of the trees and allowing itself to slide to the bottom of our lake. Then the birds fall silent. It is the time when the echoes of life bathe before going off to sleep. The countryside holds its breath. The shimmering on the water has frozen in immobility, the rings on the surface, the slow movement of the clouds, the subtleties of the colours, the shadows, the edges of everything . . . The world is a beautiful picture in a book: we are in it.

Soon, you will hear a sound like a sigh. The picture will be blurred. The trees will sway, the gentlest of breezes will trouble the mirrored surface of the lake, from this point to that other one, and we will set off. By pulling just a little more on the oars this time, whilst amongst the tree trunks, in the deepest part of the world, darkness will advance, still shy, concealed in a sort of drowsy dust, hanging above the river bank like a breath of honey.

We are returning, darling Laure. Darling Céline, we're coming back. Once again, we have seen everything. Everything remains to be seen. We will come back. Night never falls for ever. Winter always goes away one day, the snow flies off, the neighbours celebrate, we go to sleep in the morning.

The fisherman has picked up his things. He slides his folding chair over his arm and sets off. It looks as though he's going in the

C'est peut-être un père qui ne cache pas un cœur lourd sous une chemise rouge et que sa fille, aucun soir, n'attendra en vain.

As-tu froid? Veux-tu ma veste? Moi, j'ai chaud de ramer, je n'en ai pas l'usage. C'est encore un beau jour. Les jours devraient tous être plus beaux les uns que les autres. Quand le brouillard montera du lac, on sera rentrées depuis longtemps. Nous arrivons déjà près du bord.

Je souris. Toi, tu lui tournes le dos, tu ne te doutes de rien, mais moi, j'ai aperçu sa silhouette sur le ponton. Il est venu nous chercher. Il a mis le blouson que tu aimes tant.

Nous sommes rendues. Il te saisit sous les aisselles. Il nous embrasse. Il nous serre. Il dit: «Voilà ma Céline!» Plus bas, il prononce mon nom. Il t'assied sur son bras. Il verse ta figure sur sa joue. «Ma Laure ! Ma Céline ! Mes filles. Mes femmes.» Tu ne peux pas voir l'air qu'il a.

Il t'embrasse encore. Il met son autre bras autour de moi. Il frotte son nez contre le tien et, tout de suite après, l'enfouit dans mes cheveux. Il n'y a rien à dire, alors on fait semblant de se taire.

A notre gauche, derrière les bouleaux, le lac est un murmure sans rives. On marche, les trois tout emmêlés, sur le chemin de terre. On s'éloigne dans cette vapeur transparente du soir, où flotte une odeur de fumée.

same direction as us. He is perhaps a father who does not hide a heavy heart under a red shirt, whom his daughter will not wait for in vain any evening.

Are you cold? Would you like my jacket? Rowing is making me warm, I am not used to it. It is still a beautiful day. Every day should be more beautiful than the ones which went before. When the mist rises from the lake, we will have been back a long time. We are already getting close to the edge.

I smile. You have your back to him, you do not suspect anything, but I have spotted his silhouette on the landing-stage. He has come to find us. He has put on the short jacket that you like so much.

We are exhausted. He grabs you under the arms. He gives us a kiss. He hugs us. He says: 'There's darling Céline!' More softly, he pronounces my name. He sits you on his arm. He rubs your face against his cheek. 'Darling Laure! Darling Céline! My girls. My women.' You cannot see the expression on his face.

He kisses you again. He puts his other arm around me. He rubs his nose against yours and, immediately afterwards, buries it in my hair. There is nothing to say, so we pretend to keep quiet.

On our left, behind the silver birch trees, the lake is a boundless murmur. We walk, the three of us intertwined along the earth path. We walk off in that transparent evening mist, on which floats a smell of smoke.

Notes on French Texts

LEARNING HOW TO LIVE (*Fajardie*)

1. *prolo*: This is a contraction of *prolétaire*, as is *sympa* of *sympathique* at the end of the paragraph. This tendency to contract frequently used terms is a feature of modern French. Compare *fac* for *faculté*, *resto* for *restaurant*, *sensas* for *sensationnel*, etc. *Also see* n. 8, p. 213.
2. *Arts-et-Métiers*: Metro station in central Paris between République and Rambuteau on the Mairie des Lilas–Châtelet line.
3. *place de la République*: Vast square created by Baron Haussmann between 1854 and 1862 as part of his reconstruction of Paris.
4. «*Grandes Espérances*»: A reference to Charles Dickens's novel *Great Expectations*.

ALL LIGHTS OFF (*Fajardie*)

1. *l'an III*: An echo of the Revolutionary calendar, which replaced the Gregorian calendar during the French Revolution. For example, Year One of the Republic was declared as having begun with the abolition of the Monarchy on 22 September 1792.
2. *grandes écoles*: Selective higher-education colleges that function alongside, though independently of, universities. Entry is by competitive examination (*concours*) two years after the *baccalauréat*. The oldest were created by Napoléon Bonaparte to train high-level technical specialists, though many more have been founded since his time. The best known are probably the École Normale Supérieure, the Polytechnique and the École Nationale d'Administration (ENA).
3. *Kapital*: Written by Karl Marx (1818–83), *Das Kapital* is the fundamental text of Marxist economics. Published in three volumes between 1867 and 1895, it focuses on the exploitation of the worker and appeals for a classless society where the production process is shared equally.

4. *la Libération*: The liberation of France from German occupation in 1944.

5. *Mai 68*: Initially a student protest, which began at the Nanterre campus on the outskirts of Paris in March 1968, against the perceived immorality of the international capitalist order as typified by the involvement of the USA in Vietnam. Police brutality caused the movement to spread until barricades were erected in Paris on the night of 10 and 11 May. Soon after there were massive strikes and factory occupations, and the sense of people power led to a euphoric sense of a new beginning.

6. *Giscard*: Valéry Giscard d'Estaing (1926–   ) was leader of the political party Union pour la Démocratie Française (UDF), and was president of France from 1974 to 1981.

7. *Daladier*: Édouard Daladier (1884–1970). A radical socialist French prime minister who was largely responsible for the Munich Agreement and France's subsequent declaration of war on Germany.

8. *Grifton*: More commonly written as *griveton*.

9. *Calvados*: *Département* of Basse-Normandie, which has given its name to the brandy distilled from cider.

10. *Mendès France*: Pierre Mendès France (1907–82) was prime minister of France and his government was active in the prevention of the spread of alcoholism in the mid-1950s. The gradual disappearance of travelling stills, brought about by the passing of a new law preventing licences to be passed automatically from father to son, is attributable to this period.

11. *gabelous*: Literally collectors of *la gabelle*, a pre-Revolutionary tax on salt. When used pejoratively, as here, it means 'customs officer'.

12. *DS 19*: Large car made by Citroën.

13. *Prost*: Alain Prost, a French motor-racing driver.

14. *R.P.R.*: Rassemblement pour la République (RPR) is the name given to the right-wing political party which grew out of de Gaulle's Rassemblement du Peuple Français (RPF), created in 1947.

DAVID (*Le Clézio*)

1. *celle du jeune berger . . . terrifiés*: A reference to the biblical conflict between David and Goliath.

2. *jouer au ballon*: The French has a *double entendre* which has no equivalent in English that I can find. Taken literally, *jouer au ballon* means 'to play

ball', but *le ballon* also has the meaning 'breathalyzer', which is being used as an image for the glue-sniffing that is taking place here. *Souffler dans le ballon* means 'to blow into the bag'.

3. *métacarpes*: The part of the skeleton of the hand between the wrist and the fingers.

THE OCCUPATION OF THE GROUND (*Échenoz*)

1. *une cheminée . . . l'heure*: The image is that of a huge sundial.
2. *pierre de taille*: Any fine-grained stone, such as sandstone or limestone, which can be cut and worked in any direction without it breaking.

THE OBJET D'ART (*Daoust*)

1. *Clément Marchand*: Born in 1912 in Sainte-Geneviève-de-Bastican, in Quebec, Clément Marchand is a writer of short stories and poems. He was the editor of the newspaper *Le Bien Public* from 1932 to 1978. In 1985 he won two prizes for his contribution to literature, and was elected to the Académie Canadienne in 1990.
2. *Montréal*: Inland port on the junction of the Ottawa and St Lawrence rivers in the province of Quebec, in Canada. Except for Paris, it is the world's largest French-speaking city.
3. *Sherbrooke*: Metro station situated on the rue Berri and one of the stations on the line running from Rosemont in the north to Longueuil on the south bank of the St Lawrence river. The better-known rue Sherbrooke, which gives its name to the station, runs across the city from west to east.
4. *mont Royal*: The hill where the city of Montreal was founded. It was originally called Mont du Roi by Jacques Cartier in 1535, in honour of the French king François 1. This was soon changed to Mont Royal, hence the name of the city.
5. *ère paléozoïque*: The era of geological time that began 600 million years ago and ended 225 million years ago.
6. *alea jacta est*: 'The die is cast.' This is a (Latin) phrase used when one takes a bold decision after hestitating for a long time. It has been attributed to Caesar, who made the decision to lead his army across the river

Rubicon and into Rome from the north, which was forbidden by law.

7. *Théâtre d'Aujourd'hui*: A theatre showing plays only in French from September to May.

8. *Louis Fréchette*: A French-speaking Canadian author born in Lévis (Quebec) in 1839, who died in 1908. *La Légende d'un peuple* is considered to be a national epic.

9. *carré*: This French-Canadian use of *le carré* is in place of the more standard *la place* or even *le square*.

10. *avant-midi*: French-Canadian word for 'morning'.

THE HUNTERS' CAFE (*Boulanger*)

1. *rose des vents*: Literally 'compass card', but to translate as 'at all points of the compass' seemed excessive.

2. *jusqu'aux pierres*: Literally 'even the stones'.

3. *Jutland*: This refers to a First World War naval battle fought between England and Germany on 31 May 1916 off the west coast of Jutland, a peninsula belonging partly to Germany and partly to Denmark.

4. *la Cyrénaïque*: An area of what is now eastern Libya. Conquered by Italy in 1912 and captured by the British in 1942, it was handed to Libya in 1951.

5. *alsace*: Alsace is a region of north-east France, with a border on the Rhine, which gives its name to the dry still white wine which is produced there.

6. *de derrière les fagots*: Literally 'from behind the sticks', hence the sense of the wine being hidden away for special customers.

7. *Soldat Inconnu*: This refers to the tomb of the Unknown Soldier, which lies beneath the Arc de Triomphe in Paris.

8. *Champ-de-Mars*: Originally a large military parade ground, it is now a large public park, with the École Militaire at one end and the Eiffel Tower at the other. In its present form the garden owes its appearance to C.-J. Formigé. Work began in 1908 and went on, intermittently, until 1928.

9. *École Militaire*: This is a fine example of eighteenth-century architecture at the end of the Champ-de-Mars furthest from the Seine. A military

academy, the building was designed by Jacques-Ange Gabriel and opened in 1760.

10. *pergola*: A covered walk with climbing plants trailed over trellis-work. The description of it being *aveugle* seems odd, therefore, and one can only assume that this refers to some form of lean-to building erected at the back of the café.

11. *Casanier*: The adjective *casanier* literally means 'stop-at-home', and describes a person who does not like going out often.

12. *courait*: The subject of this verb is *le silence particulier*. Boulanger uses the inversion to convey stylistically the all-embracing secrecy of the meeting.

13. *arrondissement*: An administrative district of Paris, in which town alone the term applies.

14. *général de Gaulle*: Charles de Gaulle (1890–1970) refused to accept Pétain's truce with the invading German army in 1940 and became leader of the Free French whilst in exile in London. His return to Paris in 1944 was one of triumph.

15. *Les Anciens*: This is more normally expressed in its full form: *les Anciens Combattants*.

16. *Champs-Élysées*: A wide, busy avenue leading from the Place de la Concorde to the Place de l'Étoile, where stands the Arc de Triomphe, a gigantic arch whose construction was ordered by Napoléon Bonaparte in 1806 in honour of the French army. The Armistice Day parades in Paris all take place on the Champs-Élysées, hence the characters' decision to take action there.

17. *pelage de loup*: Literally 'wolfskin'. The image is a combination of stealth and menace.

18. *moitié montante*: The right-hand side of the Champs-Élysées for cars driving up towards the Place de l'Étoile and the Arc de Triomphe.

19. *Le Chant du départ*: Literally 'the song of departure'. This is a patriotic French song with words written in 1794 by Marie-Joseph Chénier (1764–1811) and music by Étienne Méhul (1763–1817).

ACCURSED NOTEBOOKS (*Cotnoir*)

1. *Shoah*: The Hebrew word for 'holocaust'.
2. *charbonnier*: Literally 'coalman', but combines with *une foi de* to mean 'blind faith'.
3. *Dachau, Auschwitz, Buchenwald*: Nazi concentration camps during the Second World War.
4. *Vergissmeinnicht*: The German word for 'forget-me-not'.

HÉLOÏSE (*Germain*)

1. *Héloïse*: In her youth Héloïse was the lover of Abélard and the mother of their son, Astrolabe. When his seduction of, and secret wedding to, Héloïse became known, Abélard was castrated at the instigation of Héloïse's uncle and became a monk. In 1129 Héloïse became a nun and eventually founded the nunnery at Paraclete, of which she became abbess. Her letters to Abélard reveal that she had a strong and, at the same time, pious character. Abélard died at Châlon-sur-Saône in 1142 and was buried at Paraclete. Héloïse was buried beside him in 1164.
2. *Edmond Jabès*: A poet, born in Cairo in 1912, who moved to Paris in 1957. Generally considered to be a mystic whose words misrepresent the nature of reality: for him, only paradox can give meaning.
3. *Apocalypse*: The symbolic and mystical last book of the New Testament, said to have been written by St John the Evangelist, though there is doubt about this. It is more usually known as the Book of Revelation, and looks forward to the second coming of Christ. In Chapter 6, when the seven seals of the book of destiny are broken, war, revolution, plague and famine are unleashed, personified by the Four Horsemen.
4. *caparison*: A decorative covering, usually for horses, which has its origins in protective covering for warhorses.

THE CHARACTER (*Escomel*)

1. *zamezégarées*: This form of neologism is almost untranslatable.
2. *Carco*: His full name was François Carcopino-Tusoli. He was a French

writer (1886–1958), the author of poems, memoirs and novels, of which the best known is *Jésus la Caille*.

3. *Apollinaire*: Guillaume Apollinaire was the name taken by Wilhelm Apollinaris Kostrowitzky (1880–1918). The author of *Alcools* (1913) and *Calligrammes*, he led symbolist poetry in new directions until it became the precursor of surrealism. In addition, he was a strong supporter of the Cubist painters.

4. *Pierrot*: A traditional pantomime character, always dressed in white with a whitened face.

5. *Clichy*: *Chef-lieu*, which approximates to 'county town', of the Hauts-de-Seine *département*, to the north-west of Paris.

6. *mordus-sanglants*: Mordu is the past participle of *mordre*. The image *mordus-sanglants*, therefore, is one of the kisses being like bites, which draw blood.

7. *Prévert*: Jacques Prévert (1900–77) wrote poetry for the common man. His work was basically oral, often sentimental, and usually scornful of authority, whilst singing the praises of the oppressed. His best-known work, *Paroles*, was published in 1946 but he was also a writer of film scripts, of which the most famous is *Les Enfants du Paradis*, directed by Marcel Carné in 1945.

8. *mélo*: A contraction of *mélodrame*. *Also see* n. 1, p. 207.

9. *Invalides*: This was a vast hospital that could accommodate 7,000 disabled soldiers. Built between 1671 and 1676, it is perhaps now best known as the last resting place of the remains of Napoleon Bonaparte.

10. *Montparnasse*: Best known as a district where artists and writers congregate.

11. *Bottin*: A telephone directory of Parisian telephone numbers.

12. *quatre sous*: A sou is a unit of money that now exists only in idiomatic expressions such as *je n'ai pas un sou*, meaning 'I'm broke'. To give some context, in the late eighteenth century, when it was still in circulation, 4 liards = 1 denier, 12 deniers = 1 sou, 20 sous = 1 livre. It was said that a man needed 300 livres a year if he was to live in reasonable comfort.

13. *Orphée*: Orpheus, son of Apollo, married Eurydice, who died from a snakebite. He went down to Hades to bring her back, and her return to life was granted on the condition that he walk ahead of her, without looking back. He broke his promise and Eurydice was irretrievably lost.

Orpheus was such a good player of the lyre that wild animals were calmed by his music.

14. *daguerréotypes*: Early photographic prints, called after the inventor of the technique for producing them, Jacques Daguerre (1787–1851). The first daguerreotypes date from 1838.

15. *les fleurs du mâle*: A reference to a collection of poems by Charles Baudelaire (1821–67) that was first published in 1857. *Les Fleurs du Mal* records the search by man for an ideal that he can never attain, and which therefore plunges him into isolation and despair.

SELF-DESTRUCTION (*Belletto*)

1. *maison d'un étage*: The *étage* refers to the first, not the ground, floor.

2. *présent*: An Anglicism. The more usual word is *cadeau*.

3. *Robinson Crusoe*: This is a fictional account, based on what actually happened to Alexander Selkirk, of a shipwrecked sailor on a desert island. It was written in 1719 by Daniel Defoe (1660–1731).

4. *Je me précipite . . . j'ouvre*: The French text of the story is written almost entirely in the present tense, using the historic present to give greater actuality to the narrative. It seemed appropriate to use the present tense until this point, when the English past gives greater effect and speed. The interpretation of this is the translator's dilemma and the result is based on a purely personal judgement.

YOU NEVER DIE (*Gerber*)

1. *Laurentides*: An area of outstanding natural beauty some sixty miles north of Montreal. In winter there is an abundance of skiing; in summer a wide variety of water sports.

Acknowledgements

For permission to reprint the French stories in this collection the publisher would like to thank the following: Éditions de la Table Ronde for 'Apprendre à vivre' and 'Tous feux éteints' from *La Lorette hallucinée* (1996); Éditions Gallimard for 'David' from *La Ronde et autres faits divers* (1982), © Éditions Gallimard, 1982; and 'Le Café des Chasseurs' from *Les Jeux du tour de ville*, Collection Folio (1983), © Éditions Gallimard, 1983; Éditions de Minuit for 'L'Occupation des sols' (1988); L'instant même for 'Le Navet' from *L'Oeil de verre: nouvelles* (1993), © L'instant même, 1993, and 'Les Cahiers maudits' from *La Déconvenue* (1993), © L'instant même, 1993; Éditions de l'Hexagone for 'L'Objet d'art' from *Nouvelles de Montréal* (1992); Sylvie Germain for 'Héloïse', © Sylvie Germain, 1999; Éditions du Boréal for 'Le Personnage' from *Les Eaux de la mémoire* (1994), © Éditions du Boréal, Montreal, 1994; Éditions Librio for 'Autodestruction' from *La Vie rêvée et autres nouvelles* (1994); Éditions du Rocher for 'On ne meurt jamais' from *Ce qu'on voit dans les yeux d'Iliyna Karopt* (1996).

READ MORE IN PENGUIN

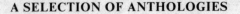

A SELECTION OF ANTHOLOGIES

The Penguin Book of Jewish Short Stories
Edited by Emanuel Litvinoff

These stories, deeply rooted in Jewish life and consciousness, reflect authentic, funny, often moving images of Jewish people in the modern world. They include some of the greatest names in modern literature: S. Y. Agnon, Saul Bellow, Isaac Bashevis Singer and many others.

Amazonian Edited by Dea Birkett and Sara Wheeler

A bold, innovative collection of previously unpublished essays from women across the world, where fiction, memoir and autobiography make their appearance on an exciting creative landscape. Writers including Shena Mackay, Suzanne Moore and Imogen Stubbs travel the globe for work, adventure, self-discovery, danger and love.

Three Entertainments Graham Greene

Containing three masterpieces of espionage, murder and betrayal: *A Gun for Sale*, *The Confidential Agent* and *The Ministry of Fear*. 'It is in the early entertainments rather than in the early novels that we may observe most clearly the genesis of Greene's mature art' David Lodge

The Penguin Book of Columnists
Edited by Christopher Silvester

'Essential reading' *Observer*. 'For journalists, the lesson of the book is that nothing succeeds like reality ... Some columns are more tragic than anything you will find in imaginative literature' *Sunday Times*

The Penguin Book of Gay Short Stories
Edited by David Leavitt and Mark Mitchell

The diversity – and unity – of gay love and experience in the twentieth century is celebrated in this collection of thirty-nine stories. 'The book is like a long, enjoyable party, at which the celebrated ... rub shoulders with the neglected' *The Times Literary Supplement*

READ MORE IN PENGUIN

A SELECTION OF ANTHOLOGIES

The Penguin Book of Women's Lives   Edited by Phyllis Rose

'A collection of outstanding – and blessedly diverse – twentieth-century autobiographical excerpts ... Here is inspiration by the cart-load – literary and emotional'   *Mail on Sunday*. 'A triumphant celebration of the spirit of women' Margaret Forster

The Regeneration Trilogy   Pat Barker

'Quite simply a masterpiece – a devastating, deeply moving account of the suffering of soldiers in the First World War and the effect of the war on those left behind at home ... Fiction of the highest order' *Express on Sunday*. 'Harrowing, original, delicate and unforgettable' *Independent*

The Collected Stories   Paul Theroux

'[Theroux] makes and remakes his own world ... throughout this shimmering, kaleidoscopic and very entertaining collection ... his dialogue is powerfully but also effortlessly accurate' *Sunday Telegraph*

The Penguin Book of the City   Edited by Robert Drewe

Twenty-nine tales of urban life by the greatest names in contemporary fiction, including Irvine Welsh, Will Self, John Updike and Gabriel García Márquez. These daring, darkly humorous stories reflect both the dangers and delights of life in the metropolis.

Three Novels   Barbara Vine

Contains the novels *A Dark-Adapted Eye*, *A Fatal Inversion* and *The House of Stairs*. 'Barbara Vine has the kind of near-Victorian narrative drive ... that compels a reader to go on turning the pages' *Sunday Times*

refresh yourself at penguin.co.uk

Visit penguin.co.uk for exclusive information and interviews with
bestselling authors, fantastic give-aways and the
inside track on all our books, from the Penguin Classics
to the latest bestsellers.

BE FIRST

first chapters, first editions, first novels

EXCLUSIVES

author chats, video interviews, biographies, special features

EVERYONE'S A WINNER

give-aways, competitions, quizzes, ecards

READERS GROUPS

exciting features to support existing groups and create new ones

NEWS

author events, bestsellers, awards, what's new

EBOOKS

books that click – download an ePenguin today

BROWSE AND BUY

thousands of books to investigate – search, try and buy the perfect gift online – or treat yourself!

ABOUT US

job vacancies, advice for writers and company history

Get Closer To Penguin . . . www.penguin.co.uk